Her Guarded Heart

LETTING LOVE IN
BOOK ONE

DAWN BACA

To my wonderful husband Jeremy,
your unconditional love and support is
my driving force. Thank you for all that you do,
and all that you are.

And to my father Wayne.
Even though I only had you in my life briefly, knowing you made
me a better person.
You are missed every single day.

Give the ones you love wings to fly, roots to come back and reasons to stay.
    — Dandelion Unknown

CHAPTER 1

An Unwelcome Announcement

August 1999
Addison

For the love of all that's holy...

Addison Tetrick blew long bangs out of her face and kneaded the back of her neck, pushing away sticky, damp tendrils of hair. Her mother had slowly killed her excitement about the study abroad program and her enthusiasm for it was fading fast.

North Carolina had skipped spring and fallen head-first into summer. Six long, hot months of suffocating purgatory. The heat rose quickly, and humidity followed as it always did. The lack of air conditioning in her mother's small rental house only added to her discomfort.

Standing near the faded brown couch where her slightly older sister sat, with her mother in a chair across from them, the room felt too small. She glanced up at the ceiling fan, unmoving. It hadn't worked for as long as Addison could remember. Sucking in a deep, soggy breath, she wiped the sweat from her face before responding.

"I'm going to school in Russia, mom."

"Russia!" Tandy exploded out of her seat. Her lips twisted into a grimace as she marched around the living room.

Queasiness roiled in the pit of Addison's stomach. She loathed confrontations with her mother. In fact, she'd spent most of her life avoiding them.

Tandy continued to mutter and pace across the room as her mouth puckered further.

Forcing a tight-lipped smile helped stifle the scream building within Addison.

"Why Russia, Addy?" Savannah mumbled.

Addison swallowed hard and faced her sister. Savannah had always straddled the fence where their mother was concerned, and it bothered Addison more than she cared to admit. Always the gatekeeper and mediator. Savannah, in a nutshell.

"Studying in another country is my dream. Russia has a long history of advancing the sciences, and now I have the chance." Ignoring her mother's scowl, she continued. "It feels like the right place for me—"

Savannah sat ramrod straight in her chair, hands

folded between her knees, her expression unreadable. Addison was preparing for another adventure. Excitement and fear collided inside of her. The tension emanating from Savannah's tightly wound posture reminded her again that it was something her sister seemed likely to never experience.

A twinge of guilt burrowed deep within her. Because of the support and generosity of her father and stepmother, she had the option to go away to a four-year university. Her sister remained at home, attending a two-year community college while working full time because their mother had bullied her into it. While Savannah catered to her mother's controlling ways, Addison worked hard to create boundaries that prevented her mother from doing the same to her. And though she struggled with the guilt that lingered around every opportunity her father gave her, she maintained those boundaries with her mother just the same.

Tandy's hands balled into fists, her face alarmingly red as she shouted, "They're communists!"

Addison rolled her eyes and focused on the peeling paint on the empty wall behind her mother. *The drama queen strikes again.* Some days, she honestly believed her mother had missed her calling as a soap opera star, instead of as a stay-at-home mother in a revolving door of marriages.

"Don't you roll your eyes at me." Tandy swatted at her ponytail. Her once-shiny ebony hair had dulled with age and lack of care. In her agitation, the un-brushed, tangled hair struggled to get out of its band. The once-beautiful debutante—the belle of the ball and most sought-after hand at the Christmas Cotillion —had lost her most entrancing traits. Tandy's fall from grace had not gone unnoticed from the society she'd grown up in.

"I'm sorry, Mama." Addison coughed, which left her voice raspy as she swiped at a fly buzzing around her ear. Her mother's continuous string of bad choices left her a bitter, tired housewife, ostracized from her affluent family long ago. Addison's grand-mother had completely turned her back on them, drawing the last line in the sand when Tandy married her third husband, Rafe—now ex-husband. Though Raleigh's father had stuck around longer than the others, her mother's attitude made it much harder to bite her tongue.

It's not my fault she's spiraled. I will not let this happen to me. Starting with Russia!

Air escaped Addison's lungs as she plopped down on the couch next to her sister, and a whoosh of dust rose from the cushion to smother her. Out of the corner of her eye, the dark, tangled mops of her two youngest sisters peeked in from the hallway, as though they wanted to come into the room. Addison's heart warmed at the brief sight of the Hobbits, her nick-name for them because of their constantly tousled hair and dirty, bare feet. She wished Quinby was there, but she spent most of her time at her best friend's house, studying. She couldn't blame her. None of her sisters had the opportunity to escape to visit their fathers like she had.

She smiled at them, relieving some of the tension in her shoulders, before directing a pointed gaze at their mother, their eyes wide at the sight of mother's disheveled appearance.

Battles with her mother had been hers alone for years. The stale air almost choked her as she inhaled, causing a hacking cough. At least Savannah wasn't antagonistic for a change.

"When do you leave?" Savannah asked.

"The end of the month—classes start at the beginning of September."

"That's only two weeks away." Savannah tugged at her chestnut hair, just a shade darker than Addison's.

"I know."

"So, there's no time to change your mind?" Tandy snapped.

Exactly. Addison chewed on her thumbnail. The idea of spending the summer with her mother's futile attempts to change her mind had prompted the delayed announcement. Savannah nudged her.

Addison bit her lip to stifle the grin, trying to escape at the goofy expression on her sister's face. Though they didn't always see eye to eye, Savannah looked and thought more like Addison than any of their other sisters. Their ages, being the closest, contributed to a big part of that. She was grateful for her presence today, and her attempts to keep the peace.

"Will you come home for the holidays?" Savannah asked.

Addison gave a slight shake of her head. "No, I'll spend the entire year there."

"Aren't you concerned about Y2K? What if it's the end of the world?" Savannah asked.

Addison flipped her hands palm-side up. "I'm not worried about crazy prophecies. They've always existed. They always will."

"You shouldn't be an ocean away if there's going to be an apocalypse." Tandy's coal-dark eyes bored into her.

This conversation would kill her if the stale air didn't first. With no circulation, the dusty room had become oppressive and claustrophobic.

"A possible computer glitch will not bring about the End of Days. If anything, it might mess up ATMs for a day or two." She eyed her mother. *Your empty checking account won't be affected in the least by a computer glitch.* Clenching her jaw, she kept the snarky responses racing through her mind to herself.

"But you'll be gone for the millennium celebrations, too," Savannah said.

"They'll be celebrating there too, I'm sure, so I won't be missing much."

Savannah rolled her eyes.

A laugh bubbled up, and Addison pursed her lips to keep quiet as some of the space between them shrank. *At least Savi doesn't hate me.*

With narrowed eyes and lips pressed into a line so tight, her mouth almost disappeared. Tandy continued to work herself up. Addison bit the inside of her cheek.

Instead of accepting the news and being supportive, her mother remained negative. "You weren't home much last year, and now you're spending a year away in a country full of communists. It's like I don't even know you anymore…"

No surprise there. Savannah's eyes grew wide, as if she could read her mind.

While her mother ranted, Addison closed her eyes and slipped her bottom lip between her teeth. She'd given the news to her father and his wife, Cassie, at dinner months before, and they had taken it well. They'd asked normal, concerned-parent questions, and offered to help with anything she needed. They'd been encouraging and enthusiastic about the fantastic opportunity ahead of her.

"You're not listening to me," Tandy said.

Addison snapped to attention. "Sorry, Mama." She dug her fingernails into her palms, a reminder to stay strong, not to let her mother get to her.

"You're never going to land a good husband if

you spend all your time traipsing around the world in undesirable locations."

That ship sailed when Grandmamma took her money and social status with her. The muscles in her back tightened as a sharp pain slid through her head behind her eyes, a telltale sign of a brewing tension headache.

Addison refused to rise to the bait. *Not everyone needs to be defined by a ring. Not that any of them are worth the gold that created them.* Addison stole a glance at the thin gold band on her mother's hand hidden by the intricate class ring her grandparents had given her at her high school graduation.

"You're being selfish." Tandy's voice was low and wheedling.

Her stomach turned; she could handle her mother's explosions. However, she was no match for the guilt trips.

"Why am I selfish to want more out of my life than you did?" Addison slid her hands under her legs and steeled herself for what she feared was coming.

Her mother advanced on her. "How dare you!" Tandy loomed above her, her face almost purple with rage, her hands whipping around in a frenzy each time she spoke.

Addison leaned back into the musty couch, out of range of her mother's hands. The movement caused more dust to escape and fill the surrounding air. "Yes, I dare. I dare to dream. I dare to go to college for more than a husband. I dare to want to make something of myself—to never have to depend on a man to support me."

Wired differently than others, Addison didn't cry at emotionally charged movies, or appropriately sad moments. Instead, she cried when frustrated or angry. Out of breath from her outburst, Addison turned away as tears welled in her eyes, which only infuriated her more.

Savannah shifted in the seat beside her.

She was in for it. Addison had never spoken to her mother with an attitude, and her mother would capitalize on her mistake.

Tandy's voice dropped to a menacing murmur as she said, "I've done my best for you and your sisters. And you act like it was nothing."

The words landed like a gut punch.

Her mother had spent years telling them that everything she'd ever done had been in her children's best interest. Remarrying quickly after each divorce, the birth of a new child occurred shortly after each to strengthen the ties. Tandy did what suited Tandy—she always had. How else did one explain four marriages and five daughters? What was best for her children had never been the primary motive behind her actions. Addison had witnessed her mother's manipulations too many times not to know that firsthand.

Don't give in. She's counting on wearing you down.

"Why is it so wrong for me to want more?" Addison asked.

"You just want to be like *her*." Tandy's voice was steely.

Here it is, the ever-bubbling hatred of her step-mother. It was irrational at this point, but her mother wasn't one to let a grudge go—even if she was the one in the wrong the entire time.

"Mama, I need to be my own person. To finish school and have a career I love. What's wrong with that?"

"If you say so. I still think this is *her* influence," Tandy said.

The front door opened and Eric, Tandy's husband, came in. The tension increased. Addison hadn't seen Eric in months and was shocked by how much he'd aged in such a brief absence. Though still a tall, broad-shouldered man, and easily intimidating, the gray streaks at his temples hadn't been there before. His light-brown hair was slick with sweat and matted to the back of his head from the baseball cap he held in his weathered hand. A ring of perspiration circled the neckline of his shirt.

Addison suppressed the urge to shiver.

Savannah's back went stiff as a board, her expression went blank, and she averted her gaze.

Eric's lip curled as he glanced into the room and spotted her and Savi. "What's for dinner?"

Addison jumped as he dropped his lunchbox in

the entryway and kicked his heavy steel-toed boots off with a thunk onto the tiled floor. The sound echoed in the enclosed space.

The small house closed in around her as he came in.

Unlike Mama's last husband, Eric wasn't verbally or physically abusive. He was just too self-absorbed for Addison's taste. A decent enough father to her younger sisters, and a good provider, he'd never bothered with the three older girls.

Of course, Quinby had been the thorn in his side from the beginning. The middle child. She'd made it clear she didn't believe they needed another father after Raleigh's father left. Eric hadn't appreciated her attitude, and so he shut them out.

"I'll order a pizza." Tandy waved her hand in the air dismissively.

With a brisk nod, Eric spun around and left the room. A bad omen. He hadn't kissed Tandy like he usually did.

Addison nudged her sister in the ribs while their mother's attention was on the retreating form of her husband. Addison leaned in and whispered in Savannah's ear, "Trouble in Paradise?"

Savannah responded with a slight nod.

Time to get the hell out before things get ugly.

The Hobbits, still somewhere down the hall, laughed as Eric greeted them. Minutes later, the pipes rumbled as Eric started the shower.

"Mama, I'm driving back to school tonight." Addison stood and walked over to her mother and gave her a light kiss on the cheek. "I'm going to say goodbye to Raleigh and Beth."

"Will you be coming back before you fly off?" Tandy asked.

"Probably not. I have a lot to do before I go."

"Humph."

Letting the conversation drop there, Addison walked down the hall and lightly rapped on the girls' bedroom door. Through the small crack, she saw them sprawled out on the bottom bunk, coloring books and crayons scattered around them.

They look just like Mama.

Other than their various last names, their similar traits—and strong resemblance to Tandy—it would be hard for outsiders to realize they had different fathers. With a shake of her head, she forced a smile and pushed open the door. This was not the life she wanted for herself.

Beth squealed, "Sissy!" Jumping up, she ran to her.

Addison swung her up, embracing her tightly, trying to ignore the oily sheen on her skin and the filthy feet that rubbed up against her.

After Addison set Beth down, Raleigh rushed up to her and wrapped her arms around her waist.

As she kissed the top of Raleigh's sweaty head, she wrinkled her nose. Her sister's hair desperately needed a dance with some heavy-duty shampoo. As usual, they were overdue for a bath. Addison sighed.

"Whoa! You two need playtime in the tub." A voice in her head scolded her. *Pick your battles. Now isn't the time to say anything.* "Be good for Mama and Savi, Bug."

Raleigh nodded as she clung to her side. "It's Ladybug," she mumbled into Addison's shirt.

"You're right, Ladybug," Addison said, hoping her voice sounded contrite beneath her grin.

"You, too, Bumblebee." Addison reached for Beth, bringing her in for a group hug.

"I will. When will you come back?" Beth asked.

"I'll see you next summer."

"How long is that? How come you won't be home for Christmas?" Raleigh asked.

"I'll be studying far away next year and won't be able to come home until it's over."

Raleigh bobbed her head. "I wish you were closer."

"Me, too." It was getting harder to maintain a stiff upper lip as Beth cried. The tears flowed freely down her cheeks as her youngest sister trembled in her arms. They were the real reason she put up with her mother's guilt trips.

"Shush, now. I'll write you both long letters and send you pretty pictures. I'll be home before you know it." Addison kissed them each again before backing out of the room. She bumped into

Savannah standing in the hallway as she closed the door.

"We'll miss you," Savannah said as she wrapped her arm around Addison's shoulder. They walked down the hall entwined.

"I'll miss you guys, too. Take care of them." Her headache hadn't subsided, and neither had the queasiness. These visits were getting harder to escape from unscathed.

"I always do." Savannah sighed. "Have fun over there."

"Thanks, sis." They hugged for longer than usual before she headed out to her car, and Savannah closed the front door.

As Addison drove away, she stole a quick glance in the rearview mirror at her mother's house, slipping farther into the background. She exhaled–her mother's drama needed to stay there.

Though already missing her sisters, if she didn't go to Russia, her mother would continue to manipulate her. She needed the distance and her independence. As the tears welled in her eyes, she slapped the steering wheel.

"My time is now. I'm not Mama. I refuse to be like Mama." Addison continued the litany the entire drive back to school.

CHAPTER 2

The Adventure Begins

Addison

A ddison shivered as she stared out the back window of her dad's car. The dark, gloomy sky had opened, letting down a torrent of rain throughout the morning. A fitting send-off if there ever was one.

At the airport, her father pulled her bags from the trunk and carried them to the terminal.

Her wet coat stuck to her like a second skin. She ran her fingers through the tangles in her dripping hair. It was an old wives' tale that rain was a bad omen; she reminded herself. Addison considered it the opposite, a way to wash away the oppression of the past and leave a clean slate for the future. After giving herself a quick shake, she checked her bags, stopping short as reality sank in. As her mood lifted, she skipped her way back to her family for one last embrace.

Her father held her in a tight hug. "Call us if you need anything."

Glancing over his shoulder, she noticed a glimmer in Cassie's eyes as she held out her arms, and Addison stepped into her loving embrace. She would miss her stepmother—her confidante. Where her mother guilted her, Cassie always supported her.

Her two mothers were polar opposites. Tandy hadn't spoken to her in weeks—in fact, only once—since Addison told her about participating in the study abroad program.

"You keep your eyes open and stay safe." Cassie wiped at her eyes, smudging her mascara.

Addison nodded and turned away. After another round of hugs, her parents left the terminal, and she headed toward her gate. After boarding her flight, she settled into her seat.

AFTER AN UNEVENTFUL FLIGHT TO FRANCE, THE FOUR-hour layover at Charles De Gaulle was exhilarating—it was one of the busiest airports she'd ever been in. She'd traveled with her father and Cassie as a child, but nothing had prepared her for the bustling activity of the Paris airport. Sipping coffee, she sat, fascinated as she people-watched at the edge of a café. She should have been exhausted. Instead, she had an adrenaline high after the all-night flight. Her nerves warred inside her. A part of her excited, a larger, more pronounced part petrified.

It wasn't until after she'd settled into her seat for the second leg of the trip that her nerves kicked into high gear. On her way to Saint Petersburg, she pinched her forearm to ground herself. She couldn't deny looking forward to an entire year away from her mother's histrionics, though she would miss her father and Cassie, and a tinge of guilt crept in over leaving her little sisters.

Addison dropped her head against the headrest and closed her eyes as the plane took off. In three more hours, she would truly be on her own for the first time in her life. Even going away to college hadn't given her such a sense of freedom. The guilt trips from her mother to visit more frequently made it difficult to remain distant and detached. When she returned for summer break, trying to avoid confrontations became harder—so much so that she pulled away. Though she returned less and less, she couldn't escape her mother's wrath. *I can't keep running away though…* She hoped that this experience would help her attain the independence she craved.

CRUNCHED IN THE BACK SEAT OF THE TAXI, ADDISON clicked away on her new camera as they drove past the enormous Hershey-Kiss-topped roofs synonymous with Russia. She snapped even more photos, passing the red and white structures of Saint Petersburg University's main building. As she changed positions to get a better view out the window, she winced as the prickling sensation crawled up her leg. So taken with the scenery, her foot fell asleep beneath her. As the cab continued down the road, it became clear that what appeared to be the main building was a row of twelve buildings, not one. A year spent studying among the beautiful, ornate architecture from the eighteenth century—the Age of Enlightenment—was exactly what she needed. Drumming her fingers on the glass, she took in the beauty surrounding her. *I'm here. I'm really here.*

The taxi delivered her to the front of the admissions building. Standing at the bottom of the magnificent staircase, facing the massive structure, intimidated her. She tugged her sweater tighter around her shoulders before taking the handles of her two enormous purple suitcases, yanking them up the ridiculously steep concrete steps.

Once inside, she paused, out of breath, before pulling her luggage toward the admissions desk. A plump, matronly woman stood behind the counter, a smile in place as Addison approached.

Once Addison reached the counter, words flew out of the woman's mouth in an incoherent stream of rapid Russian. *What was I thinking? My Russian isn't good enough.*

Her expression must have belied her panic because the woman spoke again, slower and in English. "How may I help you, dear?" The woman's raspy voice hinted at many years of smoking.

"My name is Addison Tetrick." Her words came out in a strained whisper.

"*Amerikanskiy?*"

Addison nodded.

The woman smiled wider as she began typing furiously on her keyboard on the counter.

"Ah, Ms. Tetrick, I have you in room 332."

"Great, can you tell me how to get there?"

"It is in the dormitory on Kapitanskaya street 3."

Addison's smile slipped. "Is there a map?"

"Of course." The woman pulled out a printed map from a drawer under the counter and slid it over to her. There were large circles drawn around the administration building and the dormitories.

The map was overwhelming. "Can I walk there from here?"

"*Nyet.* You must take the Baltiysky Rail." She pointed to a circled spot on the map in the center of the paper.

Addison's gut dropped as her pulse thudded rapidly in her ears. Never comfortable with public transportation, she sucked in a deep breath. Thanking the administrator, she folded the map and put it in her purse before towing her bags out the door. Finding the train station was a disorienting and difficult experience. All the directions at the kiosks were in Russian, and they didn't accept credit cards. Grateful for the wallet full of Russian rubles, she'd stuffed what she expected was far more than enough money for a one-way passage into the booth. Snatching the printed ticket from the machine caused the corner to tear. Swearing under her breath, she pulled her luggage through the station to the platform.

After a brief, nerve-wracking train ride, then a short walk across the campus, she found the dormitory and took an elevator to the third floor. The door to her assigned room was slightly ajar, so she pushed her way in.

Dropping her bags to the floor, she turned around the minuscule area she would call hers for the foreseeable future and took in the chaos. The whitewashed cinderblock walls and small, narrow window at the far end gave a claustrophobic vibe to the space.

A willowy young woman with a bright, burgundy, stylish bob came into the room from a side door a moment later.

"*Bonjour.*" She greeted Addison in a thick French accent and thrust her hand in Addison's direction. "I'm Sophie."

"Addison." She shook her roommate's hand.

Sophie waved a hand around the cramped space. "Sorry for the mess. I spent the day shopping."

"When did you arrive?" Addison took in the boxes

and shopping bags littering both small beds—and most of the floor space between them.

"Yesterday."

"Wow, you've been busy."

Sophie blushed. "*Oui*. Any excuse to shop is good."

Addison laughed as Sophie scrambled to move the boxes around and unpack her purchases. There were bags of bedding sitting on her side of the room and brightly colored throw pillows tossed against the wall in the corner. Oversized comforters draped over each bed. Stacks of bath towels sat folded neatly at the edge of a desk under the window. A large shag area rug filled the space between the two beds.

"Do you really need all of this?" Addison asked, as multiples of everything covered every flat surface.

"Some of it is for you, too. I hope you don't mind. We can take back anything you don't like and get you something else. I just needed color. This room was *très* drab." Sophie shrugged, not meeting Addison's gaze directly.

"For me? I don't understand." *Why would she buy me all this?*

"We are going to be fast friends—I just know it." Sophie giggled. "And I have Papá's credit card with implicit instructions to have fun."

"Wow, really?" Addison had met no one her age with unlimited access to a credit card before. A part of her envied that luxury. Her father lectured her for years that his credit card was strictly for necessities.

A sheepish grin crossed her new friend's face. "Papá is still trying to make up for the troll."

"What troll?" Addison asked.

"His ex-wife. Camilla." Sophie gave an exaggerated shudder. "She hated me. Made Papá ship me off to boarding school."

"How horrible."

"Oh, boarding school was fine, though I missed Papá. And any reason not to share a roof with *that woman* was welcome."

Addison cringed. The way she said "that woman" reminded her of how her mother often referred to her own stepmother.

"Was she really that bad?" She felt guilty for even asking, considering her own mother's behavior.

"Oh, yes. Papá is a very private man, but she wanted to always go out and be the center of attention. They got into a huge fight a year ago, and she made a public scene. Their divorce was finalized last month."

Something about Sophie's story niggled at the back of Addison's mind. She recalled reading something in the supermarket tabloids about a French millionaire and his socialite wife divorcing.

"Wait a minute. Are you saying your father is Bertrand Comte?"

"*Oui*! You know him?"

"*Everyone* knows about him. He's famous."

Sophie giggled. "Oh, Papá doesn't think so."

"Considering we've heard of him in the States, I'd say he is." According to an article she'd once read in *People Magazine*, Bertrand Comte was a well-known horse breeder. With his beloved first wife, Nadeen, he built an empire comprising some of the most sought-after equines in the world.

Sophie smiled. "Camilla disliked the horses almost as much as me. At least Papá didn't send them away, too."

Addison's brow arched, but Sophie became distracted by her purchases once again. Within moments, she pulled a slinky black dress from a bag on the bed and held it up for inspection.

"What do you think of this?"

Addison laughed. "Wow, that's, um… small."

Sophie giggled. "It stretches."

"I hope so."

Sophie shook her dress out and held it up higher. It stretched out minimally. "Well, I can't wait to wear it out on the town."

"I hope it came with a jacket. You might get cold with only that on."

Sophie slid the skimpy little black number over a hanger and placed it in the closet before shaking out the rest of the bags and hanging more clothes. Meanwhile, Addison made both beds with the new sheet sets and blankets.

"Ugh. That was a lot of work," Addison collapsed on the edge of her fully made bed.

"*Oui*. But what fun! Tomorrow after classes, we can go shopping again?"

Addison looked around the room, not a single surface or space unadorned. She couldn't imagine needing more, but she nodded anyway. At least shopping would help her get accustomed to her surroundings.

Having Sophie as her roommate made adjusting to being far from home easier. Her laughter was infectious, and Addison felt a kinship with her she hadn't felt with anyone since she was a child.

"Hey, where are you?" Sophie asked.

"Hmm. Just thinking how lucky I am to have you as a roommate."

"*Oui*. I'm *magnifique*." Sophie pranced around the room, flipping her hair in the air.

Addison grinned and rolled her eyes. "We should get to bed early to be fresh for school in the morning."

"It's our last night of freedom, so we should go out and celebrate," Sophie suggested.

"Thanks, but I'm exhausted, and *I loathe morning classes.*"

"Oh, please." Sophie dropped onto her bed and crossed her legs. "We won't stay out all night. I just want a chance to unwind a little."

Addison mustered up a laugh she didn't quite connect with.

Addison could feel her resolve slipping. Sophie was right—this would be their last chance to explore before school started, and then she'd have her hands full with homework.

SOPHIE PLACED TWO SMALL GLASSES OF VODKA ON THE tall table where they sat while Addison scanned the crowd and chewed on the inside of her cheek, determined not to show her discomfort. *Why did I agree to this?*

Hot pink and purple rays of light bounced off the walls of the dark room. The music pulsed, causing the table to vibrate and slosh vodka onto the scarred melamine veneer.

Sophie picked up her glass and saluted her. "*A votre santé.*"

Addison lifted her glass and smiled before downing the drink. She shuddered as the potato spirit burned through her.

Across the room, a group of men hooted and hollered. Engrossed in conversation, he stood in the middle of their circle, waving his hands. Laughter erupted from the men, capturing the attention of several females in the club, including Addison. A dark-haired man with strands of untamed hair sliding down his forehead glanced over and caught Addison's eye. He had a strong, square chin, but it was hard to make out his other features in the darkened club.

Sophie waved a hand in the air before her face.

"*Allo?*" Sophie giggled.

"Sorry, Sophie. You were saying?"

"What has got you so distracted?"

"Nothing," Addison replied, glancing across the room.

Sophie turned her head toward the group of men as their laughter increased. "Ah, I see."

"See what?" Addison asked, her eyes wide.

"I see a young man staring back at you. He seems to be just as distracted."

Addison's gaze flew to the other side of the room and zeroed in on the mysterious stranger. As their eyes met again, a zing traveled up her spine. Startled, she shifted in her seat and forced her attention back to her new friend.

"Are you ready to call it a night?" The vodka was already giving her heartburn.

Sophie rolled her eyes exaggeratedly. "*Oui*, let us go back."

They gathered up their jackets quickly. Addison cast one final, longing glance in the direction of the handsome stranger before following Sophie out of the bar. I don't have time for boys... She was here to study, learn about Russian culture, and cement her independence from her mother. She was not here to date.

CHAPTER 3

Catching Up

Sergei

S ergei Petrova ran his hand through his hair.

The dark room suited his mood. Distracted and not really up for socializing, the vodka in his hand-held little appeal. The group of men he was with laughed and slapped each other on the back, absorbed in their stories as his mind wandered.

His friend, Pyotr, had dragged him away for drinks on the last night before term started, continuing his mission to turn him into a social butterfly. Though he smiled and laughed when appropriate, he longed to get away from a crowd, preferring smaller groups and less noise.

After completing his undergraduate studies in

Yekaterinburg, he was glad to be home. Over the past four years, he had returned home only during the summer months, since the distance had been too great to travel for shorter visits. That year, he'd spent the summer with his family and moved into his dorm room yesterday.

It had been hard on him—he hadn't wanted to go to school so far away, but his father had insisted. His parents wanted him to become more independent. In his heart, he knew they wanted what was best for him. They hoped it would help ease his fear of abandonment and purge the overwhelming anxiety plaguing him since childhood.

A flash of the strobe light blinded him for a moment, reminding him of another flash from long ago. His mind took him back to that seven-year-old child standing on the sidewalk, waiting for his family to join him. His sister fidgeted in her booster seat as his parents tried unbuckling her. A loud boom shook the ground and knocked him off his feet, followed by the window breaking behind him, showering glass onto his head. Through the ringing in his ears, the smoke billowing around him, he could make out people screaming, babies crying, sirens screeching in the distance. He woke up the next morning in the hospital. His parents and younger sister were gone. A bomb exploded in the restaurant where they'd planned to dine. Memories of his biological parents had faded as years replaced the images of their faces in his mind. The Petrovas took him from the hospital and adopted him, showering him with love.

Shaking the memories from his mind, he gazed around the room. The corners held dark secrets, while the dance floor was bathed in bright red and purple circles from the strobe lights above.

Across the room, on the other side of the dance-floor, someone caught his eye. A woman with wild dark curls tugged on her tight-fitting black dress before climbing up onto the tall barstool. She crossed her legs, revealing a pair of thigh-high stiletto boots. The metallic bracelets on her wrist gleamed.

She seemed out of place. Uncomfortable, even. He couldn't look away, even though he couldn't see her clearly. The dimly lit room left everything in shadows, hues of pink and purple bounced off the walls.

A moment later, another woman wearing an even shorter tight black dress, and even higher-heeled stiletto shoes, joined her with two small glasses. She set them down on the table.

Even from where he sat, it was clear the two women were entirely out of his league.

The first girl lifted her glass and swiftly drank the contents. He couldn't help but be transfixed by her graceful movements. Her laughter floated through the air, and even through the buzz of voices around him, he heard her pretty well. He couldn't be sure, but he got the distinct impression she was watching him as he observed her. He smiled.

More laughter erupted around him. Turning his attention back to his friends, with great effort, he returned his focus to his friends, fighting the urge to glance back at the mesmerizing woman across the bar.

A short time later, he glanced back and noticed the two women were nowhere in sight. *Not like I would approach them if they were still here, anyway.* With a sigh, he drank the last of his vodka.

It cannot be her. It is not possible.

Sergei stopped dead in his tracks at the first glimpse of her profile. How he recognized her, he couldn't say. Her straight hair brushed across her shoulders. She was there in the flesh, only a few feet away, inside a classroom.

He stared from the hallway, stalled on his walk to a different class. *It is her!* But there was little about her that resembled the woman in the club.

Her flushed cheeks came close to the shade of the deep-red sweater she wore. It brought images of fresh Sangria to mind, and his mouth watered for the fruity wine. Her mere presence befuddled him. Frowning, he felt lost. He checked the sign next to the door-frame. *She is a student? Here?* The peal of her laughter through the doorway reached into his heart. There was no mistaking that laugh. Coherent thoughts vanished. He had definitely fallen under her spell.

I have to know who she is. Even if it meant enrolling in a class, he didn't need.

The following week, Sergei found himself sitting in a classical literature class that he hadn't intended to take. He lacked the nerve to speak to her. Each class passed as he observed her from afar. The way she tilted her head to the side and how her face lit up enthralled him. The sound of her giggles was like the melodic rippling of a bubbling brook.

I can't just sit here and stalk her. There was only one option. *Introduce myself. Oh, God.* His stomach lurched with dread. He imagined all the things he would say, and he wondered how to make her see him.

The heat crawled up his neck as her friend's voice floated over to him. The petite French girl had caught him staring. Before he could look away, the mystery girl's eyes met his. A spark traveled down his spine, linking him to her. His breath caught in his throat. He rubbed his clammy hands across his jeans.

What is wrong with me? Why does she affect me like this?

"Class dismissed," the professor said, finally. Moments later, people were talking and rushing past him. As she walked out the door and away from him, a sweet scent lingered behind. His pulse roared in his ears.

Sergei's friend, Pyotr, elbowed him, pulling him from his thoughts of her.

"Come on, lover boy, let us get out of here."

"Funny."

"Are you planning on talking to her before the end of the year?" His friend made kissy noises and laughed.

"Who?"

Pyotr cocked a brow as he smirked.

Sergei shifted in the seat. His knees pressed up against the underside of the desk and the scarred wooden top seemed unwilling to release him from its clutches as he wrestled his way free.

"I plan to talk to her."

"But this year is the question. She will get away if you do not move faster."

"She is not a stray cat."

Pyotr's smirk remained in place. "No, she is a beauty, though, and I am sure you are not the only guy who fancies her."

Sergei nodded. *No kidding.* His stomach flopped. He couldn't argue that point.

"Well, then?" Pyotr said.

"Do not be a pest. I will talk to her next week."

Pyotr gave him a knowing look, reminding Sergei of his friend's shock when he appeared in the class a few weeks after the start of the term.

Sergei had tried in vain to explain the situation and the woman who had taken him by surprise.

Pyotr had been amused.

He had never expected to see her again. And

then, suddenly, she was there—passing through the corridor, bending over to retrieve a pen from the floor. Her hair slid across her face before she tucked it behind her ear. It was such a fluid thing, yet so sensual. As he redirected his path toward her, someone grabbed her arm and pulled her into the classroom. But her laughter echoed through the hall behind her. By the time he reached the doorway, she was on the other side of the room, seated, and deep in conversation with the other woman from that night. He was drawn to her in ways he couldn't explain. The sheer power of the magnetic attraction left him stunned, and he soon signed up for Literature 101. The following week, he bumped into Pyotr as he entered the classroom for the first time.

He watched her during the lectures, even maneuvering his seat to get the perfect view without being caught. He listened to her soft voice as she answered the professor's questions or asked her own. He just needed to gather the nerve to talk to her.

When she walked by him, the scent of her sweet, fruity shampoo filled his nose.

Shaking his head, he grabbed his bag from the floor, and the two men headed into the hall.

Years of having a singular focus on his studies left him ill-prepared for the sudden onslaught of emotions and the physical pull he felt for the woman. His brother Viktor's warnings from secondary school rattled in the back of his mind—some warnings he saw little reason to listen to because he couldn't imagine letting her slip away. Others, like the time Viktor once told him, "You will see. One day, a woman will cross your path and leave you breathless," struck closer to home. *And now she had.*

CHAPTER 4

Admirers

Addison

The term started in a whirlwind.

Addison hardly noticed as summer slid into autumn. Classes filled her days, and exhaustive study sessions took up each night, so much so that she was surprised to see her calendar said it was nearly the end of November. Taking a moment from her homework, she opened her computer to catch up on emails. The most recent displayed Tandy's typical impatience. In fairness, her note had been sitting in her inbox for a few days, but her mother never respected that she might have other obligations. She read the message begrudgingly.

Addison,
You haven't called me or responded to my last two

emails. You've already been gone two months. If you don't write to me soon, I'm going to call your school.
Mom

A tinge of guilt slipped in, but with classes in full swing, she lacked the energy to respond to her mother. The previous emails had been brief—nothing about her sisters, nothing specific at all—just random missives, nothing requiring immediate attention. Firing off a quick email saying she was fine and busy with classes, she shut down her laptop and sighed. She needed to get to class.

EXHAUSTED FROM ANOTHER LONG DAY, IT CAME AS A welcome reprieve when her literature professor dismissed class early. Addison stood, stuffing her laptop and notebooks into her bag. As papers slid off her desk onto the floor, her roommate leaned over and whispered to her.

"Looks like you have an admirer," Sophie said.

Addison's head popped up.

"Don't look now."

Addison scanned the room and caught the eye of a broad-shouldered man peeking in their direction over his books three rows to the left behind her. His gaze felt like a gentle caress. He looked familiar and his blush made her insides dance, so she offered him a small smile. She'd never noticed him in class before, which was a surprise considering those dimples and soft brown eyes. They made for a handsome package.

"Stop staring. You're being obvious." Sophie shook her head.

Addison smiled again at the dark-haired man, then turned and stuck her tongue out at her friend. Her hair masked her face, so hopefully, only her friend was on the receiving end of her unladylike behavior.

Sophie roared with laughter as she held out Addison's runaway papers.

Addison grabbed them out of Sophie's hand and stuffed them into her bag. A quick glance up. Heat filled her cheeks as the man peeked at her with a shy smile.

There was something about his smile.

After she shrugged into her jacket, she followed Sophie to the door, her shoulders slumped from the heavy bag. She was spent, grateful to have finished her last class for the day. She needed to go back to her dorm and send a more thorough note to her mom. They would celebrate Thanksgiving in a few days, and her mother would be furious if she delayed much longer.

THE DAYS BLURRED TOGETHER, AND THE WEATHER WAS getting colder. Seated in their usual spots in literature class, shivering, Addison wished she wasn't so close to the door.

Sophie nudged her. "He's watching you again."

Addison groaned. "You make it sound so sinister."

"Or romantic," her friend replied airily.

"You're so French."

Sophie giggled. "*Oui*, we French certainly know about love." She batted her eyelashes and waved her long, delicate hands in the air.

Addison swatted a rolled-up paper in her friend's direction, missing her by inches as Sophie leaned away.

The professor walked in, and class began, cutting off any further playfulness.

Ninety minutes later, she stuffed her notes into her book bag and stood. Glancing up, her admirer wasn't in his previous seat. *Damn, he's not here.* She rolled her eyes. *And so, what if he was? Not like I've got time for a boyfriend, right?* Distracted by his absence, and her internal monologue, she trudged behind Sophie, looking down at her boots, and bumped hard into an immovable object.

It wasn't an actual wall. Though he was indeed big enough to qualify. Looking up quickly, Addison stumbled back, the weight of her bag pulling her down as muscular arms shot out to steady her.

"Sorry," a thick Russian-accented husky voice said.

"It was my fault," Addison stammered, glancing

away as heat rose in her chest, crawled up her neck, and filled her cheeks. *Smooth, Addy, real smooth.*

"*Amerikanski?*"

Addison nodded.

His eyes sparkled as he smiled. "I wanted to ask for your help." He shuffled to the side of the door as Sophie came back in.

"Oh." Sophie grinned impishly.

The man turned to her friend and stuck his hand out. "Sergei."

"Sophie. And this is my friend, Addison."

"Nice to meet you… I am having a difficult time in class," he said abruptly.

Addison smiled softly as she glanced at Sophie. She could almost see the gears turning behind her roommate's gleaming eyes. Matchmaking? *Not on my watch.*

"Sophie could tutor you," Addison replied quickly. "She's brilliant. And she speaks Russian better than I do." While there was this small nagging feeling in her stomach at the fact that she was giving up the chance to get to know him, he was far better off with Sophie.

"*Da?*" Sergei's eyebrow rose as he turned to Sophie.

Out of the corner of her eye, she saw Sergei's shoulders slump slightly as he faced her friend.

"Hmm. Sure." Sophie twisted a piece of hair around her finger.

"Where should we meet?" he asked.

"The Chaykhana is usually quiet in the afternoons."

"*Da.*" Sergei bobbed his head.

"Tomorrow at four?"

Sergei bobbed his head again. "*Da.*"

"I'll see you then."

"Tomorrow. Four. Chaykhana." Sergei mumbled to himself as he backed out through the door.

When he was just out of hearing range, Sophie huffed, "What did you do that for?"

"Do what?" Addison pulled the fur collar of her coat tighter around her neck.

"He's been staring at you for weeks."

"It was probably you he was looking at," she retorted blithely.

Sophie let out a string of expletives in rapid French that would make a sailor blush.

Though Addison wasn't exactly fluent, she understood enough.

Her friend's face twisted into a grimace as she stared at Addison. "You should be the one studying with him."

Addison shook her head. "It makes more sense for you to tutor him."

"How can you not see his interest in you?" Sophie's voice held a note of incredulity, making the heat rise in Addison's cheeks.

"I'm here to study, not meet a man."

That wicked glint was back in Sophie's eyes. "Ha!

He'll be asking you out by the end of the month. C'est vraie!" Sophie's conviction, with her strong comment "this is true" at the end driving her point home, almost shook Addison's resolve.

"You're positively diabolical."

"I try." Sophie's wide, toothy grin had Addison shaking her head.

Addison shifted her book bag on her shoulder and headed out the door, this time making it through the frame and into the long, narrow hallway.

Sophie spent the entire walk back to their dorm trying to convince her that his interest was in her, and she should study with him.

Addison refused to give in. She was there to study, not get involved, despite how attracted she was to Sergei. After they settled back in their room, Addison typed up a longer note to her mother while Sophie showered.

Hi Mama,

Sorry I haven't written more often. My roommate, Sophie, is from France. She's great and funny. School is much harder than I expected. The classes are tough here, so I need to focus on keeping up with my studies. I have classes every day and then study in groups most nights. I love and miss you all. Kiss the girls for me.

Love,

Addy

Emailing her mother reminded her of what happened when sidetracked from her responsibilities. If Mama had been in her shoes, she would have been soaking up every ounce of Sergei's attention. Which is precisely why she offered Sophie up to study with him. She was better off keeping her mind on her classes because she didn't want to end up like Tandy, on her fourth husband, with children from each.

CHAPTER 5

Friendly Interrogatories

Sergei

Sergei waited patiently for Sophie at a table in the back of the coffee shop. His materials spread across the table as he watched for her like usual. She had apologized the first few times until she admitted she was always late, and she was unlikely to change. He had laughed at how she was upfront about her tardiness, and was honest, without providing excuses. He appreciated her frankness and could respect her lack of punctuality.

He enjoyed his coffee as he considered what to ask her. Their conversations were as much about life as they were about their literature class. She was a treasure trove of information about her friend, too.

As he scribbled questions on the pad in front of

him, Sophie arrived with a whoosh of air and a soft floral scent mixed with sandalwood.

"*Allo.*" She dropped her bags on the chair across from him and slid into the seat beside it, facing him diagonally.

"*Bonjour.*"

She smiled. "Shall we speak Russian, French, or English today?"

"We could try German," Sergei said.

"*Non.* I've reached my limit."

Sergei grinned. "I have a feeling it will be a blend of the three like usual."

Sophie giggled.

"Where should we start?" Sergei asked.

Sophie looked up from her bag, her notebooks in her hand. "We should focus on comparing Dostoyevsky's works."

Sergei nodded, and after he flipped over the page with his questions, he created a list of the previously read books by the author. A few moments later, he glanced up to see her watching him. She had a twinkle in her eye. "*Da?*"

"I was wondering what questions you are going to ask me today."

"What should I ask?"

Sophie shrugged. Her face held a mysterious grin.

"Has she asked about me?"

"*Non.*" Sophie shook her head.

"I do not think she likes me." Sergei's gaze dropped to the table.

"She does. She's just stubborn."

Sergei blew out his breath. "What do I do? How do I make her see?"

"Patience, *mon ami*. That is all you can do. Be patient."

Sergei nodded. "I try."

"I know."

Their papers shoved aside as he pulled out a list of questions about Addison. The page was a mess of handwritten notes and scribbles with crossed-out questions Sophie answered to the best of her ability, and stars next to ones that she could not.

"How long is she planning to stay in Saint Petersburg?" he asked.

"As far as I know, she's here for the school year, like me."

"What other classes is she in?"

Sophie bit her lip. "Hmm. The Russian Literature class with us both."

Sergei scrawled notes on his paper as she spoke. Trying to piece together her schedule.

"I think she's in an anthropology class."

He wrote that down, too.

"And we take a horticulture class together on Fridays."

"Do you take all the same classes?"

"Only the two. I'm studying animal science. She's more plant science."

"So, her week is full?" Sergei said.

"From what I've seen, all she does is study." Sophie let out an exaggerated sigh.

Sergei laughed. "You say this as a bad thing?"

"We are young. We should have fun."

"To study is good, too."

Sophie rolled her eyes at him. "Not you, too?"

He laughed harder.

"So, Mr. Smarty-Pants, what were you doing in the club that night if all you do is study?"

"Exactly."

Sophie squinted her eyes at him. "Exactly what?"

"I study too much. My friends decided I needed to go out before the term started. So, I did."

"We may have to try that to get the two of you together."

"Do you think she will go?" Sergei sipped his coffee.

"I honestly don't know. I had to beg her to come with me that night as well."

Sergei sat back in his chair and blew out a long breath. "Does she know it was me at the club?"

"I don't think so. I never thought to mention it."

"Ah. Maybe that is why she is distant."

"Don't worry. I'll figure something out to get her to study with us next week, maybe invite some people from class to pretend it's a study group," Sophie said as she pulled her notes back in front of her.

Sergei pursed his lips and gave her a wan smile. *Waiting is so hard.*

The rest of the afternoon they spent quietly reading the assigned book, Fyodor Dostoyevsky's *The Idiot*, and working on their reports. It was all he could do to keep his frustration in check.

Now I remember why I do not date.

CHAPTER 6

Defenses
Worn Thin

Addison

Addison glanced up and caught Sergei staring in her direction. *Again?* When she lifted her face toward him, he turned away. She hadn't caught his eye since that class weeks ago. Addison had the impression he was upset with her, but she ignored it. *Is he angry I didn't volunteer to study with him?* Still convinced he was interested in something more than books, Addison continued to keep him at a distance. Besides, Sophie would be an excellent tutor, and she was happy she'd sidestepped any attempt at matchmaking by her quirky roommate.

Weeks passed, and she put it out of her mind.

"He's really smart," Sophie said.

"Who?" Addison asked distractedly, thinking of the paper they were working on.

"Sergei."

"Oh, yeah? That's good."

Sophie nudged her. "You should come and study with us."

"He doesn't need two tutors," Addison said.

"*Non*, but you could still study with us." Sophie rolled her eyes. "Like a study group."

"Are you meeting tomorrow?"

"Yes. So, you'll come?"

Addison relented. "I guess." *It should be safe enough to study together.*

Sophie cried out in glee.

THE NEXT MORNING, ADDISON WOKE TO AN EMPTY dorm room. She drank her coffee and dressed with care, not wanting to appear too dressed up for her meeting with Sergei that afternoon, but she couldn't help wanting to look her best.

She compromised with black jeans and a pullover sweater. She zipped up her boots and headed out the door, ignoring the queasiness gurgling within. The coffee, mixed with her nerves, upset her stomach.

Her classes barely held her attention, and she looked forward to the end of the day. Her nerves hummed, and her skin tingled every time she checked her wristwatch. She was sure her classmates could see her eagerness, as she was practically floating by the time class dismissed, and she headed over to the coffee shop.

Addison shivered when the warmth hit her face as she stepped into the café. The air outside had been crisp and sweet, cleansed from a brief bout of snow the night before. The aroma of Turkish coffee filled her nose, a bittersweet combination of cardamom and cinnamon, different from the Arabica beans at home. The coffee machine dripped a fresh brew from the counter against the wall. Yelena, the afternoon barista, wiped the counter down while a song by Jewel blared from the speakers, filling the room with her ballad.

A quick glance around the room showed most of the tables were empty; only a couple of people were in the café. He wasn't there. Her breath caught in her throat. That she was eager to see him disturbed her. *It's just a study date, right? No, not a date. A meeting. A study meeting.* But what if he'd canceled? Or changed his mind? And where was Sophie? Self-doubt raced through her mind as she chose a table by the window. *What the hell is wrong with me?* As she pulled out her laptop and her notepads, and set them on the surface, it was clear she was more excited about meeting him than she'd allowed herself to think. She fidgeted with her book bag as she set it under her chair.

Sergei strolled in just as she flipped open the lid to her computer.

Her heart somersaulted. She drew in a quick

breath in an attempt to appear less ruffled than she was.

He slid into the chair opposite her and dropped his bag on the floor. The bag thudded as it met the linoleum. "Hi." The word came out as a croak.

She smiled at his flushed face and his hair in wild disarray.

Addison smiled. It was a small measure of comfort to see she wasn't the only one nervous. "Hello. I'm glad you came."

Sergei gave her a quizzical glance. "You doubted?"

"I did. Sorry."

He laughed. A good, hearty laugh that made his eyes glisten. "I was afraid you would not come either."

"I wouldn't have missed it."

"Really?" he asked hopefully.

Addison glanced away, trying to cover her blunder. "I'm not sure where Sophie is."

Sergei shook his head, indicating he didn't know either. He pulled his computer from his bag and set up his side of the table.

"Should we get coffee?"

"*Da.*"

They stood at the same time, and Sergei waited for her to pass before moving in behind her. At the counter, they ordered their coffee. A plain black drip for him, a white chocolate mocha for her. After they returned to their seats, Sergei looked across the table at her and blushed.

"I am not so good in these kinds of classes," he said. His brow creased as he looked away.

"Why did you sign up then?" Addison asked. She loved reading and writing classes, often taking them as electives whenever they were available.

"To impress a girl."

Addison laughed. "That's sweet, but not very practical." Her thoughts immediately strayed to Sophie, wondering why she wasn't there. She'd called her cell phone on the walk over, but the call had gone straight to voicemail.

Sergei shrugged. "I know. She took my breath away when I saw her walking into that class. I just had to get to know her better."

Addison laughed again. He was such a romantic, an excellent match for Sophie. The hollow feeling in her gut that followed was unexplainable. "How's that working out for you?"

Sergei glanced down at the table, avoiding her gaze. "I think it is going well so far." His voice was so low she almost didn't hear him.

She stopped laughing and stared at him. *Is he referring to me?* Sucking in her breath, she continued to stare at him. He still hadn't looked up at her. Sophie had said he was interested, but she had put little stock in her roommate's romantic notions before.

"Is that why you started the class late?" The

aroma of the coffee messed with her nerves, making her stomach lurch.

"*Da.*"

Addison's heart quivered in her chest, and the butterflies flitted around. She pushed the other thoughts from her mind. *Focus, damn it! I'm here to study, not flirt. I will not follow in Mama's footsteps.* Addison blinked hard and then gave Sergei her full attention.

"So, what do you like best about the classics? Instead of the current novels on the New York Times Bestseller list?" he asked.

"I enjoy both. The classics remind me of a world before my time. Where traditions reigned, where love was pure, where society's expectations were clear."

"Interesting." Sergei took a sip of his coffee.

"I read classic romance and classical mysteries. And I read today's modern mysteries to compare them."

"But you do not compare the romances?" His question was genuine.

"The romances are impossible to compare. Today's novels are full of touching and illicit sex."

Sergei choked on his coffee. His cheeks reddened, and his hand trembled as drops of coffee splashed from the cup.

"Sorry," she said.

"The classics have sex, too." He dabbed at his hand and smiled.

"Yes, but think of Jane Austen. *Pride and Prejudice.*

It's full of stolen glances and dances that were chaper-oned by the entire community. They were huge, family-inclusive, neighbor-oriented events."

Sergei nodded.

"The way they spoke, the way they interacted, they had to fall in love with each other while virtually never having been alone with each other. They had to get to know each other's minds and temperament. Even each other's families."

"We still do that today." He peered at her over his steaming cup.

"Do what?" Heat rushed to her face.

"Get to know each other, learn each other's minds."

"True, but today's fiction doesn't give much time for that in its pages. Not that I'm complaining. I'm down for a great love story, no matter the generation."

"So, you are a romantic, too?"

"I don't think I'm in your league," Addison said bluntly.

Sergei's face fell. "I do not understand."

"I don't think I'm romantic enough to study a subject that doesn't interest me, just to meet a guy."

Sergei grinned, his previously creased brow and sad expression gone. "I never said I was not inter-ested. Just that I am not so good at it. I am better in science and math classes."

"Fair enough. So, let's see if we can change that."

Ignoring the blood racing through her veins, she determined to keep her attention on the assignment.

She flipped through the pages of the book. The assignment was to write a report based on the author's prose. Addison was familiar with Dostoyevsky's work; she was even developing a soft spot for the Russian writer.

They exchanged their first drafts and worked in silence for the rest of the afternoon. Addison caught Sergei stealing glances at her and it made the butterflies in her stomach riot. He affected her more than she wanted to admit, even to herself. She wasn't impulsive like her mother; instead, she was more like Cassie. When she married, there would be the type of connection her father had with her stepmother. A love to build on—something that would stand the test of time and weather all hardships. A relationship built on mutual respect and shared dreams, not simply a marriage of duty based on raising children. She lowered her head and, with a deep breath, forced herself to concentrate on the computer screen. *A short-lived, long-distance romance is the last thing I need. No matter how drawn to him I may be.* She strived to hold that thought through the rest of their study meeting.

CHAPTER 7

The Perfect Roadblocks

Sergei

What a woman!

Chills crawled down Sergei's spine. The woman across from him was smart and beautiful, with the voice of an angel. That moment of first seeing her in the club sitting alone in the dark, then two weeks later catching sight of her while passing through the corridor, had stunned him. His breath caught in his throat as he watched her. Though disappointed when she suggested her friend tutor him, he accepted it and plied Sophie with questions about her roommate each time they met. It had taken three more weeks, and now she sat at the table across from him. *She is remarkable.*

Things were not going as smoothly as he wanted,

but he hoped they were on the right track. He did not know for sure since this was his first attempt at romance.

Sergei smiled as Addison put away her notes. "Would you like to go to dinner?" he asked.

Addison's eyes grew wide. "I'm sorry, I can't. I already have plans."

Sergei expelled the air from his lungs. "Of course, I understand."

"Maybe some other time," she said.

Sergei beamed. "*Da.* That would be nice."

"Okay, I'll see you next week in class."

"Oh. *Da,* I will see you then."

Addison stood and pulled her backpack over her shoulder before walking out of the coffee shop.

Sergei sat there for a moment. He had not expected her to leave so quickly. She had turned him down for dinner before he could offer to walk her back to her dorm. He was confused. They had such a pleasant afternoon studying, and he was sure she would have enjoyed dinner afterward.

I must be doing something wrong. Addison pushed him away each time he moved in her direction. Any time he mentioned something not directly related to studying, she immediately redirected his attention to the assignment.

There was no mistaking his inexperience in the world of women. Having never dated, or spend much time outside of academic pursuits to socialize, he now found himself unprepared for her easy rejection.

He briefly contemplated calling his brother, Viktor, but quickly pushed those thoughts aside. He would have to wade through this new experience on his own, as inept as he may be.

Staring at his empty coffee cup, he considered going back to his dorm until his stomach growled, reminding him it was empty. No longer in the mood for a heavy meal, he ordered a sandwich to go before cleaning up his papers and putting everything away in his book bag.

Back in his dorm room, Sergei sat on his bed, the unwrapped sandwich in his lap, when Pyotr walked in.

"What do you have there?"

"Dinner."

"Enough for two?" Pyotr grabbed a chair and flipped it around, straddling it to face Sergei on the bed.

"*Da.*" Sergei handed over half of the sandwich.

"Have you talked to the girl?"

The girl. She is a woman. A wonderful angel of a woman.

"I studied with her today."

A loud whooping sound came out of Pyotr as he choked on the half-chewed bite of sandwich in his mouth. "I had my doubts."

Sergei glared at his friend, which only made Pyotr laugh harder.

"So, what are you doing here, eating a sandwich in your room?" Pyotr asked.

"I invited her to dinner, but she turned me down."

"Ouch."

"*Da*."

"Are you sure she is worth it?" Pyotr asked, then finished his half of the sandwich in two bites.

"She is. I am just not so sure she thinks I am worth it."

Pyotr tilted his head as he stared back at him. "So, when do you see her again?"

"Not until class next week."

"That is tough. Are you going to eat that?" Pyotr motioned to the half-eaten sandwich in Sergei's hand.

He looked down at his barely touched sandwich. "*Nyet*, you want it?" His appetite had deserted him as quickly as his optimism about Addison had.

Pyotr didn't even pause before taking the sandwich out of his hand and stuffing it into his mouth.

While his friend ate, Sergei imagined how differently his meal could have turned out. Beautiful Addison, seated across from him, smiling—certainly using better manners than Pyotr displayed as he chomped down the sandwich like a hog.

Despite his eating habits, Pyotr was right. He had to wait another week to see Addison again. Wait, wait, wait. Sophie told him to be patient, but for how long?

CHAPTER 8

A Growing Attraction

Addison

A week later, Addison agreed to study with Sergei again. Not to pursue him, she reminded herself, but to assist him on his assignment, of course. She offered to meet him at the library for more quality studying time. Being a Saturday morning, the library was almost empty. Most of the students congregated in the coffee shops surrounding the university when not in class.

Settling into the hard, tall-backed wooden chairs, she turned on one of the small lamps on the desk. The light illuminated a tiny circle on the surface. Small square windows tucked into the tops of the walls did little to help the darkened room. Soaring ceilings gave the room a sense of being an ancient cathedral, not a modern university library. Leather-bound books filled the shelves, silently condemning her lack of appreciation. Dust particles floated in the streams of light from the tall windows. It gave the air a thick, musty smell.

Addison wasn't fond of the campus library, with its stuffy, oppressive atmosphere and a librarian, who ruled the room with an iron fist. There was no eating or drinking allowed, and only the softest of whispers tolerated. Most of the students on campus only used the library when they needed a specific book for their research or assignments. However, she thought this location would be perfect to keep them focused on their schoolwork and less on personal conversations.

Addison's books and papers covered the surface of the table in a haphazard mess.

When Sergei arrived, he let his bag slide to the floor as he pulled the heavy chair out from under the table, scraping it against the hardwood floors. With a heavy sigh, he plopped down in the seat next to her. He was out of breath.

She laughed.

"*Shhh!*" The tight-lipped librarian directed a shrill hiss at them from across the room.

Addison grinned as she began pulling her papers from his area of the table.

Sergei's eyes widened.

Addison bit her knuckle to halt the giggles. Expulsion from the library wouldn't be a smart move.

The sounds coming from their laptops as they

powered up got them a stern look from the librarian. Sergei went in search of the reference books they needed for their papers while she read his latest draft. When he returned, the librarian was not far behind; a scowl etched on her face.

The librarian kept her eagle eye on them all morning. Every few minutes, she prowled around the room, making a pass near their table. Laughter welled up within Addison each time. Though they spoke little, and only in the lowest of whispers, there was little doubt the librarian had seemingly not forgiven their earlier transgressions.

Addison's stomach gurgled. Sergei's head shot up as he stared at her, and she couldn't fight the laughter. "Sorry. I skipped breakfast."

"I can hear that."

"Shush!" the librarian said.

Sergei bit his lip.

"Are you hungry?" she asked.

"Famished."

"Me, too."

They cleared their workstations as quickly as they dared. Addison was afraid the librarian would have a coronary if they made any more noise. Sergei dropped off the reference books on their way out.

Her stomach let out another sound, and she winced. *So much for sticking to the books, huh?* She sighed and followed Sergei. *Hey, a girl's gotta eat. Still doesn't mean this is a date; we'll multitask. Eat and work on our reports.*

They trudged across campus to *Chaykhana*, the rain-soaked ground squishing beneath their boots. The icy air was sharp as it scraped through her nose, throat, and lungs. It was only a little less painful on its way out, with white puffs forming with each exhale. Despite the cold, the brief trek didn't seem to dampen the heat blooming inside of her. There was an unexplainable pull towards Sergei, who walked slightly behind and beside her.

Once inside, she took in the warm air. It was a relief to shed her heavy, sodden parka and drape it on the coat tree.

Sergei did the same before he walked to an empty table across the room. They set up their computers again and pushed them aside. When they had ordered food and had cups of hot coffee between their fingers, Sergei looked at her eagerly.

"What is your major?" he asked.

"Botanical and environmental sciences."

"Not literature?"

Addison grinned. "Dual major in the two sciences, and a minor in literature."

"An interesting combination."

"I've always loved flowers and plants. Growing up, I had an amazing green thumb, so this direction felt right. Becoming a botanist seems like a natural path."

"And the literature?"

"I love to read. It was a great escape as a child."

"I have always been interested in more theoretical science, like physics."

"My family scoffed at my choice of studies, but this is where my heart is." She stole a quick glance at him. Would he, too, ridicule her passion and her academic focus? Her heart skipped a beat as he smiled at her. It was nice to talk to him. She didn't have to ready her defenses like she did with her mother. *Ouch.* It hurt to admit that, even to herself.

They ate sandwiches and drank copious amounts of Turkish coffee while working on their reports for most of the afternoon. After three hours, Sergei stretched his arms and yawned.

"Would you be interested in a walk?"

"It's freezing outside." An involuntary shiver wracked her body.

"We can walk the halls," he offered instantly.

She straightened in her seat, her back protesting the hours of inactivity while studying. *Moving around would be nice.* "That sounds good." Addison packed up her laptop and books while Sergei cleared off their table.

The bitter weather discouraged any desire to linger outside, so they strolled through the long hallways inside the campus. The temperature inside wasn't much warmer, though. Even with all the warnings, nothing could possibly prepare someone for a Russian winter. Russia was a world of its own. As much as Addison hated the cold and the wet, sticky snow, her excitement at spending a year there outstripped it all. Dreaming of visiting Russia often as a child, she hadn't hesitated to sign up when her professor suggested it. She only regretted her decision when the cold made it hurt to breathe. She huddled in her parka and stuffed her gloved hands into her pockets.

As they walked, Sergei was full of information and funny anecdotes about the paintings, statues, and the people they represented.

"See this bump on his nose?" He pointed to the bust of a man on a pedestal in front of her.

"Yes, it's very faint."

"They had to file off the mole after the sculpture was done."

"You're kidding."

"I am." Blushing, he glanced away.

Addison laughed, puffs of air coming out of her. Sergei's sense of humor was infectious. Try as she might to resist, she was drawn to him like a moth to a flame. She felt safe with him, this stranger in a strange land.

Russia was turning out even better than she'd imagined. The people, the food, the culture—it all amazed her. There was an urge to pinch herself every once in a while, just to make sure she was actually there. And then there was Sergei.

Glancing up at him, his gaze pierced her for a

moment before he smiled and looked away. The way he stared at her made her nervous. He was an unusual combination of shy introvert and abundant overconfidence. The way he was so sure of himself one moment, yet quiet and timid at other times, intrigued her. *So, he's intrigued by me, too. But so, what?* Looking away, she mentally flogged herself. *A romance is the last thing I need.*

"Ruble for your thoughts?" he asked.

"Is that all they're worth to you?" The words tumbled out, and she glanced away to avoid his eyes.

Sergei shrugged. "*Nyet*, but that is all I probably have in my pockets."

"Ah, I see." She smiled. Their banter was preferable to staying in her dorm room, studying by herself.

"Unless you'll consider dinner proper payment." Sergei grinned at her again.

Addison struggled with the conflicting thoughts in her head. The man fascinated a part of her, while a looping dialogue in her mother's voice played in the background, telling her that getting involved with a foreign man was a mistake. She could just hear her now. *He's a Communist. He doesn't speak clear English.* Addison fought the urge to roll her eyes at the commentary Mama would make if she saw her at that moment, strolling with abandon.

"Do you eat Greek?" Sergei asked.

"Yes."

"There is a nice place at the end of the street."

Addison nodded. She was familiar with that restaurant.

It's just dinner. Not a date.

It took every ounce of strength to ignore her raging thoughts and focus only on Sergei as they walked down the block of cafes that offered a wide range of choices. The daylight faded as Addison admired the dancing shadows against the buildings.

The warm air greeted her with feather-light caresses to her frozen skin. The little shop was quiet when they entered, as it was before the usual dinner hour.

As they sat, Addison slipped off her coat and draped it on the back of the chair while Sergei spoke with the waiter.

"A bottle of your Pinot Noir and a dish of hummus, please," Sergei stated. The waiter nodded and left to put in his request.

They perused the menu while they waited for the wine. Addison had frequented the establishment in the past. It wasn't as foreign to her as everything else around her, so when feeling homesick or over-whelmed, she came in, and after a glass of wine and dinner, she felt like herself again. The warm atmosphere with the murals of the Greek islands on the walls, the low lighting, and the usually crowded tables gave her a sense of inclusion. It reminded her of the Greek restaurant at home her father and Cassie frequented. I couldn't think of them and not miss them.

I wonder how the Hobbits are doing?

Is Eric still around Mama's?

How is Savi holding up? I need to check my emails.

Her guilt trip disappeared when the waiter returned with their wine and appetizer. After they placed their order, Addison sat back as Sergei poured them a glass of wine. The fresh pita bread was warm in her fingers as she breathed in the scent of garlic hummus, then popped the piece into her mouth. The hummus was gritty on her tongue.

"What is your favorite color?" he asked.

"Lilac."

"That is very specific."

"I like the pastel shades of most colors best. Purple is my favorite overall."

He nodded.

"And yours?"

"Red."

"Just red. Not a specific hue?" she teased.

"Ruby."

"Why Ruby?"

"The first time I watched *The Wizard of Oz* as a child, her ruby red shoes fascinated me."

"Dorothy's shoes. Really?" Addison grinned.

"We did not have a television at home in Germany when I was young. So, I loved to spend my free time at my classmate Viktor's house. One evening, the Petrova family sat down and watched the movie. I remember the shiny shoes."

She'd never met a man who ever noticed shoes before. Her father only noticed how many shoes her stepmother had because of the room they took up in the closet. And her stepfather only noticed things because of the money her mother spent without his approval. The image in her mind of a little boy infatuated with colored shoes warmed her heart. *Knock it off. Getting sappy over shoes is ridiculous.*

Sergei looked up at her. "Do you realize that all of our conversations today have been in Russian?"

"No," Addison said in English.

Sergei laughed. "You speak it quite well when you are relaxed and not thinking too hard."

He was right. She was speaking his language without realizing it. The more time spent with him, the more comfortable she became. *Crap. Not good. Not good at all.*

After dinner, Sergei walked her back to her dorm. At the main entrance, her whole body froze as he leaned into her. She started to close her eyes for a kiss when he reached down and took her hand in his. He brought it up and placed a chaste kiss on the back of her glove.

"Goodnight."

She swallowed the lump in her throat. "Night. Thanks for dinner."

Addison grinned as he turned and walked away,

his body huddled into itself as he walked back to his dorm. Sergei was old-fashioned and a gentleman. In the time she'd known him, he'd never tried to steal a kiss, giving only shy glances when he thought she couldn't see. He never made inappropriate comments or rude gestures when she was around. It was as if he had popped out fully formed from a page from Mr. Darcy's storyline. He certainly was dashingly handsome enough. A part of her liked him more than expected. The other part of her instinctively knew it was a dangerous game to play. It would be far easier if he behaved like less of a gentleman. If he were a typical bad boy, she could walk away, ignoring any interest she might harbor. She had no patience for immature boys trying to steal kisses or simply amuse themselves with her. But faced with men like her father, someone who exuded stability and security, a part of her wondered if maybe things could be different for her. Unlike the men her mother habitually married, Sergei reminded her of a cliff overlooking the sea. It took its daily beating in its quiet, subtle way, waiting for the raging sea to calm its fit of temper. Welcoming the chance to soothe its frothy tantrum. For her, this was worse. She wasn't sure she could walk away if she needed to. The calm, steady character she sensed in him called to her.

After her shower, Addison crawled into bed and stared at the ceiling. Sophie came in, full of laughter and questions and giddy, but she didn't seem to be inebriated.

"You missed a good party. What were you doing?" Sophie dropped her purse onto the chair near her bed.

"We studied in the afternoon, and then we had an early dinner at Papachino's before he walked me home."

"Did he kiss you?" Sophie's voice was wistful.

"My hand."

"Really? How proper." Sophie giggled.

"He is," she replied defensively.

"Well, maybe he will next time. There will be a next time, right?" Sophie dropped her high-heeled boots onto the floor with a thud.

"I think so. We set nothing up, but I hope so."

"Ah, young love." Sophie sighed. She slid her wrinkled black pencil skirt down next to her boots. Her lacy black bra followed from under her bright red top, leaving her standing there in only a T-shirt and panties.

Grinning, Addison picked up one of the square throw pillows on her bed and tossed it at her. "You set this whole thing up; that's why you didn't show last week. You louse!"

Sophie caught it in midair with one hand, hugging it to her chest, then collapsed onto her bed in a fit of giggles. "*Oui*. He is interested in you, not me. I told you that."

Addison shook her head and laughed before she rolled onto her side and snuggled deep under her blankets. Sophie crawled into her own bed and turned off the light. She was fast asleep in seconds. Addison's mind whirled with snapshots of Sergei. There was no longer any doubt. She was in over her head and sinking fast. *Pull it together. If you don't, you'll end up married with kids before you know it. Just like Mama.* The voice in her head chastised her for acting like a love-struck teenager, making sleep even harder to attain late into the night.

THOUGH SLEEP HAD BEEN ELUSIVE THE LAST FEW DAYS, she woke excited to see Sergei in class. She dressed in her usual jeans and pullover and swept her hair back in a clip, adding a touch of concealer under her eyes to hide the dark circles lurking there.

The hours sped by while she looked forward to their literature class. Once seated in class, she waited for Sergei to appear. Sophie arrived, dropped into the chair next to hers, and chatted away while Addison continued to seek his familiar face. The bell rang its loud clang, but he was MIA. For weeks, it felt like he was everywhere she looked. After seeing him in class every week, and then agreeing to study together, his absence was a sharp contrast. It hadn't occurred to her to get his phone number since she saw him every week in class, and then the last two days studying together.

The class was excruciatingly slow and couldn't hold her attention. Her thoughts drifted to Sergei. He hadn't mentioned missing class when she saw him last. Though she hadn't asked, either. There was a void, and not just in his empty chair. *Come on, Addison. You're here for class, not for him. Remember?*

The following week she rushed to their literature class, hoping to see him peeking over her textbook every few minutes for a glimpse of his broad shoulders, or mop of dark hair. Even after the bell rang, she continued to seek him out while trying to appear engrossed in reading. She left class feeling dejected, telling herself it was for the best. *Get a grip. There's no time for a romance that will end in a few months, anyway.*

Directing her focus toward the lectures and taking notes seemed a battle of wills, and each day, the chasm in her heart widened even more. Her head told her she shouldn't care, and his absence shouldn't affect her like this, but her heart had developed an agenda of its own.

By the third week, when she had accepted, he was no longer a fixture in her life; she came into class and found him standing by her usual chair, talking to Sophie. Her breath caught in her throat. She had adjusted to seeing his empty chair in class, and suddenly he stood in front of her. A wide grin appeared on his face as she came toward them. Could it be possible? Had he missed seeing her as much as she'd missed him? She shook her head, unwilling to go down that road. *It doesn't matter.*

It was too soon. She barely knew him.

"Hello," Sergei said. His face reddened.

"Hello." Addison's voice came out in a croak.

"I missed the last two classes. May I borrow your notes to catch up?"

Addison nodded, a fierce rejection flowing through her. He hadn't missed her; he just needed her notes. Sophie glowered at her from her seat. "I'll dig them out and give them to you after class," she mumbled.

"Spasibo." Sergei, still smiling, turned, and headed across the room to his usual seat.

"What's with you?" Sophie hissed.

"Nothing. Just wasn't expecting to see him, that's all," Addison said.

"He asked about you."

"He did?" A rush of adrenaline filled her head, making her a little dizzy.

"You act like you haven't even noticed he was gone." Sophie glared at her.

Is she kidding? "I didn't," she replied blithely.

"You certainly didn't look thrilled to see him."

"I was surprised, that's all."

"Well, he was expecting to see you. So, you'd better kiss and make up after class." Sophie gave her a pointed look.

"We don't kiss." The words rushed out before she thought them through. She took in her friend's exasperated expression.

Sophie eyed the ceiling and blew out a long breath. "What am I going to do with you?"

The professor walked in, talking even before he'd reached his podium. He looked disheveled as usual, his hair a wild array of untamed waves. His shirt was untucked, and the cuff of his left pant leg was stuck inside the edge of his sock. Images of the absent-minded professor from the movie *Flubber* sprang to mind, causing her face to split open in a wide grin.

"Shush." Addison glared at her roommate before turning to the teacher and scribbling notes as fast as she could.

A couple of times, the hair on the back of her neck tingled, and a shiver ran down her spine as though being watched. However, every time she stole a glance at Sergei, he was concentrating on the professor's lecture. Their eyes never met. Finally, the class ended, and when she lifted her gaze from her papers, Sergei was standing beside her desk, a lopsided grin plastered on his face. She sucked in a breath.

"Would you like to go for a drink?" he asked.

Addison turned to Sophie, her eyes pleading, but she received no reprieve from her friend. Her stomach dropped as though on a roller coaster. In a way, she was. She had wanted to see him, had missed him.

And yet, she continued to hold herself back at the same time.

"Hmm... okay," Addison said.

"Sophie, you would join us?" Sergei asked. He shuffled his feet; his bag slung over his shoulder, hands deep in his pockets.

"Are you sure?" Sophie's brow bunched as she stared at Addison.

Addison nodded as she glanced up at Sergei.

"Of course," Sergei said.

"I'd be delighted, then."

With a quick nod, he crooked his elbows out from his side, and the women each took an arm.

They crossed campus like that. Arm in arm, tied together, laughing as they headed to the karaoke bar down the street from school. The air stung like sharp needles pricking her skin. Addison shivered and rubbed her arms. Sergei and Sophie seemed impervious to the frigid air as they trudged along. He held the door open and ushered the women inside. Warm air enveloped her like a welcome blanket. The bleating coming from the stage was almost painful to her ears. Strobe lights filled the room with eerie colors, splashing walls, and faces alike with blues, yellows, and reds. This bar was even more uncomfortable than the club she'd gone to the first night with Sophie.

Sergei led them to a small, round table in the corner. It was closer to the stage than she liked, but it was the only empty one. They sat crowded around the small table as a petite, dark-haired server stopped by with a tray full of glasses, not much bigger than a shot glass, and a tall bottle of Stolichnaya.

"Vodka?"

"Please," Sergei said. He glanced in their direction.

Addison and Sophie nodded.

"Three," he said. The server kept her eyes glued to Sergei as she poured out three small glasses. She pressed the first into Sergei's hand. He handed it to Addison. Then the server gave the second to him, and he passed it over to Sophie. When she handed him the third glass, he laid a pile of rubles down on her tray.

"You can keep the change," he said. The server gave him a wide, toothy smile and backed away, her gaze never leaving his face.

He didn't seem to notice her focused attention, instead staring at Addison. He raised his glass and said, "*Tva-jó zda-ró-vye.*"

Sophie lifted her glass and nodded. "To your health."

Addison followed them and held up her glass. Their glasses clinked, and everyone downed their vodka in a single shot.

The music pulsed out of the speakers surrounding them while the singers on the stage rotated in and out, different songs playing. With effort, Addison tuned out

the music and focused her attention on the conversation at their small table. Though not fluent in French
or Russian, she knew enough to follow most general
conversations, which came in handy around Sophie
and Sergei.

"Where have you been hiding?" Sophie asked in
rapid French.

"I was ill. So, my family convinced me to come
home," Sergei responded.

"For the entire week?" Addison was baffled. The
idea of taking a week off school to visit her family was
a foreign concept. She might have considered it to
visit her father and Cassie for peace and T.L.C., but
certainly never her mother if she was hoping for any
R and R.

"Of course. I had not seen them since this
summer. I came from another school farther north, so
I did not visit often. I needed to go home so they
could see for themselves."

"See what?" she asked. Sophie kicked her shin
under the table. Addison glared at her.

"See that I was okay. The twins were worried
about my cold."

"How old are you?" Sophie asked.

"Twins?" Images of Sergei having children filled
her thoughts. A pang of uncertainty reared its ugly
head. The idea that he had children with someone
else gave her an empty feeling in her gut.

"Twenty-three this year," Sergei answered Sophie

first, before turning to Addison. "My youngest siblings. I am the oldest, a few months older than Viktor. Our family is close."

A phone call would've been nice. Addison swallowed hard before nodding. *Stop being ridiculous.* They were just friends, not a couple. She bit her tongue as her anxieties raged within.

"Another drink?" Sophie asked.

"Addison?" Sergei looked at her for her answer.

Addison hesitated before responding. "Sure, one more. I've got to get to bed soon."

Sophie giggled. She often teased Addison about her early nights.

"Okay, one more." Sergei's hand was in the air, beckoning the server. She repeated her process from before, then smiled and sauntered away.

They lifted their glasses up and with another clink. Sergei said, *"Za fstryé-tchoo."*

"To friendship," Sophie repeated in English. With her Russian being far more fluent than Addison's, her translations helped with the slang and common phrases.

Another involuntary shudder coursed through her as the vodka warmed its way to her stomach. She wondered if the sharp taste and heat of the spirits ever improved. In the back of her mind, Addison noted that the conversation had bounced from English, French, and Russian in smooth transitions.

Sergei's company was enjoyable. Addison liked

that he had included Sophie not only in the invitation, but in the conversation as well. Yet the way he spoke French with Sophie gave her pause. She could imagine them as a couple, and that made her heart skip a beat. She hadn't wanted to admit it—and she would die before letting Sophie know how much she had missed him while he was away. But she had. His absence had been like a hole in her heart, tearing wider each day he was away. *I'm going to end up just like Mama. If I'm not careful, everything I've worked for will be derailed. How did I get myself into this mess?*

CHAPTER 9

A Story of Romance

Addison

Exiting the bar, Addison tightened her coat to block out the cold. Sergei shrugged off his leather jacket and wrapped it around her shoulders as he escorted them back to their dormitory.

"I can't take your jacket from you." Her teeth chattered beneath her tightly pressed lips.

"I cannot very well ask for a second date if you freeze to death, now, can I?" he said.

She gave him a sideways glance to see if he was joking, but his face was serious.

"Tha—Thank you," she said. Her body wracked with tremors beneath his heavy coat.

Sergei nodded.

"And what about me?" Sophie laughed.

"Ah, *mademoiselle,* come, we will warm you as well."

Sophie's brow rose as Sergei lifted the edge of his jacket and motioned for her to lean in close to Addison.

Addison lifted her arm, inviting her friend to share the jacket with her, the frosty air biting into her skin. Sophie snuggled into her side and wrapped an arm around her waist. Sergei then draped the jacket over her shoulder and draped his arm around both women, bringing them closer together as the three of them walked as a unit down the path.

Addison's mind couldn't seem to formulate words, and the trembling made it harder to talk, so she just listened to Sergei's and Sophie's easy banter.

When they reached the dorms, Sophie slid from her position and used her key to unlock the main door.

Addison pulled her side of the jacket off and handed it back to him. When his hand touched hers, a jolt of lightning passed through her, and she shivered, though not from the cold air.

As he slid the jacket back on in a single fluid movement, her heart skipped a beat. No matter what he did, he oozed grace and masculinity. She looked away to keep her wits. His closeness took her breath away. The way the scent of his cologne filled her nose muddled her senses.

Sergei took her stiff hands in his warm ones, infusing her limbs with a small amount of heat. An involuntary shiver wracked her body as he kissed the back of her gloved hand like before.

"Study together tomorrow?" he asked.

"I would like that." Addison nodded.

"Goodnight, lovely ladies."

"Goodnight," Addison said.

"Thanks for the drinks," Sophie called out from just inside the building.

He gave a quick bow and then headed into the night.

Addison leaned against the doorjamb for a moment, intoxicated by the way his hips moved as he strolled down the sidewalk. Pulling his collar up around his neck, he zipped up his jacket and stuffed his hands deep into the pockets. Addison sighed as butterflies did a jig in her stomach. Watching him, it was clear he was more affected by the cold than he'd let on, yet he'd still given his jacket to her without hesitation. His presence affected her more than she could admit if the warmth radiating from her belly, was any sign. Shaking her head, she turned and followed Sophie into the building.

THE NEXT DAY, ADDISON AWOKE LONG BEFORE THE alarm went off. Her scattered thoughts had made sleeping difficult. She rolled over and stared at her still-slumbering roommate. Sophie slept like the dead, her breathing measured and regular. Addison envied her.

Sergei was on her mind again. Nothing new. Over the last few weeks, he'd invaded her waking thoughts and dreams. It frustrated her she couldn't get away from him. He was there in person, and when he wasn't, her head filled with thoughts of him. *Am I that hung-up on him? Is this how Mama felt with all her men?*

With a soft sigh, she moved her weary bones to the showers down the hall. The hot spray pounded against her head and shoulders; the steam woke her up and eased the kinks in her neck. Throwing on her robe, she wrapped her wet hair in a towel and wandered back to her room.

Sophie's bleary eyes stared at her from the coffeepot as Addison closed the door behind her with a click. She lifted a cup in Addison's direction.

"Please," Addison said.

Sophie poured the liquid into two oversized mugs before handing one over.

"Thanks." Addison inhaled the steaming brew. It filled her lungs and cleared the cobwebs from her mind.

The sun peeked through the blinds as they sipped their coffee.

In a moment of ridiculous insecurity, Addison faced Sophie. "Are you sure you aren't interested in him?"

"Don't be foolish. He only has eyes for you."

"You're so at ease with each other. I can't help but imagine you as a couple."

"That is because you put me in your place as his study partner."

"I shouldn't be getting involved with anyone."

"We are young. We are free. We should get involved with anyone we fancy." Sophie's hands were a flourish of movement as she spoke, accentuating her words.

"I wish it was that simple."

"It is *mon amie*. It is. You're the only one making it complicated."

"Sophie, it's different for you. You're rich."

"What does that have to do with anything?"

"To have any chance of independence, to travel, to see the world—to be something other than a wife and mother—I need a solid education and a degree." Addison waved her hands in the air.

"So?"

"So, falling for a man, in a place I'll be leaving in a few short months, makes no sense."

"Who said anything about love?" Sophie asked.

"Oh, Sophie. I'm not like that."

"Oh, *mon amie*, I think it's time for you to learn." Sophie winked at her. "I should have told you before now. I already have a boy at home. Claude. Someday I will marry that stubborn fool."

"Then why are you here in Russia without him?"

"To make him miss me and appreciate me more."

Addison didn't respond. Instead, she stared out the window as Sophie slipped out of their room to shower. She dried her hair and pinned it back, brushing on a little mascara and lipstick for color. Though she wore little makeup daily, the urge to make herself up today was strong. Her insecurities seeped in, and the makeup would boost her confidence.

She was cramming books and folders into her bag when Sophie returned.

"Give me a moment, and we can walk to class together."

Addison nodded and picked up around her area, sneaking a glance at Sophie's typically messy side of the room.

When Sophie was ready, they hurried across campus together toward the science building. They separated once inside, with Addison heading into her cultural anthropology class and Sophie to her pharmacology course. Addison struggled to focus on the professor's lecture as her mind drifted to Sergei, pulling his collar tight around his neck the night before. His windblown dark hair poked out against the leather coat. She had the urge to smooth it down for him as she watched him walk away, and the desire hadn't lessened overnight.

The day passed quickly, and she was grateful to be

walking into her last class—another she shared with Sophie. The medicinal horticulture course was one of her favorites, making her distraction even more frustrating.

The clock's slowness was aggravating; every time she glanced at it, the hands seemed to never move.

The professor dismissing class caught her off guard. Sophie snapped fingers in front of her face to get her attention. "*Allo?*"

Shaking out of her reverie, she glanced up at her friend. "Where did the time go? I just looked at the clock, and it said it was five after three."

Sophie scrunched her face in confusion. "It's four o'clock, and class is over." She tapped her wristwatch.

Addison glanced up at the clock on the wall. It hadn't moved—it still said five after three. Well, it was good to know that time hadn't stood still after all. Just the clock had.

With a sheepish grin, she piled everything into her bag and stood. She was glad the day was over and eager to get to the coffee shop to see Sergei again.

The two women walked out of the classroom together before parting ways. Sophie headed to the movies while Addison rushed across campus to meet Sergei.

Seated at their usual table, his back to the door, his head down, engrossed in what he was reading. The coffee shop was quiet. Noticing there was no coffee cup next to him, Addison stopped by the counter and ordered their coffees before coming to the table.

"Hi," Addison said. She set her bag down on the chair across the table and then dropped into the empty one beside it.

Sergei looked up with a start. "Hello." His eyes were unfocused. He closed his magazine with a slap and slid it over.

A moment later, the barista came to the table. She smiled as she placed the two cups of coffee on the table.

"Thank you," Addison said.

"*Spasibo*," Sergei said before reaching for his cup.

"*Pozhaluysta*." She nodded and walked away.

"What had you so mesmerized?"

"I was reading about the Hubble telescope. I look forward to seeing what they find."

"Astronomy?" Addison asked, her brow furrowed.

"A hobby. During the summers, we camped, and my father and uncle pointed out the constellations to us."

"My father did that when we went camping, too." Addison smiled at this shared experience. As a child, she had loved lying out under the vast sky, watching the shooting stars.

"We should visit Pulkovo together," Sergei said.

"Pulkovo?" Addison asked.

"The Observatory."

"Oh. That would be wonderful."

"How about tomorrow night?" There was a wistful look on his face.

"A date?" Addison's breath caught in her throat. *Oh, Lord help me.*

"Yes," Sergei said.

Addison paused before replying, "I'd like that very much."

"Great, I will pick you up at five o'clock. Dinner before we go to the observatory?"

Addison nodded. Her throat was dry, and her chest tightened. Breathing was painful.

"We will be out late." He grinned.

"Okay." Addison smiled at his reference to her early nights. Suddenly, for a date with Sergei, she wouldn't hesitate to stay out until the sun came up. *Watch it, girl, it's a date, not anything else. Just chill, already.*

"How is the paper coming?" she asked, hoping the change in topic would slow her frantic heartbeat.

"Slow. Will you look at it?"

"Of course. Let's trade," she said.

He hit a few buttons and slid his computer across the table to her. She did the same. While she reviewed his, he could look at hers for inspiration.

His writing style was very enlightening. He looked at things differently, not the simple dialogue or narration, but deeper, searching for the author's motives behind his choice of words. Twenty minutes later, she looked up. He stared at the computer screen before him. Looking down at her half-finished cup, she sighed and excused herself. After ordering them fresh coffee, she headed to the ladies' room.

Sergei was still reading her screen when she returned. Sipping her coffee, she scribbled some notes on her notepad to help give Sergei more ideas on where to direct his attention for his paper.

"I think you have a sort of poetry and symmetry in your report. I envy the way you see the deeper meaning of things."

"Thank you—I hope it is enough." Sergei glanced over and picked up the new coffee cup.

They traded laptops back, and she tore off the page she'd been writing on. "Here are some ideas that might help."

Sergei nodded as he read the paper. "You have such pretty writing. It is easy to read."

Being left-handed like her father, her penmanship mattered. The delicate compliment moved her.

"Thank you," she mumbled.

They worked in silence while Sergei read the rest of her notes. After he set it aside, he pulled out some white sheets of paper and slid them across the table. A quick glance at the list before her made her grin.

"Thank you, these will be helpful."

Sergei had provided her with a basic list of Russian slang that would help her understand the language more, even if she still needed plenty of practice before she could pronounce many of the words on her own. At least she wouldn't feel at such a disadvantage when others spoke around her.

Folding the pages in half, she slid them into her notebook and laid it on top of her laptop before slipping the stack into her backpack. Sergei cleared his things off the table and put them into his bag. He stood and reached for her hand. Together, they walked out of the coffee shop with fingers intertwined. They walked across campus to her dorm, and he kissed the back of her hand once they reached the outer door.

"I will pick you up tomorrow at five."

"I look forward to it."

"Goodnight," Sergei said. He turned, and pulling his collar up, headed back across the quad to his dormitory.

Watching him walk away made her stomach lurch. His tight jeans molded to his well-formed rear end. When he was out of sight, she backed into the doorway and headed to her room with a sigh. She lay on her bed that night, thinking of Sergei. They had been studying together for weeks now, and tomorrow they would have their first actual date. She wondered if they'd share their first actual kiss tomorrow. The idea of his full lips pressed firmly against hers filled her with longing.

She had never met anyone like him before. In

high school, she had taken dates to the school dances, but never settled for a single boy. There had been no inclination to pursue anything further than a casual friendship, or to alter the path she'd set upon toward independence. In fact, most people made her impulse to flee stronger. *But not Sergei…*

CHAPTER 10

A New Adventure

Sergei

S ergei took a deep breath as he sat in his dorm room, waiting for the clock to move. Addison didn't expect him to pick her up until five, but he was so nervous he was ready before three. As he sat at his desk, attempting to finish his homework, his attention wandered. The words on the pages faded as his vision blurred.

A warm feeling spread through his gut as he thought about his plans for the evening. He hoped Addison would love Pulkovo as much as he did. Growing up, the observatory gave him hours of pleasure. The entire Petrova clan had visited it often. The world opened to him there, where he came to understand how huge and fascinating the universe was, standing under the clear night sky. Each constellation, planet, or comet he witnessed through the eye of the telescope mesmerized him.

The observatory grounded him, and it was in its hallowed walls and open sky dome that his appreciation of science and astronomy grew into a lifelong passion. Unlike his siblings, whose interests ranged from accounting to linguistics, following his heart had led him to the sciences.

"What are you doing?"

Pulled from his reverie, Sergei looked up. "Sorry, I was studying," he said.

Pyotr gave him a knowing look. "Studying, huh? What were you reading?" A sly grin crossed his face after Sergei looked down at the book and back up again.

"What brings you home mid-afternoon?" Sergei shook away the fog.

"Work closed early." Pyotr walked across the room and tossed his jacket onto the bed. "I thought you had your date tonight."

Sergei ignored the mischievous glint in his friend's eyes and nodded.

Pyotr stripped off his dirty T-shirt and threw it into the corner. He rummaged in the closet for a moment before yanking a new T-shirt off a hanger and pulling it on.

"What are your plans?" Sergei asked.

"Heading to the club. You?"

"Pulkovo."

"Sounds boring."

Sounds perfect. Sergei rolled his eyes. "Addison does not strike me as a barfly."

"But the observatory?"

Sergei shrugged. "We were talking about astronomy, and she looked interested."

"Like I said. Bor-ring." Pyotr laughed.

"Get out of here." Sergei tossed a pencil in his direction.

Pyotr laughed again before doing an exaggerated bow. "Later." With a dismissive wave, he slipped out the door.

As the door slammed shut, Sergei glanced over at the clock on the wall. It was half-past three, and there was no chance of him getting any homework done that afternoon. His nerves were on edge, and his mind distracted. With a snap, he shut his books and set them aside. He grabbed his leather jacket and headed out the door.

Driving into town, he filled up the gas tank before he pulled into the car wash. He maintained his vehicle and kept it immaculate. But because he did not have people in it often, he decided it would be nice to have it freshened up for his date. In reality, he just needed to get out of his room before he went crazy.

Glancing down, he saw the digital display on the dash blink back at him. It was now a quarter to five. He pulled into the parking lot closest to Addison's dormitory. As he strolled across the quad, the setting sun left red and orange streaks in the sky. He reached the main entrance just as Addison exited the building. *She is so beautiful.* He wiped his clammy hands on his jeans and reached his hand out to her.

CHAPTER 11

First Dates

Addison

A ddison stepped out of the main door of the dormitory as Sergei walked up—dressed in black jeans and a black cashmere sweater under his usual leather bomber jacket. He looked even more handsome and mysterious than usual. *Good thing I stuck with the jeans.* She'd donned black jeans and a purple angora sweater under her heavy down parka to keep it casual for their first date. Her tall black leather boots would help keep her legs warm, while her jacket stopped well below the waist. Though her blood raced through her veins, she was determined to appear unaffected by him.

"Hi," she said.

"You are punctual, unlike Sophie." He laughed.

His warm, solid fingers tightened around hers

while they walked to the parking lot. When they reached his old Lada Riva, a faded blue compact car, he opened the passenger door. "Your chariot awaits," he said.

"Thank you," Addison said as she slid inside.

He smelled of citrus and something like eucalyptus, but she couldn't put her finger on it. Whatever the blend was, it intoxicated her. She closed her eyes and breathed in as he closed the door.

The drive from the school to the observatory would take a little over half an hour, considering there wouldn't be much traffic on a Saturday evening. Sergei reached over and took her hand, holding it while he drove. Her heart skipped a beat as his warm hand covered hers.

"Do you like Chinese food?" he asked.

"Yes."

"I know the best place. Close to Pulkovo."

"Perfect," Addison said.

Sometimes it felt as though she couldn't find the right words to have a simple conversation with him, and other times, it came naturally. *God, I suck at this whole dating thing.*

As they drove, the radio played Pachelbel's "Canon in D." The soft music muffled the sounds of the beat-up road and crunching snow below them. Sergei drove slowly, though each bump and pothole rattled her bones. January had brought a light snowfall. The fluffy powder had just begun falling the day before. It was pure white on the ground and up the embankments. The pristine glow of the setting sun bounced off the peaks and surrounded them.

Addison sucked in a breath as Sergei's thumb caressed her knuckles. The tender motion shot fire through her.

She peered through the glass at the breathtaking white-capped trees taking in the beauty outside.

When they arrived at the Chinese restaurant, Sergei jumped out of the car and rushed to her side just as she opened the door. He helped her out and then stuck his elbow out for her. They walked into the restaurant entwined. His closeness made her pulse race. She was sure he could hear it.

After they sat and the tea was brought to their table, Sergei leaned across the table and said, "They have amazing dim sum here."

Addison had never eaten dim sum before, usually sticking to her favorites back home. "How about you surprise me?"

Sergei nodded.

She took in her surroundings. The dining area bustled with activity. Families filled many of the tables surrounding them. Spurts of conversations mingled with the soft sounds of the water fountain in the entrance. Waiters walked around the room with enormous platters, stopping at various tables where patrons selected items from the tray.

"What are they doing?" she asked.

Sergei poured the tea into their small cups before he responded. "Passing out the dim sum. They come to your table and tell you what they have on their trays, and you can select what you want."

"Hmm. Interesting. I've never seen that done in a restaurant before. Only at weddings."

"Weddings have dim sum?"

Addison laughed. "No, some weddings I've attended have waiters pass around hors d'oeuvres while you're waiting for the reception to start."

"I know what you refer to now. *Da*, this would be similar, I believe."

Addison sipped her tea. It was a unique flavor unfamiliar to her. "What kind of tea is this?"

"Oolong. It has a hint of jasmine as well."

Addison took a quick whiff of the steaming cup in her hand and grinned. She recognized the flowery scent at once.

A short, older Asian man stopped by their table and pulled out his pad. Pen poised, he looked expectantly at Sergei. He wrote furiously on his tablet as Sergei ordered. Then the waiter smiled, bowed, and retreated.

Addison sipped her tea and people watched to distract herself from the pull she felt toward the man seated across from her. *I can't just stare at Sergei all night!* The families laughed with their small children, while others selected items from the passing waiters. The nerves she thought she'd tamped down danced around in her stomach. She hadn't been on a date in a long time. Then again, she hadn't been interested enough in anyone, either.

"Are you an only child?" he asked.

"I wish…"

Sergei chuckled. "I understand. I have four siblings."

"Tell me about them."

"You first."

"Okay, I have a sister who's two years older than me, Savannah. Then, we have three younger sisters. Quinby is fifteen, and Raleigh and Beth are eight and four, respectively."

"That's a huge age gap."

"We all have different fathers, except for Savannah and Quinby."

"Oh, I understand now." His brow creased. "Wait. I thought Savannah was older than you, and Quinby was younger?"

"That's right."

"But they share a different father than you?"

"It's a long story." Addison shook her head. It wasn't an explanation she wanted to give on a first date.

"We have time," he said.

"Nope, it's your turn now."

"Okay, Viktor is the same age as me, and then Mikhail and the twins are younger."

"How are you and Viktor the same age?"

"Ah, that is a long story..." Sergei's lips twisted into a mischievous grin.

"Cute. Seriously, though."

"I am adopted."

"Oh, I'm sorry—I didn't realize."

"I do not remember my first parents much anymore. I was very young. I know my father was a professor. The rest of that time is now a blur for me," Sergei said.

"Where are your biological parents?"

Sergei sipped his tea as he glanced over the cup at her. "They died in an explosion with my sister when I was seven."

"So young." Addison felt her eyes well up for the small child who lost his family.

"*Da.*"

"Was this when you lived in Germany?"

"*Da.*"

"How did you meet your adoptive parents?" Addison dabbed at the moisture in her eyes with her napkin.

"My father worked with Nikolai. I took classes with Viktor."

"So, they adopted you in Germany, and brought you back to Russia?" Addison sipped her tea. The curiosity was killing her.

"*Da.* I was born here. They have been good to me."

"You sound surprised."

"Sometimes I am. They have four children of their own," Sergei admitted.

"But they still had room in their hearts for you."

Sergei nodded.

"Was it hard to leave Germany and return to Russia?"

"I never thought about it. Living first in Germany for eight years, then in Belarus for two, I am familiar with the adjustments that must come, just as you have experienced them this year. While you knew you would be here a brief time, as a child, I never knew if or when I would return to Mother Russia to live. My family immersed itself in the environment and cultures of our host countries. We adapted."

"Sounds like so much fun."

Sergei gave a nonchalant shrug.

"Growing up, I lived in between two homes. I was always torn. Half of me wanted to be at my dad's and Cassie's, and the other half needed to be with my mother and sisters. They fought over me in court almost my entire childhood. There was always tension and guilt. It wasn't nearly as exciting as your child-hood," Addison said.

"I am sorry. I cannot imagine my parents ever fighting like that."

"It sucked because my mother expected me to stay close to her."

But not anymore… I'm here, aren't I?

Sergei shook his head. "Nikolai encouraged us to

go away to university, not to stay close to home. He wanted us to become more independent."

"Are they happy that you've come close to home again?" she asked.

"After four years away, very happy."

"Four years?"

"I attend Saint Petersburg for my master's."

Addison hadn't expected that. She had assumed he was also in his third year of school.

The waiter stopped by their table with a large round tray and set the edge down on the table.

Addison looked to Sergei for direction.

"It is her first dim sum. Could you tell us what this is?" Sergei asked the waiter. The Asian man bobbed his head before describing his items.

"Hmm. Sounds delicious."

The waiter placed two small round balls on each plate and, with a bob of his head, backed away with the tray.

She speared a piece and popped it into her mouth as Sergei continued to talk. She closed her eyes, and a soft sigh escaped. "These are delicious," Addison murmured.

Sergei smiled. He wiggled his face as he played with his chopsticks, trying to scoop up sauce with them, and had her in stitches. She laughed so hard the people at the next table stared at her and made her glad they weren't in the library. The stuffy librarian would have had a conniption.

She was enjoying her time with him. He was so unassuming, and she liked he was introducing her to new things as well. It felt like an adventure each time they were together. They would become great friends, she was sure. But only friends; nothing good would come of anything more.

Waiters often appeared with new trays. The conversation remained easy and never stalled. Addison moaned as she tasted the pineapple bread. It was a slice of paradise on her tongue.

Sergei laughed at her as she closed her eyes and swallowed.

"You enjoyed it," he said.

"Delicious. Thank you."

Sergei glanced at his watch. "We will need to get to the observatory soon."

Addison nodded and popped the last piece of pineapple bread into her mouth as Sergei grinned. After he paid the bill, he stood and reached for her hand. Once securely tucked into his, they exited the restaurant together as they had arrived.

Once he pulled the car onto the road again, Addison turned to him. "Thank you for dinner. That was fantastic."

Sergei reached for her hand and brought it to his lips. "My pleasure," he murmured into her palm.

Addison's pulse raced as his lips brushed a soft caress against her skin. He continued to hold her hand as he drove, intimacy filling her stomach with flutters as the soft sounds of Miles Davis filled the small space around them. *Only a friend, Addison. Only. A. Friend.*

He parked in front of the main building, helping her out of the car. Then, tucking her hand under his arm, he led her inside. He pulled a folded document from his inside coat pocket and handed it to an elderly gentleman in a red uniform. The man opened the paper and ran his eyes down the page before handing it back to Sergei with a smile.

"Mr. Petrova, would you like to tour the museum before or after the show?"

"Before, if you do not mind."

"Of course." The man gave a slight nod before walking away, leaving them to walk around the building on their own.

"How does he know your name?"

Sergei smiled. "I practically grew up here."

Addison nodded, confused. He hadn't mentioned spending much time there before. The more time with him, the less she felt like she'd learned. He reminded her of an onion with his various layers of mystery.

Sergei held her hand as they walked through the halls. Large photographs of constellations, planets, the Milky Way, and the International Space Station hung on the walls. They paused at each one, taking a moment to observe the magnificent beauty depicted in the colorful and detailed pictures.

Standing in front of a massive image of the Aurora Borealis, Addison raised her hand towards it.

"Have you ever seen this?" he asked.

"No, you?"

"Not yet. Someday I will," he said.

Glancing at her watch, she was surprised to see thirty minutes had passed while they toured most of the wing.

"Would you like to see the telescope now?" Sergei asked.

"Yes, that would be great."

"There is a unique history to one of the larger telescopes here. The one we are going to use it is a German Zeiss refractor that was supposed to go to Italy."

"Then how did it end up here? Did you guys steal it?"

Sergei laughed as he bobbed his head. "I guess we did."

Astonishment filled Addison's face as she gasped.

"Spoils of World War II."

Addison shrugged. "Oh, well, that makes sense."

Sergei grinned. "Hitler promised it to Mussolini, but we captured it instead. Then we kept it after the Nazis tried to invade us."

"Seems like a fair price to pay."

Sergei chuckled. "We thought so. Let us go see it. It is quite beautiful," he said. "Not as amazing as the first two refractors here in the past. Pulkovo once hosted the first two-largest telescopes in the world during their times."

"Wow, that's outstanding."

"Our contribution to astronomy is remarkable." A note of obvious pride filled his voice.

Sergei led her down the hall, past more amazing images of the night sky, before making their way into a huge domed room. Wooden slats covered the ceiling of the dome. There was a massive opening in the center of the ceiling like a giant sunroof, and the enormous telescope had an unfettered view of the stars above.

A middle-aged man stood beside it, his back to the room. He turned to face them as they came closer. He opened his arms wide, and Sergei stepped into them. They hugged, and the man patted him on the back.

"Welcome back; it's been too long."

"Yes, *Dyadya*, it has," Sergei said.

"How is the family?"

"They are well. You must visit."

"*Da*. I will soon."

"*Dyadya*, this is Addison. Addison, this is my Uncle Yuri."

"It's a pleasure, my dear." Yuri clasped her hand in his enormous paws and gave it a gentle shake. "It's nice to meet you."

Yuri wrapped his arm around Sergei's shoulder. "Come, see what I've got."

Addison fell into step as the two men got closer to the telescope.

As Sergei stepped up and peered through the telescope, he sighed. "*Krasivaya.*"

"I thought you might like that," Yuri said.

"Addison, come look." Sergei motioned for her to come closer as he backed away from the eyepiece.

Addison stepped up, peered into the eyepiece, and gasped.

"That's amazing. What is it?" She looked up and over at Yuri.

"That, my girl, is the M1, or the Crab Nebula. It is one of the most widely known supernovas."

"What's a supernova?" Addison asked. She was familiar with constellations and the basics of astronomy, but she wasn't an expert.

"A dying star," Yuri explained.

Addison's brow rose as she stared at the two men.

A grin crossed Yuri's face as he took in Addison's expression and explained. "When a star explodes, the gas and dust inside spread across the sky."

"And that's what that is, gas and dust?" Addison continued to stare.

"Yes," Yuri replied.

"I've never seen anything so beautiful," Addison said.

"Yes, it is quite a spectacular sight," Yuri agreed.

"Can I see it again?" Addison gestured to the telescope.

Yuri grinned. "Yes, please." He waved his hand toward the telescope.

Addison peered through the lens again, enjoying the bright colors. It was hard to fathom the brilliant sight was light-years away. She took in the amazing spectacle through the lens before she stepped back to make way for Sergei to look again. *He's so thoughtful. What an amazing experience!*

They continued to take turns while Yuri regaled her with stories of Sergei's youthful shenanigans. "… And one time Sergei was watching his brothers while Lena and Nikolai were at the hospital. The twins had come early, so in the middle of the night, they left their oldest in charge until I could get there. I was visiting Lake Lodoga for the weekend, so I was hours away."

"It was the middle of the night. Wasn't everyone asleep?" Addison asked.

"You would think." Yuri laughed.

"They weren't?" Addison glanced up at Sergei's broad shoulders, his back to them, his attention only on the night sky.

"I arrived at three in the morning. The three boys were in the kitchen, the kettle was on, and Sergei was at the stove scrambling eggs," Yuri went on.

Addison laughed. "How old were they?"

"The twins are five now, so Sergei had to be about fourteen, maybe fifteen."

"Why were they awake?"

"Mikhail was afraid. He'd had a nightmare and went to crawl into bed with his parents. And when he found the bed empty, he cried. Woke the others up. So, Sergei did what his mother would do."

"Make tea?"

"Yes, and eggs."

Addison giggled.

Sergei came and stood beside her. "It is late. We should get back."

"Of course."

He reached out his hand and lifted her to her feet.

"Come back and visit an old man sometimes," Yuri said.

"Soon. I promise," Sergei said.

Yuri gave his nephew a hearty hug before turning his attention to Addison. "I hope to see you again soon."

"Me, too." She hugged him and kissed his grizzled cheek.

Sergei took Addison's hand, and they headed out to the car.

"Did you enjoy the supernova?" he asked.

"Yes, it was beautiful."

"They are my favorite to watch in the sky. Even better than shooting stars."

"I can see why." Addison leaned back in the seat and stretched her legs. They were cold, and the warm air pouring from under the dashboard eased some of the stiffness setting in.

When they reached her outer dorm door, Sergei leaned in and kissed her cheek. A zing coursed through her body at the warmth of his lips. Addison turned her face toward his, and he kissed her again, just a light press of his lips to hers. She leaned into him and deepened the kiss, tingles moving through her body before he pulled back, still holding her hand. He reached up and wiped a snowflake from her cold cheek, his warm hand sending heat through her whole body.

"Thank you for tonight. I had a wonderful time," she said.

"I did, too."

"Night."

"Goodnight." Sergei gave her a little bow before turning toward his car. Addison could barely feel the ground beneath her feet as she practically floated up to her dorm room. The kiss had been even better than she'd imagined.

Oh, crap. I'm in deep now.

CHAPTER 12

Confessions

Sergei

Sergei set his textbook aside. Cabin fever was setting in. Finding his morning classes canceled left him without his usual routine. The dorm room was clean for a change, and his homework couldn't distract him from his thoughts of Addison and their date to the observatory. Holding his cell phone, he pressed the digit for the first number in its memory. Pressing it tight against his ear, the line rang once before connecting.

"*Zdravstvuyte.*"

"*Mamochka,*" Sergei said.

"*Syn,* what is wrong?" his mother asked.

"Nothing is wrong, *Mamochka.*"

"Calling on a school day? You should be in class."

"I need your advice." Perched on the edge of the chair at the small desk, he fiddled with a pencil.

"There is a girl." Not a question, but a statement. His mother could read him like a book.

"*Da.*"

"Yuri called."

Ah. And there he was, giving his mother psychic abilities again. He laughed.

"You should bring her home," she said.

Sergei paused. "I do not think she is ready."

"Are you ashamed of your family?" His mother's tone grew crisp.

"*Nyet.*"

"Of her?"

"Of course not." The pencil between his fingers snapped in half. Frustrated, he dropped the pieces on the desk.

"Then bring her home so that we can meet her."

"That may be rushing things," Sergei said.

"If you look at her the way Yuri says, it is time," his mother responded.

"What do you mean?"

"If you are going to date an American, your family should get to know her."

"Why is that?" Sergei asked.

"You have never shown a serious interest in a girl. For you to be drawn to someone so different from your culture, your homeland, she must be special."

He couldn't argue with that logic. "I think she is the one."

"Bring her home, and I will tell you."

Sergei laughed again. "Do not go scaring her away."

"Sergei Niklaus Petrova, if this girl is worthy, your family will tell you."

Sergei chuckled. "I will bring her for a visit soon."

"See, don't you feel better getting that off your chest?"

Sergei chuckled. "*Da, Mamochka.*"

"Good, now go to class, and we will see you and your girl this weekend."

Sergei hung up the phone, shaking his head. He should have expected his mother's pointed request to meet Addison. However, there was a distinct unease in his gut about telling Addison he wanted her to meet his family. He couldn't recall the last time he had brought a girl home, even just a classmate. *This will be interesting.* Her mention of Addison being an American reminded him she expected to leave at the end of the term—unless he could convince her to stay. *But how? I had better come up with something fast.* In a sudden twist of fate, she had dropped into his world and filled his heart with peace. She was his match in every way.

STUDYING AT THE COFFEE SHOP, HE WAITED FOR Addison with clammy hands, which he wiped on his jeans. He started sweating and became nauseated every time he thought of asking Addison to visit his parents. His mother was expecting them in a few days, and Addison still did not know. How to invite her to a family dinner without scaring her away continued to elude him.

Addison slid into the chair across from him and smiled at him.

"How are you today?" he asked through a dry throat.

"Good, and you?"

"My mother wants to meet you." The words rushed out of his mouth.

"Excuse me?" Addison started coughing.

"My mother asked me to bring you home for dinner with the family."

"It's too soon." Addison's face paled. Reaching over, she grabbed his coffee cup and took a huge gulp of the steaming liquid. "Ahh! That's hot."

Sergei watched her set the cup back down with a sheepish glance in his direction. Her face was now red and blotchy, and her eyes were full of moisture.

"I'm sorry," she said.

"I should not have dropped that on you. I meant to explain first."

"How long have you been planning this?" Addison asked.

"Not long. I talked to her this morning."

"Today?" she squeaked. Addison closed her eyes and took a deep breath.

The silence made his nerves tingle worse. *What is she thinking?*

"As soon as I talked to *Mamochka*, she wanted to meet you."

"I can't."

"Why not?" Sergei glanced at her.

Addison's eyes looked glazed as she stared at him. "Why are you talking to your mother about me?"

"*Lubov moya*, do not be nervous. You will like her. You will see."

"Sergei, we're just friends. You shouldn't be taking me home to meet your parents."

He stared at her. *We are more than friends.* "It is just dinner, Addison. Even friends come to dinner with my family." His gut clenched at the misdirection. Addison's tension was palpable, and he would do anything to ease it for her. He didn't want to scare her away, even if he saw things differently. "Please come. My family are good people."

"I don't do family-type events well. I don't even like doing them with my family," she whispered.

Sergei couldn't imagine not being close to family. Even adopted, he had an undeniable connection to the people who had taken him in and loved him most of his life. It was clear he would need to work harder to understand where the disconnect lay between Addison and her family.

"Please say you will come." Sergei held his breath.

The moments ticked by in silence while Addison continued to look around the room, not meeting his eyes.

"Fine."

"*Spasibo*." Sergei let out the breath trapped in his chest.

"Don't thank me yet. This might be a huge mistake."

Sergei grinned. He had faith. *Everything will be fine.*

CHAPTER 13

Homecoming

Addison

A week after their first actual date, Addison's nerves were tight with anticipation. She sat at her computer, staring at the screen. Things were moving so fast, and she wasn't sure of anything anymore.

Opening her email, she figured a quick update to her family would be in her best interest.

Mama,

Hope the family is well. School is going fine. Busy as always. My friends, Sophie, and Sergei, keep me busy with our study groups.

Love,

Addy

Addison attached a couple of pictures of the snow-topped roofs around campus. Her favorite was one that resembled a white-chocolate Hershey Kiss sitting on the top of a building.

Sending that email to her mother didn't ease her nerves, though it eased her guilt. She wasn't ready to tell her mother about Sergei. Then again, she wasn't sure she understood herself. Sitting there with her email open, she mulled over her feelings, deciding she needed to sort that out.

> *Cassie,*
>
> *Thinking of you and Dad and missing you both. School is busy, but fun. Sophie is the best room- mate I could ask for; she has the coolest French accent. I met a boy. His name is Sergei. We've been studying together for the last month. I like him. He took me to see the observatory last week. Today he's taking me to meet his family, and I'm a little nervous.*
>
> *Give Dad my love.*
>
> *Love,*
>
> *Addy*

After sending her second email, she logged out and finished getting ready. Sergei was taking her to meet the parents. *His parents.* She wasn't ready for it. It was one date—a great one, no doubt—but a single date. Parental meetings were meant for deep, serious, committed relationships., not budding romances. *I'm going home in six months.*

But now she had agreed to meet his family. The look on his face and the way he'd asked made her feel for a second like this wasn't such a big deal. But that second passed, and her guts went into mutiny.

Sergei was chatty during the drive, talking about school, their classes, and their friends. He looked handsome, like he did on their first date, but her nerves were too shot to focus on what he was saying. It was a lot of talking with little actual information. The only thing she knew was that his parents lived on the outskirts of Saint Petersburg.

Addison covered her face with her hands. When he said things like "my love," especially in Russian, the butterflies in her stomach went wild. She was going to be sick. Her simple blue jeans and black mohair sweater suddenly made her feel underdressed for meeting his family. Unsure what to expect, she'd dressed casually, tied her hair back in a ponytail, and added a touch of makeup.

In a moment of self-conscious doubt, she yanked the band from her ponytail and tugged her fingers through her hair, hoping it would compensate for everything else.

An hour later, Sergei pulled the car up to an immaculate-looking manor with large front windows. The white-washed fence and gate glittered in the fading sunlight. Snow covered the large grounds around the home as far as the eye could see. The snowy tree limbs gave her the impression she'd stepped into a postcard. It was beautiful in a softly stated way. Her stomach dropped somewhere around her feet. She hoped she didn't trip over it while making her way to the door. *Oh God, why did I agree* with *this?*

Sergei helped her out of the car towards a young couple standing before the modest stone house, holding hands. Addison shivered as the wind whipped around them. Even the parka couldn't keep the chill at bay. Her feet slipped on the icy pavement below. She grasped Sergei's arm to stop from sliding to the ground.

"I've known you a month," Addison said, "and you whisk me off to meet your parents." She shook her head, choking down her fear.

"They will love you, I promise." Sergei's smile filled his face, and his eyes lit up.

Addison sucked in a deep breath. Never having been a big family person, throughout high school she'd avoided meeting the families of the boys she dated and only brought her prom date home to meet her mother because she'd had no choice if she wanted to go.

"*MAMOCHKA* MADE AN ENORMOUS FEAST—EVERYONE came," Sergei said. He gave her hand a soft squeeze.

"Everyone? To meet me?" Addison sputtered. She stared at Sergei as horror filled her.

"Yes, my brothers are here for dinner. So are their girlfriends." Sergei fidgeted.

"No pressure," Addison muttered.

The door flew open, and a young boy flew out. "*Mamochka's* been cooking all day." He skidded to a stop in front of her. "Wow. She's beautiful."

Heat filled Addison's cheeks as she sucked on her bottom lip.

"Behave. Alexi, this is Addison," Sergei said. Releasing her hand, he stepped up behind her.

Alexi stuck his tongue out at his older brother, reached up, and put his hand in Addison's. Before they could take a step toward the house, a young girl came skipping out. She stopped in front of Alexi and Addison and smiled.

"She's pretty, brother," she said.

"Yes, Zara, she is. Say hello to Addison," Sergei replied.

Zara hid her face behind a dark mop of curls, suddenly shy.

"Hello," Addison said.

"My name's Zara. I'm a twin," the little girl said. She peeked through her hair.

"You are? That's pretty special." Addison smiled down at the beaming little girl.

A moment later, a man about their age stepped

out of the house. He extended his hand to her as he strode toward her.

"You must be the lovely Addison we have heard so much about. I am Viktor." He shook Addison's hand and gave it a gentle squeeze before he released her and ruffled Alexi's hair. *"Mamochka's* waiting for you." He looked over at Sergei.

Sergei gave him a pointed look.

Viktor shrugged in response before he turned on his heel and returned through the open door.

Zara giggled, and Alexi laughed. Zara slid her fingers into Addison's empty hand while Alexi tugged on her other hand to follow him. The twins' eagerness and enthusiasm reminded her of Beth and Raleigh.

Sergei brought up the rear.

Addison's stomach flipped as the children pulled her forward. She took another deep breath. The house was straight out of a storybook. The curves in the slate roof and the gabled windows enthralled her. She stood on the cobblestone driveway that sloped into a walkway leading to the enormous carved wood door. The scene gave everything a picturesque quality.

The way it had been lovingly put together reminded her of her father and Cassie's house. When she was a child, they had taken an old, abandoned plantation and turned it into a beautiful home.

Sergei's parents' home seemed even older and more charming. She stepped inside the door and warmth emanated around her. Family photos covered the top of the polished, black-enameled piano, and old tapestries hung on the walls. The spacious family room was inviting.

A woman's voice startled Addison from her reverie. "Welcome. We are glad that you could come break bread with our family."

Turning, she saw a woman far younger looking than she had expected. A crisp white apron around her waist covered a long, dark-blue skirt.

"*Mamochka*." Sergei kissed his mother on both cheeks, enveloping her in a big hug. "Something smells delicious."

"*Knish*, *vatrushka*, and *stroganov*."

"My favorites." Sergei kissed his mother's cheek again before releasing her.

The woman grinned. She extended a hand to Addison. "I am Lena."

Addison released Zara's hand to accept Sergei's mother's hand. It was warm in hers.

"*Mamochka*, she's so pretty," Alexi gushed.

"Alexi, go bring your Papa in from the greenhouse."

"Yes, *Mamochka*." Alexi dropped Addison's hand and tromped off, his head hanging down.

"He's upset because Sergei doesn't visit much, and he never brings pretty girls home," Zara whispered.

Oh no, this is worse than I thought. This isn't normal.

"Zara, go wash up. Supper is almost ready," Lena said.

The little girl nodded and left the room, her head drooping like her brother's.

"Come to the kitchen. There is tea."

Sergei's mother led the way into the large kitchen. The stone hearth in the corner had a small fire going. The room was a cozy scene straight out of an old classic film. An enormous stainless-steel teakettle whistled on a large, old-fashioned stovetop. Sergei's mother moved around her kitchen, busying herself with pulling cups out and sliding the kettle off the fire.

Sergei pulled Addison over to one of the largest butcher-block-style tables she'd ever seen and slid out two chairs at the far side for them to sit. He held out her chair before he took the one next to hers.

His mother brought over two steaming mugs and set them down in front of them. The aroma of mint and chamomile teased her nose. After a moment, Lena sat down across from them with another cup. Her warm smile relieved some of the tension that had been building between Addison's shoulders. The ease of Sergei's mother reminded her of Cassie. The kindness of her welcome, unlike anything she could expect from her own mother.

Alexi burst into the room with Sergei's father in tow. He was a massive man, with broad shoulders and hints of silver hair at his temples. He held a bowl of green onions in his large hands.

"Hello." The man's warm smile helped relax her further.

"Papa, I told you she was pretty," Alexi gushed.

Heat returned to Addison's cheeks as the man turned his gaze on her.

"Yes, Alexi, you did." The man set the bowl on the counter before coming to stand next to Addison's chair. "It is a pleasure to have you in our home. I am Nikolai."

Addison accepted his extended hand. Her hand disappeared into his huge ones, which were softer than she had expected considering his size.

"Mikhail and Oksana just pulled up." Viktor came in from a side door. He slipped a heavy wool jacket on as he spoke. "I'll be right back; I'm going to pick up Marina. Need anything while I'm out?"

"*Nyet, syn*, be safe. Dinner will be ready on your return," Lena said. She lifted herself up from her seat, kissing his cheek on her way to the stove.

Sergei's father slid into a chair at the head of the table. A moment later, Lena returned with another steaming mug of tea for her husband.

"*Spasibo*," Nikolai said. He patted her hand as it briefly rested on his shoulder. This tender sign of appreciation reminded her of her father and stepmother.

Alexi sat in the seat closest to Sergei while Zara slipped into the empty chair next to Addison just as two teenagers came blundering into the kitchen. They were laughing loudly but halted when the boy almost mowed Lena down.

"Sorry, *Mamochka*," the tall, scrawny, dark-haired boy said. His hair was a mess of ebony curls that draped over his forehead. The girl stood slightly behind him.

Lena rolled her eyes and swatted at the boy with the dish towel hanging over her shoulder. He moved deftly away, grinning like a schoolboy.

With the attention directed at Sergei's mother and one of his brothers, the girl slipped into the room and dropped into one of the empty chairs at the table.

Lena turned back to the stove and pulled more cups from the cupboard. Her hands flew with such ease that Addison couldn't keep up with her movements. Within moments, more steaming mugs were on the table.

"I'm Mikhail, and this is my girlfriend, Oksana." He flipped his hand in the girl's direction, seated beside him. She beamed in return.

His voice overlapped as everyone tried to talk at once, a melody of voices vying for a position. They started in Russian and then moved to perfect English when she stumbled over some of her responses. The questions came at such rapid-fire pace; she had little time to answer one before another came at her.

"Leave the poor girl alone," Lena said. She directed a slight smile at Addison before she stood.

Addison returned her smile, grateful for the ally.

"Alexi, Zara, go wash up—supper is ready." Lena wiped her hands on her apron and headed back to the stove.

CHAPTER 14

Acceptance

Sergei

S ergei smiled as the twins darted out of the room. His mother approached, patting his shoulder before leaning down and ruffling his hair. As she stepped away, he felt something heavy pull his pocket down. Glancing up, he saw his mother give a slight nod; he caught a twinkle in her eyes.

A lump formed in his throat. He patted his pocket, and the edges of the square-shaped bulge within became distinct. Though not positive without looking at the object, his gut told him his mother had just given her approval of Addison.

Nikolai's mother had worn a beautifully designed cocktail ring on her right hand. Shortly after his family died, and the Petrova's brought him home to live with them, he'd met his new grandmother and had admired this ring. It was his first memory of her.

His eyes pooled with tears as he recalled her first words to him.

"You are one of us now, my boy. And one day, this ring will belong to you if you would like."

Sergei had beamed at her simple acceptance of him into her family. *"Da, Babushka."*

The short, rotund woman wrapped him in one of the tightest, warmest hugs.

From that moment, he never doubted this new family was his. *He was home.*

RELIEF FLOODED THROUGH ADDISON AS THE conversation turned from her, and Viktor asked if anyone had caught the last Futbol match.

"Supper is ready—clear off the table and set it."

Everyone stood and scattered. One boy brought placemats, another grabbed dishes. Alexi and Zara came skidding back to the table, holding worn cloth napkins and flatware in a whirlwind of motion. Within minutes, where she sat was transformed into an elegant dining table. Brown embroidered placemats and faded red napkins sat on the table at each seat, and flatware lay on the folded napkins. Mikhail set a stack of white ceramic plates in the center of the table next to a large metal trivet. The thick block of wood had seen many family meals, Addison was certain. The formal dining table in the other room looked lovely but lonely in the big house. It was clear the family congregated in the kitchen at the butcher-block table more than anywhere else in the house. Although it was a snug fit with everyone together, it was cozy. Unlike dinners at her home, which were usually tense and uncomfortable.

As the bustle of activity died down, Viktor returned with his girlfriend. They took up the last remaining spaces at the table. While Lena filled the table with dishes heavy with food, Sergei and his father talked about his classes. His mother served them plates of food and the kids dug in. Addison looked up to see Lena give the twins a death glare. They turned their heads away so quickly their mother missed the expressions that crossed their faces. Addison took a quick sip of tea to hide her smirk behind the cup. She knew those glares well. It brought back memories, good ones. Her grandmother was famous for them. When they were children, they used to call it the skull-face look. Her grandmother was not amused. She thought of her maternal grandmother sometimes. Even Grandmamma's uptight nature was a blessing compared to having no family ties at all.

"How long have you studied the Russian language, Addison?" Nikolai asked.

Pulled back into the conversation, Addison faced Sergei's father. "I took two semesters before coming to

Saint Petersburg." The silence that followed filled her with dread. *Is my Russian not enough? Am I not good enough?*

Nikolai smiled and nodded.

"What brought you to Russia to study?" Viktor asked.

"My Russian literature professor suggested a year abroad to strengthen my language skills."

"Russian literature?" Lena glanced up at her.

"One of my electives in my second year." Addison speared another piece of *stroganov*.

"Is that your major?" Viktor asked. He snuck a glance at his mother.

"No. I'm studying botany."

"Ah, another science geek. Like Sergei," Mikhail said.

Addison nodded.

"Where does the Russian literature come in?" Viktor asked.

"Passion. I love books. So, I've always taken classes in historical and classical literature. English, French, and Russian are some of my favorites."

"*Mamochka* is a professor of Russian literature," Mikhail said.

"Was, *syn*. That was a long time ago."

"When did you stop teaching?" Addison asked.

"When we came back to Saint Petersburg. I taught for a brief time, then I retired after the twins were born."

"Was that after you lived in Germany?"

"*Da*, East Berlin."

It went unsaid that they had come back after the wall came down, and East Germany no longer existed. Addison wondered if it was a sore subject for Sergei's parents and made a mental note to ask Sergei later.

"What are your plans after graduation?" Nikolai asked.

All eyes turned to Addison.

"I still have another year after this one." Addison hadn't given much thought about life after college. It was hard enough keeping her mother at bay. She hadn't spent nearly enough time mapping out her future. A steady career would be necessary—something to promise her financial independence. There was no way she'd let herself get stuck in loveless relationships like Mama had, with no freedom to support her children. *My future will be doing what I want, living my life how I see fit. Not Mama. Not according to what a man wants—*

"I'm going to marry her," Sergei said.

CHAPTER 15

Confusion Reigns

Addison

"What?" Addison sputtered.

Zara beamed.

Everyone at the table burst into the conversation. *He's going to marry me? Since when? How? Just... What? Marry me?*

"He's crazy," Addison choked out.

"So, it seems," Viktor agreed.

Sergei's grin widened. His eyes sparkled with laughter.

"Are you sure? She does not look convinced," Mikhail questioned.

"I have no doubts." Sergei shrugged.

Excuse me!

"What if she says no?" Alexi whispered. Sitting next to her, though his voice was so soft under the raucousness of voices, it could've been a shout as the room grew quiet and all eyes turned to her.

"Why would she?" Sergei's tone was so serious his brothers laughed.

We haven't discussed this. Does he remember the part about me only being here for a few months? That my life and family are in a different country?

His parents continued to sit at the table without saying a word. She couldn't be sure they approved of this sudden turn of events.

"What have I gotten myself into?" Addison muttered under her breath. She held her hands up.

Lena patted her shoulder. "You will be fine, *moy rebenok.*" She exchanged a silent glance with her husband across the table.

"Where's the ring, brother? Did you give her a ring?" Zara asked, her approval and uncontained excitement evident as she bounced in her seat.

He reached into his pant pocket and pulled out a clenched fist. With shaking hands, he leaned over to Addison. He whispered, "I hope you like it," and slid a cold band of metal onto her finger. Looking down, she could see nothing beneath his large hand enveloping hers.

"Let's see!" Zara squealed.

Pulling her hand from his, Addison spread her trembling fingers and stretched her arm out to the center of the table. Her voice caught under the boulder in her throat.

The women crowded around her. They oohed and aahed as each held her hand and inspected the ring.

Mikhail whistled. Viktor pounded Sergei on the shoulder.

Her first real look at the ring came after the family had each gotten a glimpse. It was an enormous, dark-green, teardrop-shaped stone resembling an emerald, with three large prongs holding it in place. The band had a pink tinge to it. She hadn't seen anything like it before. Two rows of tiny white diamonds surrounded the green stone. The same tiny white diamonds sat nestled in the scrollwork on both sides of the band. The ring was breathtaking.

"That is *Mamochka's*," Zara said.

The conversations stopped as they turned to Sergei's mother.

Nodding, Lena stroked the cheek of her youngest. "This was Nikolai's mother's," she said, "and now it is yours."

"It's beautiful," came Addison's raspy reply. She didn't recognize her own voice.

"Is that chrome diopside?" Marina asked.

"You have a good eye," Lena said. At Addison's puzzled expression, Lena explained. "Chrome diopside, sometimes called a Siberian Emerald, though not an emerald at all, is a rare mineral from the Siberian Mountains, only mined during the summer months. It is a national treasure to our people…"

The room started spinning. Her stomach churned, and her breath hitched. There was a ringing in her ears, drowning out the garbled conversation around her. Beating against her ribs, her heart raced in an effort to escape its confines. A film covered her vision, her sight blurry. An urgency built within her to flee. To escape. All moisture left her mouth, and her swollen tongue filled every space, cutting off access to air.

Somewhere near her, she heard Nikolai's voice, his deep baritone, penetrating the fog.

"I do not think she is well," Nikolai said.

There seemed to be a flurry of activity around her, but she remained in a claustrophobic bubble.

"She needs water," someone said.

"No, she's hyperventilating," another voice said.

A small paper bag was thrust into her hand, and Sergei lifted her hands to her face.

"Breathe, *lubov moya*. Just breathe."

Taking ragged breaths in and out, her mind slowly found purchase. She looked around, humiliation stinging her cheeks.

"Thank you," Addison mumbled.

"Are you better now?" Lena asked.

Addison bobbed her head.

"You are crazy, brother," Viktor said.

Mikhail nodded his head.

His father grinned.

"He is not. She is perfect!" Zara cried.

"You didn't answer his question," Alexi prodded Addison.

Heads swung back in Addison's direction. As the blood drained from her face, she took a shaky breath and a quick glance down at her hand. The weight of everyone's gaze seared into her. She looked up and searched out Sergei's eyes, opening her mouth, but no words came out. *Say no. Tell him you can't.* Closing it, she resorted to nodding as tears streamed down her cheeks. Defaulting to her Southern upbringing to never cause a scene. *Heaven help me, what have I done?*

The twins cheered. Sergei leaned in and brushed her lips with a feather-light kiss.

"Time for bed." Lena looked down at the youngest members of the family.

"But *Mamochka*!" Zara complained.

"Come, now." His brow raised, Nikolai's stern voice stopped Zara's protest before she gained traction.

With hugs and kisses all around, the twins sulked off to bed. Mikhail gave a shy smile and followed them up to read them a story.

"Welcome to the family," Viktor said as he kissed her on the cheek.

Oksana and Marina took turns hugging her goodbye and whispering their congratulations as they got ready to go home.

Addison was left at the table with Sergei and his parents as the house quieted down.

"We should be going, too. I have a lot of home-work to do tomorrow," Addison said.

Sergei nodded and rose from the table, holding her chair as she scooted it back.

"Thank you for coming to our home," Nikolai said. He clasped her small hand in his large ones and kissed it.

Lena stood and wrapped her in a tight embrace. "Please come again soon."

"I'll try. Thank you for everything. The dinner was wonderful, and the ring. Thank you again," she said.

"The ring is from Sergei. And we hope you love it, and him, enough to become a part of our family." Lena's voice held a note of concern, though her eyes held no recrimination.

Nikolai came around the table and wrapped his arms around his wife's waist. She leaned into him as a sigh escaped her lips.

Sergei's parents reminded her of her father and stepmother. The shy glances, the little touches, the way they held hands and spoke without words. Their love was so solid and secure they didn't need loud declarations; instead, they opted for simple expres-sions. The thing that warmed her heart the most was the way they tried to bring culture and diversity to their children's lives. So unlike Mama.

Addison bit her lip. Her eyes filled as she bobbed her head. She could find no words, so she kissed Lena on the cheek. After Sergei hugged his father and kissed his mother, he led her out to the car.

As they pulled away, Addison stared out her side of the car, watching the scenery fly by. Her mind whirled. Her stomach lurched.

"I am sorry," Sergei said, breaking the silence.

Addison turned her head to meet his stare.

"I did not mean to spring that on you." Sergei's hands gripped the wheel as he focused on the road.

"But you did. Why?" she asked.

"I had it all planned out. I was so nervous when my mother gave me the ring. At supper, it was a heavy weight in my pocket, and then the words just flew out of my mouth."

"You seemed so sure of yourself. I didn't know what to say, and your family looked so hopeful." The beautiful, delicate ring twisted in circles on her left hand.

"I am sure of you."

"You can't randomly decide to marry someone."

"You are not random to me."

"Sergei, be reasonable."

"I think I am."

"Even though we barely know each other?" Addison's jaw dropped.

"Why are you surprised? It was meant to be." Sergei caressed Addison's cheek.

Addison had never gotten the sense from him that he felt she was his "one." It seemed to move all too fast for her.

"We haven't talked about the future at all!" she said, her voice warbling.

"What would you like to talk about?" Sergei's voice was calm.

"I'm going back home in a few months, and I have another year of school ahead of me."

"I know. I want to give you a reason to stay."

"It's not that easy. I have a life in America."

"I understand. You can have one here, with me."

Ugh. He isn't usually this obtuse.

"You're Russian," she continued, disregarding his last statement.

"And you are American." He nodded, caressing her palm as his eyes remained on the road.

"Exactly. Our futures lie in two different directions." The butterflies that usually danced in her stomach whenever he touched her seemed to rebel now. It wasn't a pleasant feeling. This wasn't what she had expected from a year in Russia—or him. This was supposed to be a simple, short-term thing before she went back home to real life. Panic bubbled up within her again, threatening to choke her.

Sergei gave her a quizzical glance before turning his attention back to the road. A faint smile tugged at his lips.

CHAPTER 16

The Heart Knows

Sergei

S ergei pulled into the student lot on campus and put the car in park, leaving it running to allow the heater to stave off the chill lingering in the air. The drive back to school had been tense.

Addison slid the ring off her finger and reached out to give it to him.

"*Nyet.*" He shook his head and pushed her hand back into her lap.

She stared down at the ring in her palm.

"Listen to your heart, *milaya*," he said. He twisted in his seat and held her gaze.

"I don't know how." She hung her head as her eyes filled with tears.

"We could be good together."

"Oh, Sergei. It's not that easy. My entire life, I've

149

been torn between what my heart wants and what was expected of me. Duty always wins."

"I do not understand."

"Growing up, things between my parents were ugly. My mother never forgave my father for divorcing her and remarrying."

"I thought your mother remarried."

"Yes, many times—and yet her anger toward my father never lessened. And she hated his wife Cassie even more."

"That makes no sense," Sergei said.

"I know, but that's how it is, even now. My father is happy. My mother isn't. And I have continued to be the ball that bounces back and forth."

"She wanted him back?"

"Oh, yes, even though she'd never admit it—so she continued to punish him. And she did it through me."

"That sounds terrible."

"I didn't realize it at first. It took me many years to understand her obsession with my loyalty to her or her constant pulling me to her. I didn't see it as her way of controlling me or, by extension, my father." Addison continued to stare at the ring in her palm.

"I see." He reached over and touched her hand.

"When the court battles began, things got even worse. I was asked to choose between my parents, but I couldn't. My heart wanted to live with my father and Cassie, and all the things they were offering me.

But whenever I wavered, my mother would guilt me, demand my loyalty to her, twist things between my father and Cassie. No matter what I did, the road always led me back to her."

"But you are an adult now."

Addison shook her head. "Sergei, I chose a college out of state to get space, and yet I didn't get far. Then I came to Russia to put distance between us. Your family encourages independence. My mother has worked to smother my independence from the time I could walk."

"She cannot prevent you from marrying me if it is what you want," Sergei said.

"I've never gotten what I wanted. It's never been about me."

"We can do it together. Trust me, *mon amour*." Sergei stroked her knuckles with his thumb.

"French? Really? It's bad enough when you get all mushy in Russian," Addison mumbled.

"Darling, I speak the language of love in five languages."

"Oh, God help me," she muttered.

Sergei chuckled. His eyes were full of mischief as he raised her hand and brought it to his lips. His voice dropped to a husky whisper.

"*Ya lyublyu tebya.*" His mouth pressed against the top of her hand.

Shivers slid down her spine.

"Or *ich liebe dich*." He kissed her knuckles.

She bit her lip.

"If *Je t'aime* doesn't do it for you." He brought the tips of her fingers to his lips.

Butterflies fluttered in her stomach.

"There's always Italiano… *ti amo*." He flipped her hand over and pressed her palm to his cheek.

The butterflies rioted.

"That's only four," she whispered.

Sergei's laugh was infectious. "So, it was. I love you. That makes five, I believe." He kissed her wrist.

"Smarty pants."

"I do not know that saying." His eyes clouded with confusion.

"It's a nice way of saying smart ass."

"Oh." Sergei blushed.

Sergei rested his hands on her cheeks, and with a gentle tug, pulled her face to him. When they were nose to nose, he kissed her. The soft pressure increased as she responded to him. He slowed, then stopped the kiss and peered into her wet eyes.

"I have no doubt you are where I belong. The rest is just details."

She shook her head, taking his hands with her movements. *Details.* He made it sound so simple.

"Yes. Details. They can be worked out together."

"My living in America and you living in Russia are not simple details."

"You will stay in Russia with me." Sergei's face was serious as he delivered this statement.

"No."

"But you must."

"I will not trade being controlled by my mother, to being controlled by a man." Addison stiffened in her seat.

"It is not like that," Sergei said.

"It sounds like it to me," Addison said.

"I want us to be together."

"Sergei, I can't stay in Russia. Not even for you."

"Okay, *milaya*. Okay." His voice was soft, but held no recrimination.

He had said nothing about coming to America with her, and she didn't want to push him. To ask him to give up his home, his culture, and his family when she'd just admitted that she wouldn't do the same for him wasn't fair.

Tears rolled down her face as she imagined saying goodbye to him in a couple of months.

His thumbs wiped away her tears and stroked her wet cheeks. "Do not cry. Everything will be fine. You will see."

She bobbed her head as more tears flowed unabated. She was falling in love with him, something she'd never thought possible. Leaving him would rip her heart apart. But she wouldn't stay.

"Now put on this pretty ring so you can see how much I love you." Sergei took the ring from her palm and slid it back onto her finger.

"How does a ring show me that?" Addison snuffled.

"I gave you a family heirloom, and you still talk of leaving me in Russia. I think it is self-explanatory." Sergei grinned.

It made little sense, but she was too exhausted and emotional to argue with him. She'd have to sleep on it and figure it all out in the morning.

Sergei kissed the ring on her right hand before cupping her face and kissing her deeply again. "There, now all is right in the world."

He walked her to the main door of her dorm, kissing her gently on the lips. "Until tomorrow." He kissed her again and turned and headed back down the walkway.

Addison took a long, hot shower, hoping to relieve the tension in her shoulders. Once in her room, she slipped into an oversized nightshirt before crawling into bed. The exhaustion and emotions of the day caught up with her, and as her head nestled on the pillow, the blackness of the room engulfed her.

The nightmare came. Just as it always did when she was stressed or felt trapped. She never aged in the dreams, always a little girl of about seven or eight.

Her mother was on one side, pulling on her arm to bring her closer. "You don't love me. If you loved me, you would be loyal."

On the other side of her stood Cassie. Her arms folded

across her chest, a look of exasperation on her face. "Your heart is big enough to love everyone in your life. You don't have to choose. It isn't disloyalty for you to love other people as much as you love your mom."

"Don't listen to her. She's just trying to steal you away from me." The tugging continued, her arm getting heavy even in her dream.

"Addison, you're a strong, independent, young woman. Follow your gut——" Cassie said with slow deliberation.

"You act like you want to be just like her." Her mother's bitterness was evident, even in the recesses of her mind.

The dream zoomed, and suddenly Sergei was across from her. She stood in the center of a triangle, surrounded by her mother, stepmother, and Sergei.

"You will marry me, lubov moya. *You must," Sergei said.*

"You can't marry someone like him. That isn't how I raised you."

Back and forth, the tug of war never ended. Not even in her dreams. Her entire life, she'd been torn between loyalty and the desire to spread her wings. There wasn't room for both, as far as her mother was concerned.

CHAPTER 17

Proclamations

Addison

Addison pulled the pillow over her head to block out all the noise her roommate was making. She was in no hurry to face the day, even as Sophie cheerily sung to the radio.

"Your date went well last night," Sophie said.

Sophie sat perched on the edge of the bed; her weight pulled Addison to the side.

"Hmm." Addison twisted her body to free her arm from being pinned under Sophie. Shifting the pillow from her face, she opened one eye to find her friend's face practically hovering above her.

"Looks like you're engaged." Sophie laughed.

"Engaged?" Addison popped upright in bed and stared at her, confusion muddling her mind. "No."

Sophie leaned away, hanging her hands over the

side so the steaming liquid wouldn't spill all over the bed. "According to the ring on your hand, I'd say it does."

Addison peered down at her left hand, finding it bare, turned her attention to her right hand. She gasped at seeing the large teardrop ring Sergei had given her the night before. She would like to say she'd forgotten, but in her bleary-eyed state, she'd honestly hoped it had been a crazy dream.

"Ohh. Yes."

"You forgot you got engaged last night?" Sophie laughed.

Sophie reached out and offered one of the coffee mugs to Addison.

Wrapping her hands around the hot cup helped to clear the cobwebs from her mind. "Not exactly," Addison groaned.

"What does that mean?"

"He didn't actually propose, really. He just told his whole family at dinner he was going to marry me."

"And the ring?" The rim of the coffee cup barely hid Sophie's grin as she held it to her lips.

"It's a family thing."

"Ooh." Sophie's eyes grew wide, and her mouth gaped.

"What does that mean?" Addison lowered the cup to her lap and leaned back into the headboard.

"If a Russian man gives you a ring from his family, he's going to marry you," Sophie said.

Funny, that's precisely what he said, too.

Sophie's face was expressionless, which only caused more anxiety in Addison.

"What's the difference? A ring's a ring."

"Not to a Russian." Sophie shook her head. "Family is everything here. If he goes to a jewelry store and buys a ring, she may say yes, she may say no. But if a man gives you something from his family, it means yes."

"I'm an American. We decide who we marry."

"Humph. We'll see." Sophie shook her head, the grin still solidly in place.

"Are you saying they'll force me to marry him?"

"No, no. It just means he's serious. Not a silly, inconsequential school romance."

"Oh, God. What have I gotten into?" With a shaking hand, she raised her cup to her lips. Coffee sloshed over her rim, so she set the cup back on her lap. Ugly red welts dotted her hand, showing evidence of her clumsiness.

"Looks like you're going back as a married woman." Sophie beamed.

"I can't," she choked. "I can't get married without my family or before I finish school… to a Russian man." The words came out in a barely coherent rush.

Sophie sat on the edge of her bed and grinned at her like the Cheshire cat.

"What am I going to do?" Addison said.

"I'd suggest you talk to him."

"I tried. He keeps telling me it's meant to be." Panic rose in Addison's chest.

"Sounds like you've got your hands full."

"You have no idea," Addison muttered into her coffee cup.

"Let me see the ring before you give it back."

Addison slipped the ring off and handed it to her roommate.

Sophie whistled. "I think I'd accept his proposal just for this ring. It's beautiful."

"It is, isn't it?" Addison watched as her friend slipped the ring onto her finger and whipped it up in the air to get a better look at it in the light.

"It looks like an emerald."

"Chrome diopside."

"Oh, wow. Those are rare. You're lucky to have one such a brilliant green."

Pulling the ring off her finger, Sophie returned it to Addison, who held it in her palm, afraid to put it back on.

"So I'm told."

Sophie took the ring from Addison's palm and slid it onto the proper finger on Addison's right hand. "You don't want to lose this."

Addison bobbed her head.

"Are you going out with Sergei today?"

"I think so, but we didn't make plans. Why?"

"I could use some help on our literature essay."

"Let's go down to the coffee shop and work there," Addison suggested.

"You don't mind?"

"Not at all. You were his tutor first."

Sophie gave her a rueful smile.

"You're always welcome to join us."

"Thanks," Sophie said.

Addison slid her legs around Sophie and planted them on the floor. They sat side by side on the bed for a moment. "What am I going to do?" Addison asked.

Sophie reached for her hand, lifting the ringed finger high, and smiled. "A hunk of a man, and a stunning ring. I'd say he's a keeper."

Addison shook her head and nudged her room-mate. "Thanks, you're no help."

Sophie wrapped her arm around her. "I try." They sat on the edge, entwined, laughing, before they moved off the bed to get dressed.

WHEN SERGEI WALKED INTO THE COFFEE SHOP, Addison and Sophie sat at the usual table, bent over their computers, typing furiously and unaware of his arrival.

"Hello." Sergei pulled the empty chair out and dropped his bag on the table. Seeing the ring still on her hand brightened his mood. He could not stop the wide grin from splitting and filling his face.

"Glad you could come," Addison said.

"How long have you been waiting?" His sudden insecurity around her swallowed him.

"We've been here for almost an hour."

"We are working on the literature essays. Want to trade?" Sophie asked.

"*Da*, please."

After Sergei opened his laptop and pulled up the document in question, the three exchanged computers and resumed working.

Twenty minutes later, Addison finished and closed the lid before sliding it over next to Sophie. "Coffee anyone?" she asked.

"*Da*."

"*Oui*."

Addison stood and stretched. She strolled over to the counter and placed the order for the coffees.

"Sophie, is she angry?" Sergei asked.

"No, I think she's confused."

"I did not mean to do it that way; it was so unromantic."

"It's a beautiful ring, though." Sophie smiled.

"Does she like it?"

"I believe so."

Sergei's voice dropped. "Do you think it is enough for her to stay?"

"That, *mon amie*, I cannot answer." Sophie shrugged.

"I understand this is sudden, but I know she is my match." He put his right hand over his heart.

"How do you know? Honestly?" Sophie's gaze pierced him.

"I never cared before about a woman. Not like this."

"I agree. She is special," Sophie said.

Deep in discussion and not paying attention to their surroundings, they both jumped when Addison returned to the table.

"I have sandwich forms if anyone's hungry," Addison said.

Sophie glanced at her watch. "It's almost one. Where did the time go?"

Sergei scribbled some notes on a slip and pulled out a handful of rubles. "Lunch is on me today."

Addison wrote on hers and handed it over as Sergei backed up his chair and stood. "Thank you."

"*Merci*, that's sweet of you," Sophie said.

He gave Sophie a shy smile as he took her slip.

CHAPTER 18

Christmas Break

Sergei

Contentment filled Sergei that Addison was there with him. He was thrilled she had accepted his parents' invitation to spend the Christmas break with their family. Zara stood in the doorway, avoiding the falling snow, and watching impatiently as Alexi ran out to greet them. He tugged Addison's hand, pulling her toward the house while Sergei took their luggage from the trunk. He trudged behind them; his lips stretched into a broad smile. To see his family as ensnared by her made his heart swell.

Zara threw herself into Addison's arms as she reached the door. Addison, prepared for his exuberant sister, did not stumble as she wrapped her arm around the flying child, all the while holding Alexi's hand. His grin widened as he watched them.

She was a smooth operator. Always soothing ruffled feathers and heading off tantrums before even his mother turned around. His heart filled with pride as Addison proved her natural abilities with children.

"*Papulya* has a surprise," Alexi said, dropping his voice to a whisper.

Sergei dropped the bags by the door and grabbed his little brother, lifting him into his arms. "Tell me all about it," he said.

"I cannot," he squealed. "*Mamochka* will not say a word." He continued to squirm and squeal as Sergei carried him like a flying log, tickling him the entire way.

They walked into the kitchen, where his mother stood with her back to him. Standing in the doorway, he watched his mother stirring a pot. Most of his memories were of her at the stove. She turned and greeted him with a warm smile.

He lowered his brother in a pretend drop, eliciting more squeals of laughter, before he set him on his feet. Alexi swayed for a moment before he stood tall, walked over to Addison, and retook her empty hand. The twins led her to the table and took up seats on each side of her.

Sergei laughed. He stepped closer to his mother and kissed both her cheeks. "What are you baking, *Mamochka*?"

"Cookies." She patted his face.

"Smells absolutely sinful." He sniffed the air appreciatively.

His mother smiled and handed him two steaming mugs of tea. He carried them to the table and sat next to Viktor, across from Addison and the twins.

"…and when *Papulya* gets home…" Alexi said.

"And what about when *Papulya* gets home?" a deep voice rumbled from the door.

"*Papulya*!" the twins hooted in unison, bouncing in their seats.

His father kissed his mother's cheek.

"*Papulya*, we've been good today."

"All day?" he asked, laughing.

"*Da*. We cleaned our rooms, swept the floor, and helped *Mamochka* with the dishes and cookies."

"And how many cookies did you help eat?" There was a mischievous gleam in his eye.

"Only two," Alexi said.

"Each." Zara blushed.

Nikolai's hearty guffaws filled the room. "That is good." He winked at his wife.

Smiling back at him, she walked to the table with two cups of tea. After handing him one, she stood and rested her free hand on his shoulder.

"Tell us the surprise, *Papulya*," Alexi pleaded.

Everyone's attention was riveted on Nikolai. But before he could speak, a commotion in the hall drew their attention. There was an echo of multiple people stomping snow from their boots before Mikhail came into the room, followed by Oksana.

The greetings and laughter lasted while Lena brought more tea.

"Now that everyone is here, I can tell you the surprise. We've been offered use of the university's tickets to the Orchestra."

The girlfriends and younger kids exchanged confused glances. The smiles on the twins' faces fell, while the older ones smiled.

Sergei and Viktor seemed to be the only ones at the table able to grasp the significance of their father's announcement.

"This weekend is the opening of *The* Nutcracker," Nikolai continued.

"The Nutcracker!" the twins squealed.

His father sat back in his chair and patted his mother's hand on his shoulder.

Sergei enjoyed watching his parents' comfortable way with each other, their silent communications or easy affections with him and his siblings.

"You will wear your Easter clothes," Lena said.

Zara's previously sour continence brightened, while Alexi groaned and dropped his head onto his arm spread out on the table.

Chatter filled the air as everyone talked over each other.

Catching his eye, Addison whispered, "Sergei."

The conversations stopped abruptly, as though she'd shouted.

"I'm sorry," Addison mumbled. Her cheeks grew rosy.

"You are included, my dear, if that is your concern. Everyone is," Nikolai said.

"I don't have anything appropriate to wear," Addison said.

"I have shoes. We are the same size," Oksana said.

"I have more than enough dresses," Marina said.

"If not, Addison, we will take you shopping," Sergei's mother said.

"Oh, I couldn't…" Addison started.

"It will all work out, *moy rebenok*," Nikolai said. His tone confirmed he had no doubt as he patted her hand.

Sergei smiled at her as she just nodded. He knew she would be fine in the hands of his mother and brothers' girlfriends.

He continued to observe her from across the table as his family captured her attention and kept it throughout the evening. She grew more at ease with them, and more comfortable with herself and his family. Her eyes sparkled, and a smile tugged at her lips as the conversation flowed around the table. The twins' chatter filled the air, giving him time to reflect on how much his interests and direction had changed in the short time he'd known her. This one had captured his heart most unexpectedly. It surprised him how easily he had fallen. And how quickly. He never put much stock in love at first sight, but she had reached in and touched his soul from the very first moment.

CHAPTER 19

Family-Style Memories

Addison

A ddison could see where Sergei's conviction came from. Nikolai reminded her of her father sometimes, though she didn't have the same certainty ingrained within her that Sergei appeared to have. *I envy that.*

The next morning, after a hearty breakfast, Marina and Oksana arrived. Moments later, she was spirited off with the girls. They pulled her upstairs while the men left for the afternoon. Haphazard heaps of dresses were piled high on Zara's bed. Across the room, in the corner, stood a teetering tower of shoeboxes. They took turns trying on dresses and shoes, laughing, and giggling all the while. By the time the sun was low in the sky, the girls had each picked out their outfits and were delighted with their choices.

The following evening, everyone dressed to the nines. Sergei's father whistled at the boys as they came into the room. With a soft smile and a kiss on the cheek, he greeted each of the women. When his wife came into the room with rosy cheeks and a sparkle in her eye, he kissed her and said, "You are beautiful, my love."

Lena kissed him back. Her black velvet-topped pantsuit glimmered in the light.

A few minutes later, their large group climbed into the limousine that Nikolai had hired and headed to the show.

When they arrived at the Mariinsky Theatre, Addison marveled at its size. The majestic building was a stunning tribute to one of their most beloved empresses, Maria Alexandrovna. Like so much of Russian architecture, it had stood the test of time. More than a century had done little to mar its beauty and grace.

They scrambled out of the car into flashing lights and whirling, clicking cameras as they joined the impressive throng of people entering the theater. A young man in a red uniform led their group to the second-floor suite where Yuri sat. After everyone else settled, an older woman in a black uniform passed the adults tall crystal flutes of champagne from a large silver tray. Another woman, much younger than the first, gave the children glasses of sparkling water.

"Please enjoy the performance," the young

server said, slowly backing out of the room and pulling the heavy red velvet curtains closed behind her.

"We are in the Tsar's box," Marina whispered. The awe was evident in her voice.

As every face turned to Nikolai, he nodded. "*Da*. The Tsar's box was available for tonight's performance and gave the university access to it."

Addison's wide eyes took in the luxurious, velvet-covered seats with ornate gold edges and blood-red velvet curtains.

The attendant came back around with a box full of fancy long-handled opera glasses, passing them out. The glass lenses glittered in the dim light.

The Nutcracker was everything Addison remembered as a child. Though the performance was in Russian, she followed it with ease.

Her dad and Cassie had taken her to see the show when she was about the twins' age. Her grandparents had joined them; they had all dressed up and gone to a fancy restaurant for dinner before the performance. It was one of her favorite childhood memories. The shows and plays that they had taken her to gave her a deep appreciation for theater. From their attentive and animated expressions, there was no doubt that the twins felt the same way.

When the performance ended, Addison and Sergei offered to remain in the box with the twins so his parents could socialize downstairs with friends and colleagues. While they were gone, the twins babbled about their favorite parts.

"The mouse king was scary." Zara's voice was faint. Addison smiled as the little girl in her lap fought to stay awake.

"He was, I agree," Addison spoke into her hair. Holding Sergei's little sister tugged at her heartstrings, reminding her of Beth. Sergei's family was wonderful, and she enjoyed her time with them, but they were no substitute for her own family—and as crazy as they made her, she missed them terribly.

"He wasn't so bad," Alexi said.

Sergei looked over at Addison and winked as he ruffled his brother's hair.

Moments later, Sergei's family ushered them down to the waiting car. Alexi and Zara curled up in little balls against Lena as the limousine drove them home. They had been so keyed-up that the excitement wore them out, and within minutes had succumbed to slumber. Nikolai and Sergei carried them up to bed when they reached the house, while the rest of their tribe traipsed into the kitchen where Lena put the kettle on for tea.

They piled around the large block table, talking and laughing before exhaustion took its toll on them as well. One by one, they excused themselves and headed to bed. To make room for the plethora of guests, the twins slept on cots in the master bedroom, leaving the other five bedrooms for the older kids.

Lena set the sleeping arrangements up to make sure the girls would be comfortable for the evening.

Nerves humming under her skin, Addison slipped under the covers next to Marina. She closed her eyes and visualized the vibrant costumes and elaborate backgrounds. The play had been magnificent and the evening in the Tsar's box was magical. She knew she would remember this night for the rest of her life. Lying there for what seemed like hours, listening to the hum of Marina's steady breathing, she replayed the performance in her mind. The last thoughts that crept in before sleep took her were of Clara and the prince dancing.

CHAPTER 20

A Winter Wonderland

Sergei

Sergei loaded the trunk with their bags. They would meet his brother Viktor along with Viktor's girlfriend, Marina, at the resort to go skiing for the weekend. It had been years since they had skied at Okhta Park, so Addison had easily agreed to go with them. It was their first weekend away together. She still wore his ring, but seemed to shy away from any conversations about it.

"You packed warm clothes?" he asked.

"I did, but I have no ski clothes." Addison waved her hands.

"No worries, Marina has a suit. We'll rent your boots and skis."

"I can't take her ski suit. Won't she need it to ski?"

Sergei chuckled as he held the door open for her.

"Any excuse to buy a new outfit for the trip is a welcome gift."

"Oh, in that case, I don't feel so bad," Addison laughed.

He shut the door with a smile and headed around to the driver's side. "The drive is not long; I'll keep it slow in the snow."

"Why didn't we drive together?" she asked.

"Viktor and Marina go back to Moscow after this weekend."

"Okay." Addison snuggled into her seat.

Sergei turned on the radio, drowning out the sounds of the tires crunching on the snow... his nerves on fire. He'd never gone away with a girl before. He wasn't sure what Addison expected either, since his experiences with women were so limited.

"If you need anything, we can stop at a store on the way."

"Thank you."

Sergei sighed, struggling to find the right words for small talk. His tongue got all twisted in his teeth, and his mind wandered when she was near.

"I am looking forward to a weekend away."

"I am, too. Thank you for inviting me. It's been a wonderful holiday."

"My family adores you."

Addison gave him the sweetest smile, causing his heart to skip. "I like them, too. They're easy to be with."

"I do, too."

She turned her attention out the passenger window without responding. He tried to ignore the sting when she pulled away from him. Being with her was a dance. Sometimes she took a step forward and met him in the middle, and other times she took a step backward, just out of arm's reach. He needed to step up his game if he wanted to keep her.

The time passed quickly, and he pulled into the resort an hour later.

After opening the door to the suite, they found Viktor and Marina already there, cozy on the couch. Sergei dropped their bags just inside the door. Viktor jumped up and strode toward the open doorway between their rooms to give him a hearty hug as Addison moved into the room.

"Brother!"

"How was the drive?" Sergei asked.

"We left early, missed the snow. You?"

"Did not leave early. Did not miss the snow."

Viktor gave a loud guffaw and slapped Sergei on the back. "You are here. Relax, come join us."

Marina stood and joined them in the center of the room. She embraced Addison in a warm hug before handing her a steaming mug. "Cocoa. To warm you."

"Thank you." Addison took a seat in one of the overstuffed wing-backed chairs. Sergei took another.

"We should take a walk before dinner. Show the ladies the grounds," Viktor said.

"Sounds good."

"We will hit the slopes tomorrow morning," Viktor said.

"Sounds great," Marina agreed.

"I'm not a strong skier. I'll need a refresher course," Addison said. She looked at Sergei, her eyes pleading.

"I will take one with you," Marina said.

"There you go. Sergei will join me on the slopes while you take lessons, and we will meet for lunch," Viktor said.

Sergei lifted his mug. "Addison?"

"Yes, that would be great."

"Good. Our reservations are for six."

After they finished their cocoa, the quartet wandered the vast resort until the sunset, before meandering through the halls of the hotel.

Sergei kept hold of Addison's left hand while they walked, often touching her fingers, or caressing her palm. He avoided her right hand with the ring on it, to not bring attention to it or to cause her to think of anything other than their weekend together. He was as nervous as a schoolboy, terrified she would regret her decision.

This was moving way too fast—he would be the first to acknowledge it. However, there had been no one before who made him feel like he did when he thought of her, when he looked at her. The way his heart beat faster when she laughed. He had never had much interest in anything outside of his studies. For the first time in his life, everything was different. All because of her.

They returned to their rooms to clean up for dinner.

"Addison, would you like to shower first?" he asked.

"I showered this morning, so go ahead. I'll just touch up my hair and makeup."

Sergei nodded and closed the bathroom door behind him. The hot shower soothed his nerves. He dried and dressed quickly in black slacks and a light-weight sweater before padding back into the room barefoot.

She was a vision in a pair of gray wool pants, tucked into her black knee-high boots, and a pale purple sweater that made her cheeks glow. She'd pulled her hair back with a gold clip at the nape of her neck.

He felt himself stiffen and had to turn away. He sat on the edge of the bed and focused on his socks and shoes, willing his member to relax. Never in his life had a girl affected him like this.

Contrary to the confident way he hoped he appeared to Addison—through a lot of work—he was terrified. The past month with her had been a test of his self-control. Always trying to be a perfect gentle-man. To be perfect for her. Always so sure of himself... of her. If she ever knew the depth of his insecurities regarding most everything other than his academics, she would be disappointed. His determination was firm; he would not scare her away now.

With a deep breath, he stood and let out a sigh of relief at the ever-so-slight loosening of his pants as the fabric adjusted itself. He was grateful she was unaware of his situation as he held out his elbow to her. She took it, and they walked out of the bedroom together.

THEY WERE LED TO A SMALL TABLE IN A COZY CORNER of the dining room, next to the floor-to-ceiling windows overlooking the slopes.

Wine flowed, and the food was exquisite.

"Remember the last time we were here? We were still in high school," Viktor said.

"The twins were so young. Their first trip, I believe," Sergei said.

"*Da. Mamochka* had her hands full with them. Then Mikhail talked you into taking that slope, and you broke your arm."

"Served me right for showing off." Sergei picked up his wineglass.

"*Mamochka* was so mad at you."

Pausing with his glass near his lips, he nodded. "Yes, she rarely loses her temper, but if one of us gets hurt, she goes all mama bear."

Viktor laughed. "Yes, she does."

Dinner was full of laughter and more tales of

their childhood shenanigans for Addison and Marina. Viktor had everyone in stitches with his stories. When it was over, Viktor and Marina excused themselves with a wink and a nod and left them alone to finish their dessert and coffee.

"Addison?"

"Yes?" Her eyes met his after a brief hesitation.

"There is no pressure, *dorogaya*. I want you to enjoy this weekend."

"I am."

"I am glad you are here with me."

Addison nodded as her attention flitted away from him.

He took a deep breath to tamper his frustration. He hated when she pushed him away. *She just needs time.*

"Ready to go up?"

"Yes."

He helped her from her chair and together they took the lift back to their suite.

SHE WENT INTO THE BATHROOM TO CHANGE INTO HER nightclothes while he slipped on a pair of pajama bottoms and crawled into bed. He left only the night-stand lamp on to light her way.

When she came out, he smiled, a book in his lap.

Sergei leaned over and pulled the covers down on her side of the bed. Her slow steps around the room to her side of the bed made him nervous. He could see that she was unsure.

She slid under the blankets, pulling them up to her chest. He set the book aside and pushed the light switch off. The room plunged into darkness. He scooted down into the bed and lay immobile, afraid he may scare her. Reaching his hand out over the covers, he laced his fingers with hers and rested it between them. He closed his eyes and willed himself to loosen his tense muscles.

THE NEXT MORNING, SERGEI WOKE WITH A START. Addison had moved over during the night, and her head rested on his chest. Her hand was under her cheek, and gentle snores came from her.

His entire body reacted to this unexpected intimacy, and it took every bit of strength he possessed not to move. His head on the pillow, eyes on the ceiling, her cheek on his chest, his whole body hummed. Sergei had never experienced this before.

Addison rolled over and curled up on her side, her face away from him. She appeared oblivious to the arousal he battled. Sucking in a deep breath, he slid out of bed, careful to not wake her. Carefully padding his way to the bathroom, he closed the door with a click and locked it behind him. Flipping the shower to the coldest setting, he dropped his pajamas on the floor and stepped under the cold spray. His eyes popped open as the icy needles pricked his skin.

Sergei stood under the frigid water, letting his morning erection wither. After he washed his hair, he turned off the water and dripped for a moment. He hadn't thought to bring clothes in with him. Not comfortable walking into the bedroom with just a towel, he stood in the shower stall, letting the water slide off his body as he debated his next move.

A light rap on the door snapped him out of his reverie.

"Sergei?"

"Yes?"

"Are you almost done? I need to use the bathroom."

"Give me just a minute."

He jumped out of the shower and yanked his pajama bottoms over his wet body. He threw the towel over his shoulders before jerking the door open.

Addison stood on the other side of the doorway, shifting from one foot to the other. He had barely moved out of her way as she plowed past him and shut the door.

He chuckled and shook his head before sitting on the bed to dry his hair. She came out a few minutes later. *No good morning. No kiss.* He hoped this was not an omen of the day to come.

"Sorry." Her embarrassment stained her cheeks pink.

"No problem. Go ahead and shower. Take your time. I am fine out here."

"Thanks." Addison rifled through her bag before carrying a pile of clothes into the bathroom and shutting the door again.

Sergei's body was almost dry as he pulled off his soggy bottoms and hung them on the chair. He toweled off and then draped the towel over his pajama pants.

He slipped on a set of thermals, then his ski suit, before donning his heavy boots. Satisfied he hadn't forgotten anything, he headed out to the sitting room. His brother was already there, sitting on the couch.

"Marina's getting ready, so it will take a while," Viktor said.

"Addison, too. Do you have coffee?"

"Yes, a pot was delivered already."

"Oh, thank you."

Viktor laughed. "Rough night?"

"You have no idea."

Viktor's brow rose, but he kept his questions to himself. Sergei was grateful. His brother flipped on the television to a Futbol game, and he dropped onto the couch beside Viktor, who poured him a cup of coffee before they leaned back to watch the game.

Thirty minutes later, Marina joined them, and five minutes after that, Addison poked her head through the side door.

"Any coffee left?" she asked.

"Sorry, I don't think so," Sergei said.

"Should we go down to breakfast, then?"

Marina bobbed her head as she headed for the door. Addison followed her before they could even shut off the television.

They took the elevator down to the restaurant on the first level. The rush of people having already departed for the slopes left plenty of open tables near the window to choose from.

The waiter set a pot of coffee and four cups on the table before taking their order.

Sergei laughed as, one by one, they each ordered a bowl of kasha and a boiled egg. It hadn't been discussed, but their appetites appeared to be well-matched. He poured the steaming brew in each cup while Marina passed the cups around.

The view out the floor-to-ceiling windows was magnificent. The white powder on the slopes was crisp and glowing in the morning sunlight, the lifts already full of people who'd gotten an early start.

"The beginners' lessons should be a couple of hours long. Will you be fine on your own while we ski the bigger slopes?" Viktor asked Addison.

"Of course. Marina, are you still planning to join me?" Addison asked.

"*Da*. Plan to meet up at one o'clock for lunch?" Marina suggested.

"Where?" Viktor asked.

"How about the great hall by the fireplace?" Sergei asked.

"Perfect," Marina said.

The waiter brought their meals, and they dug in with hearty appetites.

THEY SPLIT UP AN HOUR LATER, AFTER EVERYONE HAD been fitted for their skiing equipment. The women followed the guide to a small section at the side of the hotel. Dozens of small man-made hills, no more than five feet high, surrounded them.

After lessons on the techniques of slowing and stopping and how to fall gracefully—a task Addison didn't master—they were let loose on the hills to practice. She followed Marina to one of the larger hills farthest away from the group.

"You should go first," Marina suggested.

"Promise not to laugh," Addison said.

"Only *with* you, never at you," Marina promised.

With a slight bow, Addison headed to the other side of the hill. The snow was packed tighter on the backside, and it made it easier for her to climb to the top. She glided down the slight bump. She looped around her new friend and came to a perfect stop on her other side. After a quick high-five, Marina made her way to the slope and did the same. She did a little spin at the end, coming to a stop in front of Addison, facing her.

"Show-off."

Marina laughed.

The women practiced for another half-hour, Addison's speed and confidence increasing. Addison stood on the top of the hill, preparing for her descent, when the whistle blew, signaling the end of the lesson. Attempting to best her last maneuver, she spun around Marina with a whoosh. And landed on her backside. Skis up in the air, her bottom planted firmly on the ground, Addison swore.

Laughing, Marina skied over to her and, legs braced, extended her hand. "Are you hurt?"

"I don't think so, but I think I'll take these off now, just in case." Addison snapped the skis from her boots and let them fall into the snow. After Marina pulled her up, she picked up her skis and followed Marina's sashaying form to the equipment rental shop.

Her legs felt wobbly in her heavy snow boots, but she was determined not to appear weak.

Sitting next to the massive fireplace facing the windows, they sipped their cocoa. A short time later, Addison was feeling a little numb.

"These are smooth," Addison said. She giggled as she sipped her third cup.

"It's the peppermint schnapps." Marina grinned.

"No way." Addison gulped.

Marina was eyeing her suspiciously.

"I didn't... hadn't realized..." Addison was trip-ping over her words.

"Oh. I thought you knew."

"Nope... Oh boy." Addison giggled again, just as the men joined them.

"You got her drunk?" Sergei asked.

"Accidentally, I promise. The cocoa was spiked. This is her third." Marina wore a sheepish grin, which caused Addison to giggle again.

"I suggest we skip lunch and put this one to bed for a nap," Sergei said.

Addison nodded her head.

They traipsed to the elevator while she leaned heavily on Sergei for support and direction.

Once they reached the suite, Viktor and Marina plopped on the couch while Sergei directed her to their bedroom. She swayed as he sat her on the edge of the bed. She leaned in and tried to kiss him, missing his lips, her mouth landing on his nose instead, and banging her head against his.

"Ouch," she giggled.

Sergei rubbed his thumb across the spot on her forehead, where they connected in a soft caress.

"Oh, that feels good." Her voice sounded funny to her ears.

Sergei sighed and went into the bathroom for a cold cloth. After closing her eyes to keep the room from spinning, she vaguely remembered leaning back and a damp hand towel being placed on her brow.

When she woke, the room was dark, with only a small thread of light coming from the bathroom. Sergei snored softly at her side. Wiggling her toes, she struggled to recall taking off her shoes—she couldn't. Flat on her back, her face turned in his direction. The slow movement of his chest as it rose and fell held her in thrall. He fascinated and terrified her at the same time, bringing to the surface emotions she had never experienced. Addison felt safe when he was near, while at the same time panic swirled inside of her.

It was too much too soon.

He was exactly the kind of man she could see herself marrying. Later. A long time from now. But he belonged in Russia, and she in America. Relationships like theirs were too complicated. Shaking the conflicting thoughts from her head, she rested her palm on his chest, and his heat radiating into her hand.

Resisting the urge to kiss him, she slipped out of bed and headed for the bathroom. After washing her hands and face, she made her way out of the bedroom to see if Marina and Viktor were awake. Pushing the door open a little further, she stepped into the living area where the other couple snuggled on the small two-seat couch, watching a movie.

Marina noticed her first. "How are you feeling?" she asked.

"Stiff and starving."

"I imagine so. We skipped lunch and supper. Should we order room service?"

"Yes, please."

"Did I hear someone say room service?" Sergei entered the room with a wide grin.

"Where there is food, you will always find my brother." Viktor pointed at the binder on the table.

Sergei picked it up and sat down in one of the large leather wingback chairs. "Sandwiches?"

"Sounds great," Marina agreed.

"Addison, how is your head?" Sergei asked.

"Fine actually. The nap helped," Addison said. She settled into the other wingback chair.

Sergei read aloud the list of specialty sandwiches in the room service catalog before heading to the corner table that held the telephone and placing the order.

Returning, he chose the long, overstuffed couch across from his brother instead of the single chair, and smiled at Addison. He patted the seat next to him, a questioning look in his eyes. She returned his smile and moved to the couch. He wrapped his arm around her shoulders and held her close, warming her body with his.

Marina flipped through the channels until she reached a station that played older American movies. *Romancing the Stone* was on, and they settled in to watch.

Caught up in the sexual tension between Kathleen Turner and Michael Douglas, the time had passed quickly. Addison's stomach rumbled. The sound pulled the attention from the movie, and all eyes turned to her Viktor chuckled while Marina giggled. It put a crack in the hormonal charge of the room.

A hard rapping knock announced the arrival of supper. Sergei slipped from behind her and strolled over to answer the door. The service boy in the crisp navy uniform pushed the cart into the center of the room. With a nod and a handshake, he left. After closing the door, Sergei joined the other three hovering around the cart, preparing to pounce on the tray of food.

Marina filled four ceramic mugs with the steaming tea, emptying the first pot. The aroma of mint filled the air.

"This reminds me of tea with my grandmother when I was a child," Addison said.

After the plate of sandwiches was demolished, Addison snuggled into Sergei's embrace as the movie played. Sergei had one arm wrapped around her shoulders, holding her to him, while his other hand caressed her fingers. His touch was feather-light and sensual. Distracted by his touch, her mind wandered, wishing he had touched her entire body, not just her hand.

Her heart beat so hard that she was sure everyone could hear it.

After months of hesitation and fear, her reservations of being with him fled with the butterflies in her stomach. She couldn't put her finger on when they left her, but as he touched her and her skin prickled with gooseflesh, desire built within her.

By the time the credits rolled, Marina's head was tucked into Viktor's neck, and she was fast asleep. He slid out from behind her and lifted her with ease.

"Goodnight. See you in the morning," he said. He carried her into their room, and with his foot, closed the door behind him.

Addison went into their room to prepare for bed while Sergei rolled the remains of their dinner into the hall for pickup.

In the bathroom, she stripped quickly. She scrubbed her face and rubbed her favorite scented lotion into her hands, up her arms, and across her chest before combing her hair and pulling it over her shoulder. Her heart sped up as she slipped the ankle-length, long-sleeved cotton nightgown over her head, letting it roll down her body.

Sergei was propped up against a pile of pillows with the covers draped haphazardly across his waist. The lamp on his nightstand gave off a soothing glow.

Her breath hitched in her chest as she came into the room and shut the bathroom door behind her with a soft click.

Blood thrummed through her veins as she slipped into her side of the bed.

When he reached for her, she inched closer to him and rested her head on his chest. Her right hand trailed a circle over the thin smattering of velvet curls on his chest, while the green stone in her ring sparkled in the low light. It remained on her right hand for now, simply because she was still torn more than anything else.

Sergei took his finger and set it under her chin, lifting her face to meet his. He stroked her cheek, bent his head, and kissed her. It was a gentle kiss, with no undercurrent of demands or expectations.

She stretched her face up closer to his and deepened the kiss.

He sighed, bringing a smile to her lips. His breath carried the sweet scent of mint. He slipped his tongue into her mouth and teased hers. He nipped her bottom lip, causing it to swell as blood flowed into it.

Her heart beat a fast-paced rhythm. The rush of adrenaline coursing through her made her ears ring. Her eyes rolled back as he continued to tease her and ignite a fire within her.

He pulled her body onto his in a single fluid motion, never slowing his kiss.

Her mind muddled as he continued to caress her cheek with his thumb, leaving trails of gooseflesh where he touched.

His tongue battled hers for dominance and possession as he continued to assault her senses. He combed his fingers through the strands of hair that fell over her shoulder and pulled them away from their faces. This delicate touch sent shivers down her spine. He planted warm kisses on her eyelids, followed by each cheek, and then came to her mouth. After a chaste peck, he deepened the pressure, tantalizing her senses.

Her nerves tingled with each kiss.

With gentle tugs, he inched her nightgown up against her body. His hand slid under the hem, and rubbed the bare flesh of her legs, moving methodically up her waist, briefly sliding across her bottom until he reached the center of her back.

She moaned.

Caution had abandoned her, along with all previous reservations about getting involved with him. Her only thoughts were of his touch and the way her blood hummed under the heat of his fingers. She had a raw desire for him to continue invading her most intimate places. The tugs continued as his tongue plundered her mouth. Once the cotton gown met just below her breasts, he paused and kissed her nose.

"Should I stop?" His question came out in a husky whisper.

"No." She kissed him, nipping his bottom lip as he had done to her. The sharp intake of his breath convinced her she had done it right.

"You are sure?"

"I'm sure."

A soft sigh escaped as he slid his hand down her bare back. Her skin burned under his touch. She lifted her body off his chest and yanked the garment over her head, tossing the wadded bundle onto the floor beside her. Her nipples tightened in the cold air.

His eyes widened as his gaze roamed her naked body. The smoldering glance warmed her skin. He rose to meet her and pulled her against his warm chest. As he kissed her, she wrapped her arms around his shoulders, moving closer to him. Giggles exploded out of her as he flipped them over so fast their entwined bodies bounced on the plush mattress. Pinning her beneath him, he leaned over, twisting their bodies, and with a flick of his wrist, clicked the lamp off, filling the room with darkness. As he covered her, his bare chest sliding across hers, blood pulsed in her veins.

Her hand skimmed down his bare back to his firm buttocks, and up again in lazy figure-eight motions.

He groaned as she drew patterns across his skin with her fingertips.

Sergei's lips grew demanding as he kissed her, eliciting more passion from her.

Her body hummed as he stroked her flesh. Her fingernails dug into his shoulder blades as her nerves vibrated.

His pace increased until she cried out with a need that left her weak.

Her eyes rolled back as he continued to caress her and kiss her.

Sergei paused as he filled her. "Addison?" Confusion and concern filled his faraway voice.

Her breath came in spurts as her body continued to tremble.

"*Milaya?*" he whispered in the darkness. His face was next to hers, his breath caressing her cheek.

"Hmm?" She didn't think she was capable of speech just yet.

"You did not tell me…" His voice was so low she had to concentrate to hear him.

Lying in his arms, the warmth radiated through her, lulling her into a relaxed state. Her mind fogged over with the afterglow of their lovemaking. His question wasn't immediately clear. When she realized, worry filled her. Was he angry? "Does it matter?"

"I should have been gentler."

"It's okay."

"I hurt you." His fingers traced the tears that slid out of the corners of her eyes and into her hair. He leaned over and kissed her damp cheek.

"No."

"You are crying."

"From happiness."

"Humph." Sergei released her as he rolled over and got out of bed.

Panic bubbled up in her. "Are you angry?"

"Not at you, *milaya*. Never at you."

Sergei went into the bathroom but didn't shut the door. The water ran in the sink. Then he returned a moment later, and she understood. He had removed the condom. He wasn't trying to get away from her.

The insecurities raging inside were not new to her. She'd spent her entire childhood in fear of making her mother or stepfathers angry. Though she'd experienced none of the emotions that coursed through her now. Facing this unfamiliar territory made her anxious. Still, she had every intention of going home in a few months. She couldn't bring herself to regret this night with Sergei. There was no guilt or shame about giving her body to him. She would have to deal with the situation that faced them later. *In the morning.* Talking about their futures could wait until the morning.

———

SERGEI SLID OVER TO HER AND LIFTED HER HEAD TO his chest, then covered them both with the down-filled duvet. She snuggled closer as he stroked her hair.

"I am going to marry you, you know," he whispered into her hair.

"Okay."

"Addison?" His hand trailed up her arm that rested on his chest.

"Hmm?"

"Ya lyublyu tebya."

"Okay," Addison mumbled. A soft snore followed. Sergei chuckled. She was fast asleep and would probably have no recollection of agreeing to marry him tonight. Like an arrow shot into the heart, in a brief time, she had become his world. He would have to work harder at convincing her they belonged together. *She loves me.* Giving her innocence to him told him volumes.

Holding her close, he pressed his nose into her hair and inhaled her scent. Contentment washed over him as he held her in his arms as she slept. Sleep remained elusive. Arguments and counterarguments fileted his thoughts as he methodically worked his way down the list of ways, he could convince her to stay with him. He knew nothing but that he needed her in his life.

CHAPTER 21

Revelations

Addison

Addison struggled with how to make Sergei understand her desperation to be her own person, to be independent and self-sufficient, not simply the other half of a man. In the days that followed since they'd returned from the resort, she'd considered a dozen different conversations before discarding them. She'd chickened out the morning after they'd made love. He seemed upset she hadn't told him it would be her first time. When she woke, he seemed distant. She thought she had reached him, but then the moment passed, and she didn't have the words to set things straight or the heart to hurt him after what they had shared the night before. He had given her a beautiful gift, a connection that would stay with her for the rest of her days.

Continuing to avoid the topic did nothing to change the need burning within her, and it wouldn't be easily extinguished. Watching her mother go through men had left her soul yearning for more, convincing her that emotions and passions were risky. Certainly, marrying before she had finished her education and settled into her chosen career wasn't her plan. This path, her mother's path, would only lead to heartache, recriminations, and a lifelong regret of having never achieved her dreams. Her gut told her to follow the road she'd spent her entire childhood mapping out before she let a man claim her as his.

Sergei isn't part of the plan.

The weeks following their ski weekend, study groups filled every moment outside of class. He walked her back to her dorm and kissed her each night. They had had little time alone with the new semester winding up, and their homework load increased. Conversations about their future and marriage moved to the back burner, though she continued to wear the ring. He hadn't mentioned it, and she hadn't asked him about his thoughts on the future. She knew she needed to, though her fears of becoming like her mother kept her paralyzed from broaching the subject. A coward's approach. There was no getting around that. There was bound to be a confrontation, an ugly fight, with hurtful words spewed between them when she told him she couldn't marry him or remain in Russia. Addison loathed confrontations. The aversion ran bone-deep, regardless of who they were with or what they were about. She even hated debating in class. She was going home at the end of the term. And nothing Sergei said would deter her.

Marrying Sergei, no matter how wonderful it would be, could only lead to disaster. And she wasn't prepared to accept the defeat of her dreams so easily.

With a sigh, she turned her attention back to her roommate.

"…It is cruel to keep him hanging on."

"Sophie, I'm not trying to be cruel."

"If you don't plan on marrying him, you should tell him."

"Don't you think I know this?"

"Apparently not. It's been months since he put that ring on your finger, and you are still wearing it."

She had no excuse. Other than the obvious. She continued to avoid talking to him about the future.

"Tomorrow. I'll end things with him tomorrow."

"I'm not saying you have to end things; you just need to decide."

"I'm going home in three months."

"You could stay…"

"No. That's not an option for me. I belong in America."

"If that is how you feel, tell him that."

"Fine, Sophie. I'll break up with him tomorrow. Can you let it rest now?" Addison didn't mean to get testy with her friend. She just hated what she had to do, and Sophie pushing her to do it only bothered her more.

Sophie shook her head, grabbed her purse, and without a backward glance, slipped out of their shared space and shut the door.

Addison plopped onto her bed and closed her eyes. She shouldn't have taken her frustration out on her friend. Being caught in the middle wasn't Sophie's fault. She cared for them both and didn't want to see either of them hurt. Sprawled out on her bed, she stared at the ceiling, trying to calm her irritation before she attempted to study again. She only had herself to blame for this situation.

THE FIRST HINTS OF SPRING APPEARED. SO WRAPPED UP in her studies, it felt sudden. Without warning, the shift of seasons came. Patches of melted snow littered the edges of the walkway. As the days warmed, the bitter cold no longer tore its way through her heavy clothes. Smatterings of color peeked up around them as flowers fought to break through the frozen ground. It had taken the last dregs of winter to dissipate for her to gather enough courage to face the music. The relationship with Sergei had progressed faster and further than it should have. The fault was hers, and hers alone. She should never have let him put the ring on her finger in the first place. With a pang of sadness and a glance at her gloved hand, the bump under the leather on her ring finger stared back at her accusingly. In a few moments, she would break his heart, and hers along with it. From the beginning, her gut had warned her. If she hadn't gotten involved with him, though, she would never have experienced the love or the memories he'd given her. Even knowing this would end, she didn't regret her time with him, but her friend was right. He deserved more than what she could offer him.

Other than Sergei, the coffee shop was empty when Addison arrived. She took this as a good omen, not wanting a scene in front of a room full of people. She straightened her shoulders and sucked in a deep breath, trying to slow her racing heart. Her feet dragged as though traipsing through molasses. The crack in her heart widened as she steeled her resolve to do what she came for.

Seated at their usual table, his back turned to the door, he was engrossed in reading. She dropped into the chair across the table from him. He glanced up and greeted her with a smile before he slid his magazine aside.

Her eyes threatened to overflow with tears as she took in his calm demeanor. She slid the ring off her finger and placed it on the table in front of him. Seeing this, his eyes grew wide.

"Sergei, I can't do this. I'm sorry."

"Do what, *lubov moya*? Love me?" His voice remained low, gentle even.

"Yes, but I'm not ready to get married. I'm going home in three months, and I still have another year of school before I can even consider a relationship." Her thoughts were coming out in barely coherent bursts of words.

"Addi—"

Holding up her hand to stop his speech, she tried a different approach. "We're too different. We've only known each other for a short time."

Sergei just stared at her. His eyes were wide, his lips pursed as though ready to speak.

Addison pushed on before he could respond.

"I'm no good for you… I'm damaged goods. Why would you want me? I'm nothing special." Fear of turning out like her mother, incomplete without a man and dependent, roared through her veins.

"My life is in America, and yours is here," she went on.

"Addison—"

She shook her head. "I won't give up my dreams. Not even for you. My mother did that, and she was miserable for it." She bit the inside of her cheek as her eyes pooled. She would be strong and get through this. It was for the best. For them both.

Sergei's mouth opened and closed. He looked almost like a fish out of water. His face fell. The pain in his eyes caused an even deeper crack in her heart. Sergei stared at her, his eyes peered into her soul, making her catch her breath.

She used the last thing in her arsenal. "It isn't enough to give up everything for."

As he took in her words, his hand slid across the table towards her, bypassing the ring glittering like a massive wall between them now. Even as she flung daggers at him, he reached for her. His expression was wounded. It tore another fissure in her heart. Addison jumped up from her chair, knocking it over, and fled the coffee shop.

Tears flowed freely down her face as she ran back to her dorm room. Out of breath, she slammed her door, locking it behind her.

She dropped onto her bed, curling herself into a tight ball, and sobbed until she ran out of steam. The tears dried in streaks down her face.

Images of Sergei's expressions plagued her. The moment she'd placed the ring on the table before him, when she'd told him that her mother would never accept him. He'd taken her words as he did almost everything else, silently. She expected a fiery temper, any kind of angry response. She had braced herself for it. Instead, there were no recriminations, no heated words, just his stoic expression. Her heart ached for him, but her head reminded her she needed to remain steady in her convictions. If she wasn't, she would walk the same path as her mother, and everyone would be unhappier for it.

But no matter how she tried to convince herself, his sad eyes haunted her thoughts.

Worn down by the emotions raging through her, she fell into a fitful slumber. The dreams came again. Her mother was on one side, yanking her arm, but this time Sergei replaced Cassie on the other. The arguments were the same: *You aren't loyal enough... you can love me, too...* Sergei's presence in the dream wasn't calming like it usually was. Instead, she found the tug of war raging between her mother and Sergei even more discouraging.

Two hours later, Addison woke exhausted from the lack of sleep and drained of all hope. She stretched and sat up on her bed. Sophie still hadn't returned to their room. Without giving it much thought, she reached for her mobile phone and called home. After a moment, the call connected and caught Addison off guard when it was picked up on the first ring.

"Hello?"

"Cassie?" Addison's voice came out as a croak.

"What's wrong?"

"I'm sorry this call is going to cost so much." The tears welled up, clogging her eyes and her throat.

"Talk to me, honey," Cassie said.

"I... I broke up with Sergei."

"Why?" The question was gentle and unassuming.

"He proposed."

"Ah." Cassie's voice held a note of surprise.

"But I can't marry him. What would my mother say?" Addison pressed her head back against the pillow; the phone pressed to her ear and her right hand covering her eyes.

"Addison, you need to shut up and listen." Cassie's tone sharpened.

Addison sucked in a ragged breath. The words didn't surprise her, though the harsh tone coming from her normally calm stepmother did.

"I'm trying, but I can't help thinking this is the road my mom went down. Leaving college to get married and have a family."

"Stop trying to control it. Just relax, and the answers will come. Try yoga or maybe meditation or something. Just whatever you do, don't get drunk or do any drugs."

"Of course not." She dropped her hand from her face and clutched the sheets.

"I'm just saying you want your gut sober when it talks to you."

She laughed. "That's true."

Addison rose and swung her feet off the bed, and sitting on the edge, contemplating getting up to turn on the light in the slowly darkening room.

"Are you pregnant?"

"No. Of course not." Though she expected the

question to come from her mother, coming from Cassie felt harsher somehow.

A distinct pause followed as Cassie exhaled a barely concealed sigh of relief. "Check. Do you love him?"

Addison hesitated. "I think so?" She crossed her leg and bounced her foot up and down.

"Can you imagine the rest of your life with him?" Cassie pressed her.

This gave Addison pause. Closing her eyes, she tried to picture her future. For so long, her education had remained in the forefront. Now, in the same future, Sergei's presence lingered. "I guess."

"Can you imagine your life without seeing him again?"

An image flashed through her mind, and a large, dark void loomed. "It hurts when I do," Addison sobbed.

"Then it's fair to say you love him." Cassie chuckled.

"Okay." She sniffled.

Cassie was always the calm, reasonable one to turn to in a crisis. Her unwavering support and lack of judgment made it easier to think.

"Is there any reason you can't finish school before you get married?"

If I pause for a moment, I know I'll end up just like Mama.

"He belongs here. And I come home in June."

"Have you talked about that?" Cassie asked.

"I tried. He just says it will all work out." Frustrated with herself, Addison toed the shoes on the floor by her feet.

"But you don't believe that?"

"Would you do it if you were me?" With a swift kick, she sent a shoe into the side of Sophie's bed across from hers. It dropped to the floor with an unsatisfactory thud.

"You are not your mother, Addison. You don't have to do things the same way. Do it on your terms, but be sure you're doing them for the right reasons."

"And those would be?" Addison queried. All she saw was her mother's failed marriages flashing through her mind.

Cassie laughed. "Whatever your gut tells you they are. Shut up. And listen. The answers will come."

Addison tried to laugh, but it came out as a strangled croak. "When did you know Dad was the one?" She dropped back onto the bed; her legs draped over the side.

"When I knew for certain there would never be children."

Addison's breath caught in her throat. "Wait— that doesn't make sense." *They'd been together for years by then.*

"It had been a whirlwind romance. So many important issues left unsaid."

"You would think he'd have learned not to do that after my mother."

Cassie choked. "Fair enough." A strained breath came through the phone. "So many outside issues faced us, and things moved so quickly we were caught up in the moment. I never thought about what they would mean for us."

Addison sighed. Her heart ached.

"When the time came, I was faced with a choice."

Biting her lip, Addison paused before she asked, "Do you regret it?"

"I think we should have talked about our feelings and expectations from the beginning, so it wouldn't have been such a shock later."

"I agree."

"You need to talk to Sergei. Tell him everything. All your thoughts, feelings, fears. Lay it all out in the open. Leave nothing to chance. That would be my advice. Hear what he has to say. That and listen to your gut. It will lead the way if you let it."

Another sob escaped. "Oh, Cassie. I'm so scared."

"I know, honey. It's a huge decision. But you have a good head on your shoulders; don't let anything else influence you. Do what's right for you. Take your time. Don't rush things."

"Thanks, Cassie."

"Know that we love you. Take care, honey."

"Love you, too. Bye."

After Addison ended the call, she pulled out her

laptop and began an email to her mother and sisters. It was long overdue, and the mindless chitchat would give her some distance from her other problems. She attached a few pictures to it before pressing send. She closed her laptop and shook off the urge to sulk.

Setting her computer aside, she gathered her toiletries and went to take a shower. She needed to wash the dried tears from her face and hair.

Sergei watched her walk away, his heart aching. The ring on the table glinted back at him accusingly.

He picked it up, and stared down at the green stone, as though it held all the answers. He had yearned to reach out and hold her, to comfort her. To convince her they could work out any obstacle together. But the words stuck in his throat.

They both needed space before he tried to approach her again. And he needed to put his thoughts and feelings together in a way to make her see how he felt. A wild idea popped into his head as he twisted the ring between his fingers, the sparkling stone dancing in the light. He knew exactly how to win her heart. He would take a page out of *Pride and Prejudice* and write her a letter. He pulled out his notebook and began scribbling.

To my darling Addison,

I thought I would take a moment to show you I have heard everything you have said. While I do not agree, I care enough to try to see things from your perspective.

I understand your plan to return to America. While I had hoped that loving me would be enough for you to consider remaining in Russia, I love you enough to return to your homeland with you. We can continue our education together there as easily as we have here.

My family will support us whether we are together in Russia, or move to America with a promise to visit them. I believe that in time, your family will come around just as mine has.

I do know you. I know your heart is pure and your intentions are honest, and that you make me feel as though I am home. You give my heart a sense of peace it has never known. I was missing a piece of my soul until I met you. You have eased my longing and soothed my inner core. You are where I belong. Wherever your goals take you, I want to stand by your side as you reach them.

I have no desire to keep you from your dreams. Wherever your dreams lead you, I would like to help you make them a reality.

You make me want to be a better man.
I love you. Now and forever.
Sergei

CHAPTER 22

A Long Shot

Sergei

Sergei waited in the coffee shop after class. The week had taken its toll on him. He hadn't slept well, and he could not concentrate on his studies. All thoughts diverted to her when he was not distracted. Pyotr was wise enough to remain silent about the sudden temperature change between them. But his questioning look, every time he caught Sergei's eye, spoke volumes. They studied together in his dorm most nights now, though the conversations were stunted. He found it hard to put into words a rational explanation for why he continued to covet Addison after she had made it so clear she was done with their relationship.

Addison had not even glanced in his direction. Not once. She kept her gaze focused on the front of the classroom each lecture. She beelined out of class as soon as the professor dismissed them, to make sure they didn't have the chance to bump into each other. In the past, she had taken her time leaving the room. Sophie followed her out with a shrug and an apologetic expression on her face. It ripped the hole in his chest wider.

He asked Sophie to meet him to study so that he could give her the message for Addison. An irrational fear haunted him that Addison would not accept the note from him directly. This seemed the most logical approach instead.

"Allo." Sophie dropped into the seat across from him with her usual whoosh of energy and exasperation.

"Bonjour."

"How are you?"

"I miss her," he said simply.

"I'm sorry. I believe she is unhappy, too."

"Is it wrong of me to be happy to hear that?" He wrapped his hands around his coffee cup and peered over at his friend.

"I understand. She is a complicated woman."

"Can you give her this for me?"

"Of course. What does it say?"

Sergei laughed. "That I love her, of course."

"Do you think that is wise? She's determined to go back to America."

"Da. I see now that I should have considered

going with her instead of expecting her to stay. It was the wrong approach."

Sophie grinned. "Good luck, my friend."

"I will need it."

She patted his hand, slipped the crisp white envelope into the front pocket of her bag, and, with her usual panache, stood, tossed her bag over her shoulder, and headed out the door mere minutes after arriving.

He finished his coffee, hoping that in the time they were apart, Addison would see that he loved her. And that loving him did not need to be a prison of obligations and duties, but a partnership based on mutual respect and dreams.

ADDISON LEANED AGAINST THE EDGE OF HER BED. THE carpeted floor was hard beneath her. Her back ached, her legs were stiff. Stretching, she rolled her shoulders, then her neck, before pulling her legs under her again. The restlessness continued to increase. Her concentration was scattered. She'd moved from the bed to the desk and now was parked on the floor to finish her homework. Each place had soothed her nerves enough for her to get one page of decent writing in before the restlessness kicked back in, and she lost her train of thought.

Sophie came in, slamming the door behind her,

stepping on one of Addison's textbooks opened at her side.

"Whoa. What the hell?" Sophie caught the door-knob, holding herself up as her foot lurched.

"Hi." Addison laughed. Typical of Sophie to rush in where angels feared to tread.

Letting her bag slide to the floor, Sophie perched on the side of her bed, facing Addison. "I have a note for you."

"Hmm... Just leave it on the desk."

"Addy..."

Frustration filled her as Addison looked up. Closing her notebook and slapping it on top of her textbook, she gave up. She would not get any worth-while studying done this afternoon.

"Yes?" she said. She was testy, and the guilt for taking it out on her friend sliced through her.

Sophie smiled. Addison shook her head. Her friend's patience with her had to be stretched thin, considering she'd been short-tempered and moody for weeks now. Since their last argument about Sergei, in fact, before she'd ended things.

Sophie arched a brow as she reached into her bag, extending the square white envelope to her. "It's from Sergei."

"What am I supposed to do with that?" Addison snarled.

"Read it."

"I broke up with him. I broke his heart. What more do you want from me, Sophie?"

"I never told you to break up with him. Or break his heart. Or your heart, for that matter."

"You pushed and pushed. So, I did it."

"*Non, mon amie.* I told you to be honest with him. And yourself. That is not the same."

"Whatever. There's no point dwelling on it now."

"Stop being a stubborn mule. Decide what you want and go after it. Go after him."

"I. Am. Not. A. Mule." Addison ground her teeth.

Sophie bent over and held her stomach, letting out a raucous laugh.

Addison glared at her. This only made Sophie laugh harder.

She could feel her lips sliding across her teeth. How could she stay mad at Sophie? She was the one being a jerk, while her friend worked tirelessly to lighten her crappy mood.

CHAPTER 23

Desperate Measures

Addison

Addison's heart ached from the void left when she said goodbye to Sergei, yet she found herself unable to reach out to him. Even the note he'd sent via Sophie only made it harder for her to focus. Her mood continued to be sour. She spent less time with Sophie and her study groups because of it. The certainty of her future lay in going home and finishing her education. Not that of a wife and mother. Not in Russia. Asking Sergei to alter his life to fulfill her dreams felt no less manipulative than what her mother had done to her father by getting pregnant and expecting him to give up his dreams to marry her. That wasn't her path. The days grew longer without his laughter and presence. She walked into her dorm room and bumped the door closed with her hip. Tossing her bag onto her bed, she stood in the center of the dark room, eerie shadows dancing across the wall as the trees moved in the wind outside. A soft mewling sound, barely audible, reached her. Almost like something from a wounded animal. Her skin pebbled with gooseflesh. Unnerved, she flipped the light switch and blinked rapidly as the room flooded with light. The sound came again, this time clearer.

"Sophie, is that you?" She didn't expect anyone else in the room, but it hadn't sounded like anything she'd ever heard from her vivacious roommate, so she wasn't certain.

The whimpering grew louder, coming from the closet across the room. There was a metallic odor in the air. The hair on the back of her neck rose. She rubbed furiously at the gooseflesh on her arms.

As she neared the door, she realized she hadn't seen her friend for two days. And Sophie hadn't come home the night before. So wrapped up in her own drama, she hadn't taken the time to consider how unusual that was. Even if it wasn't until the wee hours of the morning, her friend had always returned before sunrise. She'd just assumed she was avoiding her.

On the floor in the corner, curled up in a fetal position, lay a trembling Sophie, her clothes torn and bloody. Blood was smeared across the side of her face and matted into her hair. The metallic odor was much stronger now, almost palpable.

Panic tore through Addison as she dropped to her knees. As she leaned in, a sudden feeling of terror gripped her as she stared down at her friend.

"Sophie?" she whispered.

"Hmm," came a soft moan from under the matted hair.

"What happened?" Addison reached down and moved the hair from Sophie's face.

Another moan followed.

"Were you attacked?"

Sophie's whimpers turned into full-blown sobs. She jerked her head, her entire body shaking now.

"We need to call the police."

"No!" Sophie's shrill scream pierced the silence. She turned her face to Addison. Pain etched her face from this effort, and she closed her eyes again.

"You've been hurt. We need help."

"No police. They will kick me out of school," Sophie pleaded.

"Sophie, please." Addison felt her composure slipping. She took a deep breath. She needed to be strong and in control if she had any chance of helping her friend.

"This isn't America. Or Paris," Sophie said.

"Can you tell me what happened?"

"I went dancing. An underground club got raided. I got separated from my group as we ran away. I lost my way. I made a wrong turn, and there were a couple of drunk men in the alley behind the building who stopped me."

"Were you raped?" Addison croaked.

"No." It was just a whisper. "They wanted to, though. One of them started slapping me around, while another ripped at my blouse. I was pinned to the ground when another group came around the corner. Screaming like maniacs as they charged at them, they chased them off. I asked them to bring me back here."

"They just left you like this?"

"They were afraid, so I told them I would be okay."

"We can't let them get away with this." Addison was at a loss. She was in a foreign country and unfamiliar with their protocol. Not that America handled assault cases much better, but at least there she knew who to trust. Here, she had no idea.

Addison whipped out her cell phone.

"No police!" Sophie pleaded.

"Okay, no police." Her fingers fumbled with the phone as she dialed Sergei, praying he didn't hate her. She hadn't talked to him in weeks like a coward.

"*Zdravstvuyte*?"

"Sergei, I need help… It's Sophie—"

Cutting her off, he asked, "Where are you?"

"Our dorm room. 332." Until now, Sergei had always dropped her off downstairs at the main door;

he had never been to her room before. Such a trivial thought to pop into her head at that moment.

"I am on my way."

The phone went dead. Sitting on the floor, holding Sophie's trembling hand, Addison felt helpless. She'd long feared Sophie's crazy antics and partying might lead to trouble, but nothing had prepared her for this. Her friend was a broken mess on the floor. She scooted closer and wrapped Sophie in her arms, making soothing sounds while she sobbed.

Sergei arrived ten minutes later, knocking softly on the door.

"It's unlocked." Addison was afraid to let go of Sophie for even a second to answer the door.

Sergei took in the scene from the doorway and swore in Russian. He strode across the room, bent down, and scooped Sophie up off the floor.

His voice was gentle as he spoke in French calmly, overriding Sophie's protests. She quieted down as he lay her on the top of her unmade bed. "Sophie, we need to look at you and get you cleaned up," he said.

After she got herself off the floor, Addison walked over to the electric kettle in the corner and boiled water for tea, unsure what else to do. She clasped her hands to stop their shaking. Sergei pulled a small, half-empty bottle from his pocket and poured a dollop into the steaming mug Addison had clasped between her hands. At her raised brow, he gave her a lopsided grin.

Sergei perched before Sophie on his knees next to her bed, as Addison moved to sit on the edge of the bed beside her.

Sophie sipped her tea and grimaced. She pushed it away. "Ugh."

"Vodka," Sergei said. He pushed the cup back into her hands and, with a look, and she relented.

Sophie sipped her doctored tea.

Addison sat beside her and held her hand.

She explained her story again, in further detail, to Sergei in rapid French and Russian. He nodded at the appropriate moments, but remained silent until the end.

Addison caught words like "*gendarmerie*" and "*polit-siya*," but there was no context since it was all flowing so fast.

"I understand. I agree. No police. This didn't happen on campus, nothing is gained by telling them, and the school would want to protect its image and would expel you and send you home for admitting to being at the illegal club." Sergei's words were soft and low. He was honest and realistic without judging her.

Sophie nodded. Addison was grateful he understood, though she didn't necessarily agree. At least she was no longer alone in this.

"Let us clean you up a little?" Sergei asked.

Sophie blanched. Her hands shook harder than before.

"I'll be gentle, I promise." Addison squeezed her hand.

Sophie nodded, her tea sloshing around in her mug as she trembled. Sergei brought over a couple of damp cloths, and as he washed her fingers, whispering soothing sounds, Addison wiped her face, the dried blood smearing down her cheek. Sergei took the washcloth from her hand and returned with two clean ones while she smoothed the tangled, blood-caked hair back from her face. After she finished pulling her hair into a sloppy braid, Sergei handed another cup of tea to Sophie.

With a stern look that left no room for arguments, Sophie accepted the tea and drank it quietly. Her trembling subsided. They sat with her until the vodka Sergei had slipped into her tea kicked in, and her eyelids drooped. They gently slid her down and covered her with a blanket from Addison's bed.

Addison slipped off her boots and dropped onto her bed. She was drained. Physically and emotionally.

"Call me later." Sergei stood and made his way to the door.

"No. Please, stay. I'm afraid," Sophie pleaded.

Sergei's eyes searched out Addison's, and she gave him a slight nod.

"I'm sorry for being such a baby." Sophie's voice was low and weak.

"For you *mon amie*, anything. Sleep now. You are safe." Sergei kissed her brow and tucked the covers around her shoulders.

"Merci," Sophie mumbled as her eyes closed again. Moments later, Sophie's labored breathing filled the room.

Sergei kicked off his shoes and, after setting the dirty mug aside, he crawled onto Addison's bed and leaned against the wall.

He lifted his hand, beckoning her. "Come, *moy dorogaya*. Let her rest."

Addison scooted back on the bed next to Sergei. Her back to the wall, she leaned into him.

"Thank you for coming. I didn't know what to do." Silent sobs wracked her body as tears slid down her cheeks in unchecked streams.

"Shhh. I am here. I will always be here for you."

He wrapped his arm around her, and she lay her head on his shoulder. They sat like that as the sun lowered in the sky and the shadows filled the room.

"How have you been?" Addison whispered.

"Lonely. I have missed my study partner."

"I'm sorry, Sergei."

"There is no need to be sorry."

"I hurt you," Addison said.

"Yes. Fear will do that. Even to those who love you the most," Sergei said.

"I don't want to be."

"Be what, *dorogaya*?"

"Be afraid. Be hurtful. I don't mean to be."

Sergei pulled her closer to him and kissed the top of her head. Warmth spread through her.

"Ya lyublyu tebya."

"Oh, Sergei. I love you, too."

"See, now, that wasn't so hard, was it?"

"What?" Addison snuffled.

"That is the first time you have told me you love me."

"It was?" Addison was surprised. Though she couldn't remember saying it before, it seemed strange that it had taken her this long. "I'm sorry."

Sergei laughed. "There you go again."

Soft whimpers came from the other side of the room.

They both froze as they turned to Sophie. She hadn't stirred. Relaxing into his arms again, she leaned her head against his shoulder.

"What did I do again?" Addison asked.

"Apologize. You are always apologizing."

"I'm sorry."

Sergei put his face in her hair as he chuckled, this time muffling the sounds.

"Ty Moy svet."

"Humph." Addison rolled her eyes. "I'm no light."

"You are mine. Your love has brought me out of the darkness."

"I'm not sure how I managed that." Addison was being difficult; she couldn't seem to help herself.

"I know. That is okay. I have a hard time letting people in. Focusing on my studies gave me an excuse to not develop a social life." Sergei kissed the top of her head again.

Wrapped in each other's arms, talking, Addison hadn't noticed Sophie stirring. Sergei nudged her.

"Sophie, how do you feel?" Sergei asked.

"*Cochon.*"

"Oh, Sophie, this wasn't your fault," Addison wailed.

"*Non*, literally dirty. I need a bath. I smell weird."

Sergei chuckled.

"That would be the blood in your hair." Addison grimaced.

"*Choquant. Oui.* A shower is a must." Sophie groaned as she moved to get off her bed.

"Would you be able to eat if I brought you something?"

"*Oui. Affamé.*" Sophie's words came out scratchy. She reached up and touched her bruised throat.

Addison and Sergei watched in horror. They hadn't spoken a word about the vicious bruises all over Sophie's face, down her throat, and covering her arms. They had taken none of her clothes off, only washing the skin that was exposed.

"I will bring you food, something warm and soft," Sergei said.

Addison and Sophie nodded.

"I will go while you shower. I will be back before you return." Sergei slipped on his shoes and grabbed his jacket.

"Take your time; I am fine now."

Addison and Sergei exchanged glances over Sophie's head. Neither believed her.

Sergei slipped out of the room with a quiet click of the door behind him while Addison was gathering Sophie's toiletries. She grabbed their bathrobes and walked Sophie to the showers down the hall. It was late, so they had the bathroom to themselves. The privacy was exactly what they needed.

Addison helped her strip off her clothes. Sophie groaned as she lifted the sweater over her head. She wished there was another way, but she didn't want to traumatize Sophie more by ripping her clothes off. Sophie whimpered as the cloth slid down the raw flesh of her scuffed-up legs. Addison bit her lip to stop from crying out at the terrible sight while cramming the tattered and torn clothes into the duffle bag she had brought to make sure no one saw them while they were in the shower. Sophie's battered body was worse than she had expected.

Still wearing her underwear and t-shirt, Addison stepped into the largest shower stall before Sophie.

"What are you doing?"

"Washing your hair."

"I'm okay. Really."

"Soph, don't argue. Just let me help you."

"I'm fine. See?" Sophie raised her arms before dropping them again in defeat. Pain etched across her face. "Oh, Addy. What am I going to do?" Tears flowed freely down her makeup-streaked face.

Addison sighed. Sophie didn't seem to have any broken bones, just more bruises and raw skin than she could fathom. The bruises on her neck seemed the worst. They were below some abrasions where they had roughly pushed her to the ground, and where she must have fought with all her strength against them. It broke her heart to see her friend abused like this.

"We're going to get you cleaned up and fed, and then you can spend what's left of the weekend in bed, resting."

Sophie stepped under the lukewarm spray and cried out. The water hitting her wounds had to be excruciating. The soap would not feel any better on them.

Addison leaned her against the wall for support as she poured the shampoo onto the top of her head. The head wound turned out to be a superficial cut right under her hairline. It certainly bled like a more severe injury, but most head wounds did. Being a few inches taller than Sophie, she had no problem washing her hair.

Thirty minutes later, Addison turned off the water, catching Sophie as she sagged into her.

"I'm sorry."

"Don't be. I'm here for you."

"Thank you; you are a loyal friend."

"You would do the same for me."

"I would. *Oui.*"

They stood dripping in the shower as Addison gently wrapped Sophie's hair in a thick white towel. Sophie shivered. Standing in one spot for so long had drained Sophie. She struggled to remain upright as Addison dressed her.

"Ouch. My skin feels like it's on fire."

Addison stopped blotting her and looked up. "I'm sorry. I'm trying to be gentle."

"I know. It's not your fault, *mon amie.*"

"Let's get you dressed and back into bed."

Sophie nodded as convulsions continued to wrack her body.

Addison slipped a camisole over Sophie's head, trying to slide it down without touching her scratched arms. Then she wadded up a worn pair of black yoga pants and had her step into them before gingerly pulling them up over the raw skin on her legs.

Soft whimpers and long sighs escaped Sophie's lips as Addison tried to work quickly and carefully. Wrapping an oversized flowery robe around her shoulders, Addison led Sophie back to their room.

Sergei had been busy while they were in the

shower. Lavender-scented candles covered every flat surface, and the aroma of warm bread and stew filled the room. A huge steel pot sat in the center of the small table in the corner they used as a desk.

Addison took in the scene before her. Sophie's soiled bedding had been replaced. Her gaze lingered on the pile of blankets and sheets in the corner before turning back to Sergei. He gave her a crooked smile. "We can wash those tomorrow."

The way he said *we* made her heart skip a beat.

"Come, I brought wine and homemade German *Gulasch*."

"Where did you find homemade *Gulasch* and wine at this hour?" Addison looked around for the time.

"I raided Uncle Yuri's icebox."

"He was okay with that?"

"Of course. He always has a supply of *Mamochka's Gulasch*. She always makes enough to fill his freezer. He sends his love, by the way."

Addison nodded.

"He said we are welcome to spend the day at his house to do laundry if you'd like." Sergei dished out the steaming stew into three large coffee mugs.

Addison accepted one from him and moved across the room to sit on the edge of her bed.

"*Magnifique*." Sophie inhaled a deep breath.

"Sit. I will make for you."

Sophie and Addison sat down as Sergei scooped

DAWN BACA

up the delicious-smelling soup. The three dug in with gusto.

After Sophie ate a decent amount of the stew, she crawled into bed while Sergei made them cups of tea. They sat huddled on top of Sophie's bed, chatting until her eyelids drooped again. Once her chin hit her chest, Sergei took the mug out of her hand, while Addison pulled the covers over her and tucked her in.

The partially closed closet door shed the smallest sliver of light from inside, and the flickering of the candles left a soft illumination of the room.

He hadn't suggested leaving again, and she didn't have the courage to ask him to. Instead, she was grateful for his strength.

Addison pulled the blankets back and slid into her bed, holding the covers open in invitation to him. Sergei lay down on her bed and pulled the covers down on top of them. She placed her head on his shoulder and her hand on his chest, linking her fingers through his.

"I'm sorry the bed is smaller than the ski chalet," Addison said.

"Stop apologizing. You did not choose this bed, or create this situation."

Addison bobbed her head.

"You see how well we work together in a crisis."

"What does that matter?"

"Teams who pull together during the worst of times shine brighter during the best times."

"Where did you get that?"

"One of *Mamochka's* sayings."

Addison rolled her eyes to the stare at the ceiling.

"You are rolling your eyes at me. You can stop now."

Addison laughed. "How can you see what I'm doing in the dark?"

"I know you. Better than you think I do."

Addison snuggled into Sergei's chest. He rested his hand on hers, fingers entwined. The time had come for her to stop running away from him and face her fears.

"Sophie deserves justice. Not calling the police feels like we're letting them get away with what they did to her."

"They won't."

"But if we don't report her attack…"

"We have to protect Sophie first and foremost. And respect her wishes."

Addison opened her mouth to speak. Sergei put a finger to her lips. "Trust me on this."

"I do trust you. I just feel so helpless."

"Be here for her. Support her. Love her. That is what she needs from you right now."

"Okay, I'll follow your lead."

Sergei reached into his pocket and slipped the ring back onto her right ring finger, then clasped his over hers in a tight ball before he brought it to his lips.

"This is where it belongs."

Addison nodded, tears welling up in her eyes. She closed her eyes tight to stop them from spilling over. How could she turn away from a man who came running when she called without asking why? He had been right all along. This was right. He loved her regardless of her fears, and his patience brought them back together in the end.

CHAPTER 24

Moving Forward

Addison

A ddison was emotionally and physically drained. The weekend flew by, and now they were facing another Monday morning. Sergei was back in his dorm room, and Sophie was on the road to recovery. They covered the bruises on her neck first with makeup and then hid some under a thick turtleneck sweater. Sophie wore her hair down so that it flowed around her neck and shoulders in waves.

They walked to their first class in subdued silence. Sophie was no longer trembling, but she hadn't regained her exuberant confidence either.

After a day filled with classes, they agreed to return to their dorms and stay in for the night.

Addison picked up takeout for dinner and arrived in their room first.

She pulled out her computer and typed up a quick email to her mother. The time had come to tell her the news.

Dear Mama,
I hope everything is okay at home. I tried calling you, but the phone line was disconnected.
I've got some great news to share.
I'm engaged.
Sergei proposed in front of his whole family. He gave me a beautiful chrome diopside ring that once belonged to his grandmother.
I'll send pictures soon.
Give my love to everyone.
Love, Addy

Addison clicked send to make sure it didn't linger in her outbox before closing the lid to her computer and setting it aside. It wasn't how she'd planned on telling her mother, but considering how much time had passed, and especially since her father and Cassie already knew, she had been forced to act and had delayed as long as she dared.

There had been no point in telling her exactly how long ago he had proposed, or that she'd broken things off between them briefly. That they were back together and getting married was all that mattered.

She put the entire thing out of her mind as she studied with Sophie, and then they curled up in bed early, spending the rest of the night talking.

TWO DAYS LATER, HER CELL PHONE RANG. SHE'D answered on the second ring.

"Addison."

Taken aback, Addison hadn't expected to hear her mother's voice.

"Hi, Mama. Is everything okay?"

"What do you mean emailing me you're engaged?"

"I tried to call you. But I couldn't get through."

"Erik didn't pay the phone bill again. I had to get a new account. That's beside the point."

It was the *only* point, but she didn't want to start a fight.

"Who is this boy?" Tandy asked.

"I sent you emails about him before."

"What's the rush?"

"We've been seeing each other for a few months."

"Are you pregnant?"

Addison bit her lip. Of course, everyone would assume this.

"No, Mama."

"So, you're dropping out of school to get married. Are you planning on staying over there with him?"

"Of course not, Mama. I'll finish school back in the States."

"You intend to bring him here?"

"I hope to."

"He doesn't belong here. He won't fit in."

"He'll adjust." Addison crossed her fingers, hoping that this was true.

"Humph. How can you be a student and a wife?"

Addison snorted. She chose not to respond to the barb. There was no doubt her mother was itching for a fight.

Typical Mama. Once again, making excuses for never having gone back to school or holding down a regular job.

"When will you marry?"

"After I graduate. The fall maybe."

"Humph." Tandy's response came through clearly gritted teeth.

Addison knew weddings were a sore subject. Mama had always dreamed of having a big, fancy, expensive white wedding in the Southern Belle style she grew up in, but she'd eloped with her first two husbands. Her mother had voiced her adamant disapproval over the next two and had refused to support them.

Addison would never forget the rants after her father's wedding to Cassie. Or the fights with Rafe, and then Eric, about deserving her own white wedding.

"Why a used ring? Are they poor?"

Addison glanced down at the significant stone on her hand and grinned.

"They're just an average family, just like us." There was an undisguised dig at her mother there, as her mother hated to think of herself as poor. She had grown up spoiled and had assumed she would always have that lifestyle.

"Chrome diopside sounds like a cheap stone to me."

"It's a semi-precious stone."

"So not like a diamond."

"No, it's not like a diamond; it's a rare Russian stone, and it's a family ring. So, it holds a special meaning to both of us."

"What about him?"

Addison snapped to attention. "Sergei graduates with his master's in June. Give him a chance, Mama. I know you'll like him."

"Humph."

"How are the Hobbits?"

"They're not dirty, hairy creatures. No matter what you may think," Tandy snapped.

Don't start a fight. "Sorry, how are Beth and Raleigh?"

"Your sisters are all fine."

"And how are you?"

"Fine," Tandy bit out.

Addison shook her head. Her mother was getting testy. It was time to go.

"Can you give me your new number so that I can call you back? I know this call is going to be expensive, and I don't want Erik to be mad."

"Erik is always mad about something these days."

"I'm sorry, Mama."

"It's nothing new."

"I'll let you go for now, so I can go study. I'll talk to you soon." Addison hung up and set the phone aside. The conversation had exhausted her. Remaining diplomatic and on edge with her mother to prevent arguing had always been a tenuous task for her.

When Sophie returned from her last class, she wore a pensive expression.

"Addy, you must see this."

"What's wrong?"

"I have been following this blog. It gives dates for when and where the parties are and how to find them."

"Oh, Sophie, no more underground clubs, please."

"No. I'm done." At Addison's skeptical glance, Sophie raised her hands. "I promise. Never again."

Addison and Sophie stared at the screen in disbelief. A blog post showed two men's mug-shots on the top of the page, accompanied by an article.

*TWO MEN, EACH TWENTY-NINE YEARS OLD, WERE *detained for attacking tourists.*

Vladimir Pudin and Dorokhin Trukhin, both career crimi-nals, who have been in and out of trouble since their teens, are accused of aggravated assault.

"YOU DON'T THINK...?" SOPHIE WHISPERED.

"I'll ask."

Sophie looked horrified at the prospect.

Addison hugged her friend. "It will be fine."

TWO HOURS LATER, SERGEI ARRIVED AT THE COFFEE shop to meet her; she couldn't contain her concern any longer and pounced before he could sit down.

"Can I ask you a question?" The heat rushed to Addison's face.

"Of course, *dorogaya*, you can ask me anything."

"I don't want to offend you."

"That is not possible."

"Do you have relatives in the KGB?"

Sergei roared with laughter.

Addison pursed her lips and scowled at him.

Sergei's laughter subsided, and he took a deep breath. "Is any of your family in the CIA?"

"Hardly. My father is a mechanic, and Cassie plans corporate trade shows. My mother doesn't work."

"Ah, see? Not everyone has diabolical family members."

"Humph."

Sergei laughed again.

"I'm serious."

"Almost everyone in my family is an academic."

"Really?" The rock in the pit of her stomach dissipated, leaving only relief.

"Yes, why so surprised?"

"I just can't imagine everyone in my family being a teacher, that's all."

"Why not?"

"I don't know, the idea of everyone in a room full of students all day." Addison shuddered.

Sergei grinned at her reaction. "Not all are teachers in a classroom—look at my Uncle Yuri."

"He's a teacher?"

"A tenured professor of physics and astronomy."

"I didn't realize."

"He mostly works out at Pulkovo and sees only graduate students now."

"I see."

"Why do you ask?"

"We read a blog about the two guys who hurt Sophie. We wondered how they were found so fast."

"And you thought that the KGB would have had an interest in a couple of thugs?" Sergei's brow furrowed and his eyes narrowed as he watched her.

"I'm sorry. It just seemed to be an unlikely coincidence."

"I can understand that. But no, my family are all teachers. Yes, they work for the government, but not the FSB."

"FSB?"

"Yes, the FSB replaced the KGB in 1995."

"I didn't realize that."

"As for Sophie, she was not the only victim these men targeted. She just happened to be saved by a group of people already on the lookout for them."

"How do you know this?"

"It is all over school."

"Oh." Addison felt foolish.

"How is Sophie doing?"

"She spends all her time in our room studying, but I think she's getting better."

"That is good." Sergei leaned across the table and took her hand. "Let us get out of here and go for a walk."

"I need to get back and check on Sophie; I don't like leaving her alone too long."

"I will walk over with you and say hello."

"Thanks."

She waited as he gathered his things and then held his hand as they exited the coffee shop. Once outside, he pulled her into his arms and held her tight. He kissed her lips with a feather-like touch.

Addison's lips swelled under his heat.

He caressed her cheek, sliding his fingers down her neck and causing goose bumps below his touch. He kissed her again, deeper this time, exploring her mouth with his tongue as it tangled with hers.

"I have wanted to do that all day."

Blood pulsed through her veins, throbbing in her ears every time he touched her. Her insides roiled with the conflicting emotions. Wanting to be with him, touched by him, loved by him and the instinct of self-preservation to run as far as she could, as fast as her legs could carry her.

CHAPTER 25

Seasons Change

Addison

A ddison sat on the edge of the bed, laughing at Sophie as she whirled around the room in circles like a lost child.

"How can you walk away from him again without a word?" Sophie asked.

"Sophie, I've tried to be with him, and I've tried to live my life without him. I don't have the answers anymore."

"So, running away is the solution?" Sophie wiped her hands on her jeans. "There, that's done." She's eyed the luggage spread out on the bed, and the overflowing boxes on the floor.

"How can you possibly still have so much stuff? You've been giving away things for days."

Sophie giggled. "Only our dorm stuff. Not my

clothes or shoes." She waved a hand toward the suitcases.

Addison couldn't argue with that. Her roommate had brought an outrageous amount of stuff with her and regularly shopped throughout the school year. She was lucky to be flying home on her father's private jet. Addison imagined Sophie's father had set it up simply to save himself on the exorbitant baggage fees.

"You will visit me for Christmas break. We will go skiing," Sophie said.

"Yes, that sounds like fun." Addison pushed down all thoughts of the previous Christmas ski trip with Sergei.

"What about the ring?"

"I put it in the envelope with my note."

"He loves you, you know?"

"I love him, too. But Russia is his home, and I belong in America."

"He would've come with you."

"But it wouldn't be right."

Sophie just stared at her. They'd had this conversation repeatedly over the last two weeks. Nothing had changed.

"You're being foolish."

"So you keep telling me." Addison sighed.

"What most wouldn't give to have a man love them like that?"

"Sophie…" Addison warned.

"All right. All right. I'll shut up now. It's your life."

"Thank you for noticing that," Addison said. Her brow lifted.

Leaving with a clean break is best for us both.

THE TOWN CAR ARRIVED EXACTLY AT SEVEN O'CLOCK in the morning, as promised. The driver loaded their suitcases into the trunk. Their carry-on bags and smaller parcels were set on the seat between them. The stack was so high they could barely see each other.

THEY SAID THEIR GOODBYES TO THEIR FRIENDS IN their dormitory the night before while they were giving away their room stuff.

Addison had sent a card and a long letter to Lena, and one to Yuri, thanking them for everything and apologizing for not being able to stay in Russia and marry Sergei. It had broken her heart, but she felt that after all of Sergei's family's hospitality, it was the least she could do. The letter she wrote for Sergei, she left on her desk.

Once Addison hugged Sophie goodbye in the airport, she watched her friend climb the steps of the family jet and disappear inside.

She was a coward. Sitting in the lounge at the gate, waiting for her flight to be called, her heart sank to be leaving Sergei behind. At the same time, she knew it was the right thing for her future.

***

SERGEI SAT AT THE EDGE OF HER BARE MATTRESS AND stared at the pristine white envelope in his hand. His name was scrawled across the front. He came to take them to breakfast, arriving just after sunrise, hoping to surprise them with an early start. Instead, he was late.

She was gone.

Addison had left him. Forever this time. Without even saying goodbye.

Sergei,

I'm so sorry to leave you this way. I know that it's wrong of me, at the same time knowing it's better for us both if I go now. I thank you for the wonderful year of love you've given me, and I will carry those memories with me until the end of time. I needed to go. You need to stay. This is who we are, and even loving each other isn't enough to change everything about our futures.

Please don't think too harshly of me. I only wanted to spare us both more pain.

With all my heart,

Addison

Folding the paper back into shape and sliding it back into the envelope didn't ease the hole in his heart. He loved her. She loved him. And yet it wasn't enough. She'd told him that before. He should have listened. Maybe had he not been so stubborn, so sure of their love, he wouldn't be so gutted now. This would crush the twins. Loving her as much as he did. They would feel this blow as sharply as if they had been abandoned as well.

He pushed up from the bed, stuffed the envelope into the back pocket of his jeans, and headed to his dorm room. This was his last night on campus.

Maybe Pyotr would get rip-roaring drunk with him. He needed to forget her, and a night with friends was the best place to start. Facing his family would come soon enough. Tonight, it needed to be about easing his pain. About mourning her, and then letting her go.

CHAPTER 26

Turning with the Tide

Addison

A ddison found it remarkable that reviewing her final grades lacked the joy and sense of accomplishment she had expected. In truth, the exhaustion overwhelmed her, leaving no energy for celebration. Her father and Cassie made plans to take her to dinner, promising to keep it low-key with just the family, understanding she was drained from the last semester. The moment she'd returned from Saint Petersburg, she'd signed up for an increased class load. Throwing herself into her schoolwork was the only way she could think of to get over Sergei. Her mother was irritated with her again. She'd come home from abroad, visited her mother and sisters for a few days, then drove back to school to dive into the summer's session. Now at home, her mother expected her to be more available to her, but as much as she loved them, she could only handle her mother in small doses. The stress of listening to her mother's complaints or rants took its toll on her. Quinby still lived there, and Savannah often came so the girls would be taken care of. This eased a part of the guilt for not being more of the dutiful daughter her mother expected of her.

Checking her emails, she saw there was another one from Sophie, asking about the holidays.

Mon Amie, I hope all is well. I haven't heard from you. You don't answer your phone or my emails. Mon Dieu, it's enough to drive someone crazy. Are you still coming to Paris at the end of the month?
With love,
Sophie

Addison had forgotten her agreement to come to Paris for the holiday break. Her mother would be pissed, but getting away was exactly what Addison needed just now. It wasn't like she would miss Christmas dinner or anything.

She responded to her friend's email and accepted the invitation, then closed the lid to her computer. Kicking off her shoes, she slid under the covers for a much-needed nap. If she was honest with herself, it was more depression than exhaustion that seeped into her bones. Then again, the reason for both continued to haunt her thoughts. She missed him. Every. Single. Day. Leaving him the way she had was a coward's move, but she also knew she lacked the courage and faith in herself to deviate from her plans. Yet now that her undergraduate degree was completed, all that remained was the sense of loss. Someday, she hoped the hole in her heart of her own making would heal enough to hurt a little less. For some reason, she doubted it, though.

THE PHONE BY HER BED JANGLED, YANKING HER FROM her thoughts. Sleep had been just as elusive during the day as it was at night. Leaning over, she pulled the cell phone from her side table and flipped open the cover.

"Addison?"

"Sophie!" Addison's excitement at hearing her friend's voice exploded out of her.

"I have missed you, *mon chère*."

"And I have missed you. How's school?"

Addison sat up, pulled the pillows up against her back, and leaned into them.

"It is boor-ring. And your studies?"

"I finished."

"*Zut alors!* The full year? That is *fantastique!*"

"Yes, I'll cross the stage in May, but my classes are complete."

"So now you can come to Paris, and we can celebrate."

"I'd like that."

"I'll set everything up. You just make sure you check your emails."

"Yes, Mother."

"Humph," Sophie responded. "I am so excited you are coming."

"So am I."

They chatted for a few more minutes before someone in the background could be heard calling out to Sophie.

"I must go. We will talk again soon."

The line disconnected, and Addison laughed. Sophie hadn't changed a bit. Always in a rush. "Later," she said into the dead phone.

She crawled out of bed and padded her way downstairs to see what her father and Cassie were doing. Taking a nap no longer held her interest. She craved company.

Addison walked into the kitchen to find her father and Cassie wrapped in each other's arms. Her father's back was to her, his arms wrapped around Cassie as she laughed. Seeing them happy, when no one was watching, just a natural affection for each other, tore the hole in her heart a little wider. So caught up in not becoming like her mother, she tended to forget the love her father had found with Cassie. They were equals in every aspect. The respect and appreciation they had for each other were exactly what she hoped for someday.

Like a slap in the back of the head, Sergei's face filled her mind. His soft lips when he kissed her. The way his hand caressed hers while he drove. When he dropped everything to come to her because she'd called him. He would have loved her as her father loved Cassie.

With a jolt, she turned her attention to her father, who had asked her a question.

"I'm sorry. What did you say?"

"Will you be home for dinner?" Cassie asked.

"Yes, of course. Can I help?"

"Dinner is done. How about some wine?"

Addison nodded and wandered into the dining room. Her father had surprised Cassie with a temperature-controlled wine vault in the dining room during the remodel. It covered the entire back wall. Six narrow floor-to-ceiling glass doors showcased a unique assortment of wines. Grabbing a pinot noir from the center selection, she brought it back to the kitchen and handed it to her father.

CHAPTER 27

Collaboration with Sophie

Sergei

Sergei stared at the roaring fire in the parlor. Even with the blazing heat from the fire, there was a chill in his bones. The family was out running errands, getting last-minute gifts for Christmas. His mother agreed to purchase gifts on his behalf, so the twins would not be denied their excitement. He grabbed the blanket slung over the back of the rocker next to him and pulled it over his legs. A heavy funk settled over him the moment Addison had fled the country, leaving him behind, saying goodbye in a note left in her room. His family continued to support him, though he hated they shared knowing looks with each other when they thought he did not see.

With trembling fingers, he dialed her number. Six

long, agonizing months since he'd last heard her voice. Her laughter. His heart on his sleeve, he was out of ideas. There were no other options available to him. He hoped she would be supportive of his plight.

With bated breath, he waited as the line connected.

"Bonjour?"

"Sophie."

"Sergei! *Mon Dieu.* How are you?"

"I miss her!"

"I'm sorry, *mon ami.*"

Her soft voice and lack of harsh words gave him hope.

"Have you spoken?" he asked.

"Oui, she's coming to Paris at the end of the month. We're skiing."

Memories of their ski trip the year before invaded his mind. The way her lips felt against his. Her soft peach skin so easily flushed. The way his heart warmed as her fingers linked between his. The passion that stirred as he made love to her, learning he was her first. Wanting to be her last.

"How is she?"

"Tired, but well, I believe."

"Sophie, please. Help me. I should never have let her leave Saint Petersburg."

"I suppose you could have tied her up and kept her in your closet." Sophie giggled.

"You know what I mean. I should have fought for

her. Convinced her to stay. Or convinced her to let me come with her."

"She would have just fought you harder."

With a sigh, he knew she was right. "You know her so well."

"Oui, and you."

His breath hitched. The last six months had been hell. He reached for the phone at least a dozen times to call, but he did not even have her number in America. Pyotr was the one who suggested calling Sophie.

"Sergei, why don't you come? Meet us at the ski lodge, and you can talk to her. Maybe the time will have eased her stubbornness. Now that she's done with school."

"Done?"

"She fast-tracked and finished last week."

Hearing Addison completed an entire year's worth of work in a single semester told him how determined she was, and how focused she had been. He only loved her more for it.

"If she's done, then her previous objections are a moot point," he said.

"Oui, as far as her education is concerned, maybe. But she still had concerns about her mother accepting you," Sophie said.

"I am not worried. As long as I have Addison's love, nothing else matters."

"If you are sure, then come."

"Will you tell her?"

"*Non*, it will be your surprise."

"You think she may not come if she knows?" Sergei asked.

"*Oui.*"

"Oh, Sophie, I do not want to make her angry at you."

"*Mon ami,* as long as you have Addison's love, nothing else matters," Sophie said.

For the first time in months, Sergei laughed. Bordering on hysterics, he could not control it. Sophie joined in.

After a moment, Sophie said, "I will send you an email telling you when to come, and where to meet us."

Catching his breath, he said, "Thank you."

"If we do this right, maybe she will take you home from France."

The idea that maybe this time when she saw him, things would be different, and she would let him love her, filled his heart. He'd scarcely dared to hope in the months they were apart.

"Like a Christmas gift."

"Exactly, like a Christmas gift." Sophie giggled again.

"Sophie, do you think there's a chance?"

"There's always a chance. We will just have to work hard at making sure it works."

"You are a good friend. To us both."

"Let's hope she remembers that when she sees you," Sophie replied, giggling. "I will get everything ready and let you know."

"Bye, my friend."

"*Au* revoir."

He set the phone down in his lap; his attention drifted to the fire again. The gentle crackling, the orange flames licking at the edges of the logs stacked on the grate. Heat from the hearth reached out and warmed him, and for the first time in months, he had hope.

When the front door opened and slammed shut again, the noise of the twins' laughter pulled him from his deep introspection. The heaviness weighing him down had left his shoulders.

After pushing up from the oversized leather club chair, he set the blanket on the back and headed to the kitchen to see what the young ones had wheedled out of his parents.

CHAPTER 28

Skiing in France

Addison

Addison landed at Paris' de Gaul airport, this time knowing she would see more than just the airport and get a much-needed break.

In the six months since she'd hugged Sophie goodbye in Saint Petersburg, she'd immersed herself in her studies, trying to forget Sergei and how much it hurt to walk away from him. Everyone said you never forgot your first love, and she wouldn't. There would always be a place in her heart for Sergei, but to reach her goals, her education came above all else. Nothing, including her love for him, could stand in her way. Getting her undergraduate degree ahead of schedule was her reward for sacrificing love.

She missed him, though. Sometimes when she was alone without her studies to ground her, she thought of him and the love they'd shared. She was sorry she'd hurt him when she walked away without even saying goodbye, but she had tried to end things, only to wind up back in his arms again. She hadn't been strong enough to stay away, so she flew away and didn't look back. The regret haunted her, and she often played the "what if" game in her mind. It didn't matter now; the choices had been made, and they both had to live with it.

She caught sight of Sophie bouncing in place at the gate as she walked out of the gangway into the terminal.

"*Mon Dieu*, you have not changed," Sophie squealed as she hugged her tight. "Addy, this is my papa."

"*Bonjour*," Addison said.

Sophie waved her hand toward a tall, handsome man with salt and pepper hair. "Papá, this is Addison Tetrick, my roommate."

"Please call me Bertrand." He wrapped her hand inside his large palm. Warmth filled her as he shook it. "It is lovely to meet you, Ms. Tetrick. I've heard so much about you."

Addison looked from Sophie to her father. Sophie just grinned in response.

"Let's get your bags," Bertrand said.

Sophie chatted nonstop to the baggage claim. When her two large suitcases came through, the bright purple bags easily identifiable, Sophie giggled.

"See, Papá, I told you she would pack light. She is nothing like me."

"Thank the stars for that." Bertrand let out a hearty bellow.

"No one could compete with the amount of luggage you take with you," Addison said.

"Except Camilla," Sophie and Bertrand said simultaneously. They looked at each other and burst into hysterical laughter.

Addison couldn't hide the surprise at hearing the name of Sophie's ex-stepmother spoken so easily and without malice.

Bertrand glanced over his shoulder at her. "It's okay," he said. "She's gone from our lives, so it's easier, to be honest, about who she was."

Addison didn't know what to make of that, so she followed behind as Sophie's father pulled her bags to the large black town car waiting at the curb.

"We will drive up to the villa on Thursday," Bertrand said.

"Thursday? I thought we were going skiing."

"We are, but first we must show you Paris in all of its glory. It will be an experience like you've never seen."

"That will be easy since I've never been here before."

Sophie crossed her eyes at her and grinned like a fool. "We will shop, eat at the Café de Monde, and visit the Mona Lisa."

"I've always wanted to visit The Louvre."

"Good, then it's settled."

"Sophie, I can't afford one of your shopping fren-zies, you know that." Addison leaned in and whis-pered in her ear.

Bertrand let out a bellowing laugh. "My dear girl, even Camilla was hard-pressed to outspend my daughter last year."

Addison felt the blood drain from her face as she looked down at her hands folded in her lap. She knew a sizeable chunk of that bill had been spent on her and their dorm room.

Bertrand laughed again. "Don't fret. I know my Sophie. She had my complete consent to spend as she did. It makes me proud that I have raised such a generous daughter."

Addison could only stare at him in disbelief. It was hard to fathom that anyone could be that magnani-mous, especially about money.

"She takes after her mother. There was no one on earth more selfless or loving than her maman."

"I'm working on it, Papá," Sophie said with a laugh.

"Yes, my girl, you are." He leaned in and kissed her on the cheek.

"If it weren't for Nadeen's crazy attempt to make me a pauper, we would not have all we have today."

"How does that happen?"

"The horses," Sophie and Bertrand said in unison.

Addison's brow rose.

"Sophie's maman begged me to rescue the horses from the racetrack. The track was being closed, and the horses were scheduled for slaughter. The breeding business came by accident."

Addison had never heard this side of the story. There were dozens of articles published about the breeding business and the demand for his horses, but there had never been a story about its origins.

"The business just erupted from there. St. Bartholomew's foals were highly sought after, a dozen people paid deposits and signed the waiting list the first year."

"That's awesome. It's exciting to know that giving the horses a new home gave you a thriving business."

"It is our passion. We love them. Sophie learned to ride almost at the same time she learned to walk."

Bertrand regaled them with stories of the horses and Sophie's childhood the entire way to their apartment.

Addison had worried her lust for life had been lost after her incident in Russia, but Sophie was bubbly and full of laughter.

That night after dinner, Bertrand excused himself, and Sophie and Addison spent the night talking and laughing until the wee hours of the morning.

They slept in the following morning, enjoying coffee in bed before throwing on the cashmere robes Sophie had hanging on the back of her door, and going downstairs to have breakfast with Sophie's father.

Sophie's father was already sitting at the table when they came into the dining room.

"Good morning, girls. Stayed up late, I see." Bertrand gave them the all-knowing look Addison was used to seeing from her father and Cassie when she'd had sleepovers growing up.

"We had a lot of catching up to do, Papá." Sophie waved her hand dismissively.

Bertrand hid his smirk behind his coffee cup.

"Breakfast is on the sideboard."

"Thank you," Addison said. She wandered over to the long sideboard against the wall draped in crisp white linen. Silver warming platters with lids covered the surface. A Matisse painting in an enormous, intricately carved gold frame hung directly above. *That has to be one of the ugliest frames I've ever seen. What a shame.*

Lifting the lids, she found fresh fruit sausages, warm croissants, and preserves. On the far end, a stack of Limoges China perched.

After grabbing one of the pristine plates, she filled it with fruit, then added a croissant and a scoop of preserves as an afterthought. She joined Sophie at the table where a large, ornate silver coffee pot sat in the center.

Each seat was set with silk napkins, sparkling flat-ware, and Baccarat crystal water glasses.

"Today we will tour The Louvre's paintings before lunch."

"Is that all?" Addison had anticipated spending the entire day there.

Sophie poured coffee into two delicate China cups as Addison sat down. "*Mon amie,* it will be exhausting and overwhelming. The Louvre cannot be done in a single day."

"Really?"

"It would take over three months to view and appreciate each display within the museum properly," Sophie said.

"I never knew the museum had that many pieces." After slathering fresh preserves over her warm crois-sant, Addison nibbled at it.

"We will have a late lunch at *Le Fumoir* when we finish," Bertrand said.

"Sounds perfect." Addison took another sip of her coffee.

Sophie and Addison finished their breakfast, chat-ting about the newspaper, before heading upstairs to shower and change.

WALKING THROUGH THE COURTYARD ALONG WITH hundreds of other tourists, passing the water fountains between the massive glass pyramid and a smaller one on the other side, Addison took in her surroundings. People sat along the rim of the fountain talking and taking pictures of themselves and each other.

Once inside, Addison craned her neck to take in the high ceilings intricately carved with flowers and animals and leaves, each carving surrounded by a sculpted border.

Bertrand led them directly to the Renaissance section of the museum to make The Mona Lisa their first stop.

The crowd was thickest in this area. As people shoved against one another, Addison moved over to the right side, hoping to see the image after the crowd of people had thinned. The museum had taken extraordinary precautions to keep the painting safe.

After ten minutes of continuously sidestepping to avoid being crushed by the crowd, Addison was able to get closer to the temporary barrier and stand facing the portrait. The gilded frame made The Mona Lisa appear larger than the artwork actually was.

"I can understand the world's fascination with her and her enigmatic smile."

"*Oui*, she is unusual."

Addison linked her arm through Sophie's. For a moment, the two women stood in silence, transfixed by the woman in the image. Standing there before this historical masterpiece, her mind traveled back to the year before when Sergei had walked through the hallways at the university.

"Shall we move on?" Bertrand asked.

They nodded. Sophie slid her hand into her father's as he led them away. Addison turned for one last glance at The Mona Lisa, before she followed them.

They continued into the Richelieu Wing, skipping the Italian art section, instead taking in Napoleon III's apartments. After an hour of touring the rooms of the once-royal residence, they stopped to see the crown jewels. The coronation crowns were not to her taste, with the oversized stones and thick gold. They didn't hold the same power over her as the necklaces, and the matching tiaras or diadems of the French Crown Jewels did. The sparkling jewels on display were stunning. A pang shot through her. *Not as beautiful as my ring, though…*

"What beautiful sets."

"Sets such as these are called *parures*," Sophie said.

"They're amazing."

"Ridiculously heavy, I'm sure." Sophie giggled.

"That, too." Addison grinned.

After passing through the rest of the crown jewel displays, they entered the Egyptian antiquities department, which held an impressive array of statues and carvings, before entering the displays of Mesopotamian artifacts.

Exhausted, they exited the museum and walked the short block and a half to the restaurant.

Perusing the menu, Bertrand and Sophie gave their suggestions.

After they gave their orders, the server excused himself, and the sommelier appeared. A short, stout, balding man, he greeted them. *"Bonjour,* Monsieur Compte, *mademoiselles. Bienvenu."*

"Une bouteille 1995 Clos de la Roche, *s'il vous* plaît," Bertrand said.

"Magnifique la vendange."

The sommelier stepped away, returning moments later with the wine. A server set three wine glasses on the table, disappearing as silently as he appeared.

Bertrand tasted the wine, nodding his approval, and after the sommelier had poured their wine, he vanished as well.

"To lasting friendships."

"Oui." Sophie raised her glass.

Raising her glass, Addison clinked it with Sophie's, followed by Bertrand's, before taking a sip.

The wine was amazing. The subtle flavors of dark chocolate and black cherries danced on her tongue.

Lunch was filled with fluid conversation, and laughter as the wine flowed.

For a little while, Addison could escape the dark depression of missing Sergei.

CHAPTER 29

A Hopeful Heart

Sergei

Sergei's flight arrived in Chamonix-Mont-Blanc first thing on Wednesday morning. Checking in at the front desk of the five-star resort was as easy as Sophie said it would be. A gangly young bellboy led him to the rooms. After doing a quick tour of the elegant suite, he dropped his bags on the floor of one of the smaller bedrooms. He headed into the large kitchen, pulled a can of cola from the icebox, and sat in a chair near the hearth. He pulled a crumpled paper from his pocket, opened it, and smoothed it out. He reread Sophie's last message, as he had a dozen times in the last day.

Sergei,

*Addison has arrived in Paris. She is well. We will
be visiting The Louvre and doing some shopping
before we head to Chamonix on Thursday. I
expect we should be there sometime after lunch.
Check in at the desk. They have your name, and
they will give you a key to our suites.
See you soon.
Au* revoir,
Sophie

Finished with his cola, the restlessness kicked in.
He needed fresh air. After dropping the empty can in
the trash, he left the suite and headed downstairs. He
anxiously wandered the grounds. The snow continued
to fall in little white puffs around him. The massive
resort was a far cry from the little slopes that Okhta
Park had offered him. Skiing the Alps, whether in
France, Italy, or Switzerland territories, was on the
bucket list for many of the serious skiers of the world.
The resort they were staying in was situated perfectly
between the three major slopes of Mont Blanc,
Grandes Jorasses, and Aiguille du Chardonnet, in the
French region. He doubted they would visit Punta
Baretti just over the border in Italy, though it was
near enough.

While he looked around at the people wandering
around the grounds, his nerves roiled in his chest. *He
was in France.* There had been no hesitation when

Sophie had sent him the information and the plane ticket.

When Addison left Russia, a part of him died inside. At first, he had tried to accept it. He kept busy, studied, spent time with his family, and started his doctorate. Nothing helped. His heart was empty. There was no joy or fulfillment in any of his deeds. His mother's pep talk, if you could call it that, pushed him into motion and sent him to France for one last attempt to capture her heart.

Now, standing there at the bottom of the Alps, waiting for Addison to arrive, he questioned this move, terrified that once she saw him, she would run away once again. He missed her. She filled his thoughts every day. Memories of what they shared. The way she tucked her hair behind her ear when distracted. Her hand in his, head on his shoulder. How his heart sped up when she was near. He loved her. Even after all this time, he loved her. He didn't doubt his love for her. Before she left Russia, he had not doubted her love for him. Since that day, he'd questioned every experience, every emotion he felt, what he thought she had. In the end, even after all the questions, he knew his love was real.

***

ADDISON'S MORNING MOVED IN SLOW MOTION, AS THEY all were lacking a good night's sleep and hosting a hangover. The copious amounts of champagne they had drank to celebrate their last night in Paris had caught up with her.

"Sophie, what has you so anxious? You're more spastic than usual."

Sophie blushed and shared a side look with her father that Addison caught, but didn't understand.

"'Tis nothing. I only hope the ski suit I bought you fits you." Sophie's eyes didn't meet Addison's when she spoke.

Suspicion filled Addison as Bertrand gave Sophie another indecipherable look.

Observing her friend over the short hour-long flight from Charles de Gaulle to Chamonix gave her no further clue. Sophie was full of mindless chatter. She was always talkative in the past. Addison couldn't quite put her finger on the difference, but her gut told her something was amiss. She didn't focus on the words, more Sophie's distraction, and the strange looks shared with her father.

A smile tugged at her lips as the porter stowed their bags in the trunk of the town car. It had been a struggle to fit all of Sophie's bags into the limited space. Leave it to her friend to pack enough luggage for a small delegation when going skiing for a long weekend.

Addison stared out the window as they sped toward the hotel, surrounded by shining snow, an almost blinding world. Driving in the valley between the tallest mountains she'd ever seen, they passed huge hotels, their windows glowing yellow from the lights within. More of the wood-sided hotels seemed to hover in the distance, larger than life.

The white powder covered the rooflines and sprinkled over the branches of trees that lined the roadway. The white-tipped mountains loomed above the horizon, making the valley seem small and insignificant in their wake. With a stab in her heart, Sergei's face filled her mind. This time, a year ago, she was falling in love. Now she was alone, and he was gone. Her heart ached for him, but she knew nothing would have changed her mind. When she held her degree in her hand, it would be tangible proof her hard work and sacrifices were worth her efforts.

SOPHIE'S CHATTER CEASED SUDDENLY AS THE CAR pulled up to the resort. Bertrand grew quiet as well. Instinct told Addison something was brewing, but for the life of her, she couldn't figure what it could be. A young a man in uniform helped them out of the car and loaded their extensive baggage onto a luggage cart.

They strolled behind the porter and the overloaded cart as he led the way to the suites booked for them.

The tension in Sophie's shoulders made Addison nervous. Sophie walked a few steps in front of her, chatting with her father. Bertrand leaned over and gave his daughter's shoulder a gentle squeeze. Addison's stomach dropped. Her toe caught on the edge of the carpet, tripping her. She stumbled a step before catching herself. The makeup bag she carried slipped from her hand with a crash. Sophie whirled around, eyes wide at Addison's swaying form.

"*Mon amie*, are you okay?"

"Yes, I'm fine. I just slipped."

Bertrand bent over and scooped up her bag from the floor before tucking it under his arm. Addison smiled at the ease with which he held the bright purple bag. Offering her his elbow, Addison stepped up to him and put her hand into the crook of his arm while Sophie took her other hand.

The three of them made a tight unit down the large hallway.

"I have a surprise for you," Sophie said.

"I know."

Sophie's stride paused as her eyes grew wide. "How?"

"You've been acting weird all morning. I knew something was up." Addison grinned.

"You know I love you. You are my best friend."

"Sophie, you're doing it again."

"Doing what?"

"Acting weird," Addison said.

"Just tell her, Sophie," Bertrand said.

"I don't want you to hate me," Sophie implored.

"Sophie, I could never hate you."

"Promise." Sophie's voice was soft and pleading.

Addison pursed her lips. This was so unlike Sophie. And Bertrand had an uncomfortable expression, making Addison leery.

"Sophie, just spit it out, will you?" Addison snapped, the frustration and the nerves getting the better of her.

Sophie shuffled from foot to foot, once again not meeting Addison's eyes. "I-I invited Sergei." A rush of unintelligible words flew out of her mouth.

Alarms sounded in her ears as blood rushed to her head. Her breath hitched, her heart skipped a beat, and her hands got clammy as she gripped Bertrand's arm. Addison's mouth opened and closed. All she heard was his name. *Sergei.*

The next thing she saw was his face. Floating above hers in a haze. He became clearer as her eyes focused.

"Addison, are you okay?" Sophie cried.

"Why am I on the floor?" A sharp object jabbed the back of her right shoulder. "And what's poking me?"

"I think that's my purse," Sophie said.

"Why is it on the floor? Actually, why am I on the floor?"

"You fainted. And when you fell, you took my purse with you." Sophie blushed.

"Crap." Addison scrambled to sit up. In her rush,

she wasn't paying close attention, and her head smacked right into a block. "Shit!"

Sophie giggled, and Bertrand exhaled loudly.

"Addison—" Sergei said.

"You're here?" Addison sputtered.

Sergei stood and reached his hand out. Addison took it and let him pull her to her feet.

Befuddled, Addison continued to stare at his face. Drinking him in. *He's here. He's really here.*

Bertrand took Sophie's elbow and moved her to the side of the hallway. "Addison, go for a walk. We will see you back in the rooms." His eyes were lit with mischief as a grin split his face wide.

"Hmm… I don't know where they are," Addison said. She tore her eyes from Sergei's face as she addressed Bertrand.

"Don't worry, he does." Sophie nodded toward Sergei.

"Oh… Of course," Addison stuttered.

Bertrand led Sophie down the hall as the porter began pushing the baggage cart behind them.

Turning her attention back to Sergei, she saw her hand remained in his.

"Do not be angry."

"I'm not mad at Sophie," Addison said.

"Are you with me?"

Startled, Addison looked at his sheepish expression and smiled. "No, I'm not angry with you either."

Sergei's shoulders relaxed their tense posture. He

took her hand and placed it in the crook of his arm. "Let us walk. I have missed you."

"I've missed you, too."

"Congratulations are in order, I understand."

"For what?" Addison asked.

"Sophie said you have completed your studies early."

"Yes. Just this month, in fact," Addison said.

"That is worth celebrating, is it not?" Sergei asked.

"Yes, of course. I just didn't realize Sophie had talked to you about me."

"When I called her, she informed me of your visit. She told me then."

They continued to walk until reaching the grounds. He led her to a small bench off to the side of the courtyard.

As they sat and stared at the incoming guests, Addison shivered.

"Here, take this." Sergei took his coat off and slid it around her shoulders.

"Thank you." Addison snuggled deeper into the warmth of his jacket. His cologne tickled her nose, filling her senses. Filling her with longing. "Why are you here?"

Sergei twisted in his seat to face her directly. "I came to convince you to marry me."

"We've discussed this already." Addison directed her gaze to the ground.

"*Da*, twice, in fact. And then you left without another word."

"I'm sorry for leaving the way I did. It was a cowardly thing to do."

"It was rotten." Sergei nodded.

"Sergei, you know I had to go. You know why. I couldn't let anything get in the way of my education."

"Not even love?"

"Especially not love."

"Ouch." Sergei flinched.

"I'm sorry, but I've always been honest with you."

Sergei leaned against the back of the bench. "I still love you. I came to France to show you that."

"I know."

"Addison, for Christ's sake. Why are you being so difficult?"

Startled, Addison leaned away. She'd never heard him swear before.

Sergei inhaled a deep, rattling breath. "I apologize." He reached out and took her hand. "I do not curse."

"I know."

"You are the most frustrating person I know."

"I'm sorry."

"Stop being sorry, damn it, and start being reasonable."

"That's not fair." Addison yanked her hand from his.

"You love me. And I love you. It is time we stopped playing games, and you married me."

"I'm not playing games," Addison said.

Sergei slid from the bench and kneeled in front of her.

"Marry me."

I can't do this. She shook her head. "You belong in Russia with your family."

He retook her hand. "Marry me," Sergei said stubbornly.

Damn him. Addison tried to pull her hand away.

He clasped it between both of his. "Take me home with you." Sergei brought her hand to his lips.

"I can't. My mother will never accept you."

"I do not care. That is not my concern."

Addison rolled her eyes. "Now look who's being unreasonable."

"Not unreasonable to follow one's heart," Sergei said.

"Would you still want to marry me if your family didn't approve?"

"Of course. My family only wants for us to be happy."

"You are so frustrating," Addison said, her tone defeated.

"Does that mean yes?" Sergei's eyes lit up.

"Yes," Addison whispered. Tears streamed down her face.

"Really?" Sergei asked, surprised.

Addison palmed away the tears in her eyes and nodded.

Sergei sprang to his feet and pulled her into his arms, pressing his lips to hers in a bruising kiss, making her head swim. He tightened his arms around her and hugged her to him.

Addison rubbed her arms. "Can we go in now? I'm freezing."

Sergei laughed. "*Da.* Just one more thing."

"Oh, God. Now what?"

He took the ring from his pocket, tugged off her glove, slipping it onto her left ring finger. Wrapping his arm around her while she worked to put her glove back on, they trudged back into the hotel.

Walking into the suite, Sergei directly behind her, they headed toward the voices, finding Sophie and her father in the kitchen.

Sophie saw them first. "So, is it settled, then?"

"Sophie," Bertrand chided.

"Well?" Sophie asked again, glaring at Addison's hand.

Sergei chuckled. He put his arm around Addison's waist and pulled her close. "*Da.* Stubborn one, she is. But she agreed."

"*Félicitations!*" Sophie cried.

"This calls for champagne," Bertrand said as he popped the cork on the bottle of Bollinger in his hand.

"You should probably glue the ring to her finger this time, just in case," Sophie said.

"Sophie!" Bertrand chuckled.

Sophie shrugged in response.

Addison's brow rose as the color returned to Sophie's face.

Sophie came around the counter and hugged Addison, then Sergei. Her face was flushed, and her eyes glittered with unshed tears. "They say the third time's the charm!"

Sergei laughed. Addison elbowed his side, making him laugh even harder.

Bertrand handed out champagne glasses and lifted his. "A toast. To Addison and Sergei. May your love deliver you through all obstacles, bringing you joy each day. And to my daughter, the incurable meddler."

Sophie joined in the laughter.

Addison stared at the ring. She loved him. He loved her. She'd finished her degree. He came to France to win her over and was coming home with her once the weekend was over. There were no more excuses. They were getting ready for dinner, and Addison needed to call her family to prepare them.

The phone buzzed in her ear as she waited for it to connect.

"Hello?"

"Hi, Cassie."

"Addy, is everything okay?"

"Of course. Why wouldn't it be?"

"Because you're supposed to be skiing in France. So, if you're calling me, something is wrong."

"Sergei is here."

"Oh."

"Yeah, after I fainted, I think I said something like that too." Addison laughed.

"You fainted?"

"I was a bit surprised, is all."

"You're okay, though?" Concern filled Cassie's voice.

Everything is more than okay now. "He proposed again, and I accepted."

"Good. I'm glad."

"Really?"

"You haven't been the same since you came back from Russia, throwing yourself into your classes so you wouldn't have to deal with anything else. We've been worried."

"I'm sorry," Addison said.

"It's not a criticism, Addy, it's just concern."

"I know. I didn't realize I was affecting you as well."

"Bring your beau home. It's time you had your own life," Cassie said.

"My mother is going to be furious," Addison said.

"Probably. But don't think about that now. Enjoy your trip. The rest can be handled when you get back."

"Thanks, Cassie."

"Love you. Give my love to your friends. We can pick you up if you'd like."

"That would be sweet. Thank you."

After Cassie hung up, Addison set the phone aside and finished getting dressed for dinner. She would put her mother and everything else out of her mind for the weekend. Reality would interfere soon enough.

CHAPTER 30

Return to Reality

Addison

Addison's stomach somersaulted as the plane taxied into place. *What was I thinking? I've lost my mind for sure.* As they exited the plane, Sergei reached for her hand, lending her his quiet strength once again. A grin split her face as her father came into view. Seeing him there waiting for her in the crowd, a smile on his face, made her glad she'd called ahead to tell Cassie that Sergei would be returning from France with her. Cassie stood beside him, off to the side of the line of people exiting the plane. The tears in her eyes glistened as she beamed back at Addison.

Here goes nothing.

As she reached them, her father cocooned her into his embrace, squeezing the breath out of her, kissing her forehead. He released her to Cassie, who, in turn, wrapped her in a deep embrace. Her father extended his hand toward Sergei.

"You must be Sergei. Welcome," Eli said.

Sergei grasped his hand and shook it.

Eli's warm smile eased the tension that had rested on Addison's shoulders since the plane had touched down.

"Thank you," Sergei said. "A pleasure to meet you."

Cassie hugged him next.

"Let's get your bags and get out of here," Eli said.

Addison hooked her arm into Cassie's and followed her father and Sergei to the luggage carrousel.

Eli and Sergei hit it off immediately. They sat in the front of her father's Range Rover and talked each other's ears off the entire drive home. Addison listened with half an ear to their easy conversation, the tension releasing the stranglehold that it had on her lungs.

"Addison tells me you restore classic British cars."

"Among other things, yes. That's my passion."

"I like cars, but know little about them."

"That's what keeps me in business," Eli said.

"You make a fair point."

Eli laughed. "When there's more time, I'll bring you to the shop and show you around."

"Thank you. I would like that."

Addison sat in the back seat with Cassie, catching up on local gossip. Addison could hear snippets of their conversation about soccer. It was good to see her father laughing.

"Have you called your mother?" Eli asked.

"Not yet."

"Addison, you know it's never a good idea to surprise Tandy. It never turns out well," Eli said.

"I know. I just wasn't ready to explain."

"You should call her before you just bring him over," Cassie suggested.

"I will."

Grateful for the soft squeeze Cassie gave her hand, Addison returned the gesture as a way of thanks.

Once they arrived at her father's home, Cassie and Addison headed for the kitchen while Eli grabbed a couple of beers and took Sergei into the backyard. Things weren't as bad as she'd feared. *Then again, wait 'til mama meets him.*

SERGEI'S NERVES HAD BEEN STRETCHED THIN SINCE THE plane touched down. Holding the beer in his hand, he toed the snow on the ground. The white powder reminded him of home. There was snow on the ground at home in Russia, and again in France. Finding it here in North Carolina was comforting.

His breath came out in foggy puffs as Addison's

father tossed a tennis ball for the dogs. The two dogs chased the tennis ball, returned it to Eli, and dropped it at his feet in turns. Eli picked it up and threw it again. The dogs raced each other in a mad dash each time.

While in school, Addison spent months telling him about her crazy family and how she dreaded going home, leaving him unsure of what to expect. The idea of meeting them gave him many sleepless nights.

He knew she was close to her father and step-mother, and watching how they greeted them at the airport, he could understand why. They were warm and inviting, and they loved Addison. It filled their eyes, sat in their smiles and was evident in the way they hugged her tight. She had experienced love. There was an instant connection with them.

Before they left France, she laid out their plans. She explained he would meet her father and Cassie first, and later she would introduce him to her mother and her sisters. That, no doubt, was weighing as heavily on her mind as much as his. He watched her talk to Eli and Cassie. She was utterly at ease with them. He had never seen her this relaxed when talking about her mother or that side of her family. Cassie reminded him of his mother, a strong, inde-pendent woman, yet soft and nurturing of her family at the same time. From the little Addison had told him of her family, he understood Cassie to be the complete opposite of her mother. For a moment, the homesickness crept in. He wished his family was not on the other side of the world right now.

"What's on your mind, Sergei?" Eli asked.

On my mind? Nothing but fear of this woman I'm about to meet. And sadness at the family I left behind. But there was no point telling his soon-to-be father-in-law that. He would remain polite and confident, despite the war in his heart. "Sorry, distracted. You have a beautiful home."

"Thank you."

AFTER DINNER, ADDISON SAID GOODNIGHT AND WENT to her room, propped herself up against her headboard, and called her mother to check in.

May as well face this fight sooner than later.

"Hi, Mama," Addison said as soon as her mother answered. "I'm back."

"For how long this time?"

Jealousy oozed from her mother's voice. It couldn't be helped, so Addison didn't take the bait.

"Sergei came home with me."

"I can't believe you brought him home!" Tandy's voice bellowed through the earpiece. "I thought you left that boy and all this foolishness in Russia where he belongs."

She pulled her mobile phone away from her ear.

"I thought you went to France to see your girlfriend."

"I did. Sophie invited Sergei to join us."

"So, she's responsible for this?"

No, I am. I love him. That's my decision. Addison gritted her teeth and then took a deep, calming breath before answering.

"Mama, I told you the last time we talked that Sergei had proposed."

"Yes, and then you came home without him."

"I made a mistake."

"Sergei. What kind of name is that?" Tandy huffed.

"Russian," Addison said simply.

"I thought you had better sense."

Addison chewed on a hangnail. She didn't want to fight. "Mama, I'd like you to meet him."

"Fine."

"Please be nice."

"Fine, I said."

"Okay, we'll come by tomorrow." Addison flipped the phone closed and dropped it on the bed. Now she had to prepare Sergei. Having him meet her father and Cassie first was the only way to ease him into her family.

She went to bed feeling more drained than she had felt in months.

SERGEI WAS AT THE KITCHEN COUNTER, DRINKING coffee with Cassie and her father, when Addison walked in. The three of them were laughing, completely at ease with each other. She placed her hand on Sergei's back and leaned in to kiss his cheek.

"My mother is expecting us today," she said.

Cassie's eyes widened.

Eli laughed. "You should have taken Sergei straight over there first. She's not going to be happy that you introduced him to us before her."

"I didn't tell her until last night. But I wanted you to meet him. Just in case."

"In case what?" Cassie asked. Her eyes widened.

"In case he runs screaming back to Russia on the first available flight."

Cassie stifled a smirk behind the potholder in her hand.

"She can't possibly be that bad," Sergei said.

Cassie and Eli exchanged a knowing glance. After breakfast, Eli clasped Sergei on the shoulder. "Well, Sergei, it was nice to meet you. Know that you're always welcome here."

Sergei gave him a quizzical glance, but smiled. Addison kissed Cassie's cheek and hugged her father tight. Ignoring the flutters in her stomach, she took a deep breath, knowing she couldn't show weakness. Her mother could smell fear.

Addison grasped Sergei's hand and walked him out to her car that had spent the past year in her father's garage. Her fingers twisted the ring on her left hand around in circles. It was the only outward sign of her overactive nerves.

Forty-five minutes later, she pulled up to her mother's house. After she switched off the engine, she faced Sergei. He seemed at ease; his face completely relaxed.

"Addison, are you all right?"

"Yes, why?"

"*Milaya*, I have never seen you this tense. Even during exams, you were calmer."

"I love my mother, but she's an acquired taste."

"If she is anything like you, I will be fine."

"She's not. I'm more like my father and Cassie."

"Oh." Sergei's expression belied his concern as he stared at her.

Addison leaned over and kissed him. He deepened the kiss, his thumb stroking her cheek and distracting the butterflies in her stomach.

She pulled away, ending the kiss. "Let's go. I don't want to keep her waiting. It'll only worsen her attitude."

Sergei's brow lifted. He leaned in and kissed the tip of her nose.

ADDISON SENSED THE SOUR MOOD IN THE AIR ALMOST immediately after she walked through the door, instantly regretting the decision to bring Sergei over.

Glancing around the family room, her mother was nowhere to be found. Her two youngest sisters were wrapped in each other's arms on the couch, crying. Savannah sat stone-faced on the chair in the corner.

"Savi, what's wrong?"

"Eric moved out today."

"Shit!"

"Addy, bite your tongue." Her sister gave a pointed look toward the younger girls on the couch.

"I talked to Mama last night. She didn't say anything about them fighting."

"Eric left ten minutes ago. Mama wasn't expecting him to leave today."

"But she was expecting him to leave?" Addison asked.

"I don't know. But he came home from work and packed his bags. He told her he rented an apartment and wanted a divorce," Savannah replied with a shrug.

"Have they been arguing lately?"

"I don't know. I've been busy with work and school, so I haven't been home much."

"Hmm," Addison mumbled.

Sergei stood off to the side, slightly behind Addison, like a rock. Her hand was in his, quietly sending her support with his presence.

Savannah looked past Addison, noticing Sergei for the first time.

"Savi, this is Sergei." Addison twisted to give her a

better view. "Sergei, this is my oldest sister, Savannah."

"Hello, Savannah," Sergei said.

Savannah nodded in response. She stood and stepped toward Addison. "Today's not a good day for Mama. I wouldn't recommend sticking around." She extended her hand to Sergei. "It's nice to meet you." She shook his hand before turning back to Addison. After kissing her on the cheek, she whispered, "I'm glad you're home."

"Addy, don't go," Beth wailed, tears and snot running down her face.

"Please stay." Raleigh wiped at her nose.

Addison went to the couch and kneeled in front of her youngest sisters. She hugged them to her and kissed their tear-streaked cheeks. It broke her heart to see them like this. Eric was the only father either of them knew. Raleigh was so young when Rafe left, she barely remembered living with him. "I'll come back tomorrow, okay? Let's give Mama a day to be sad."

"Promise you'll come back tomorrow," Raleigh begged.

"Yes, I'll come for lunch. Would you like that?"

Beth squeezed her tight before letting go and nodding. Raleigh sniffled.

Addison stood and kissed the tops of their heads. She reached for Savannah's hand. She gave it a small squeeze before reaching for Sergei's hand and leading him out of the house. So overwhelmed by their grief, the little ones probably hadn't even noticed Sergei's presence.

Once in the car, she slammed her palms against the steering wheel. "Damn it."

Sergei twisted in his seat and faced her.

"I'm sorry. I was already dreading today. But, damn, I hadn't seen this coming."

"Eric is your stepfather?" he asked.

"Yes. He's Beth's father."

"I see," Sergei said.

"They weren't getting along when I left, but I figured it was just another phase."

"They fought often?" Sergei asked, his brow creased.

"Not as much as her other husbands, but yeah."

"I am sorry."

"Damn it." Addison pounded the steering wheel again. "Damn it all to hell."

"*Dorogaya*, it will be fine."

"I need to call my dad."

Sergei's face clouded.

Addison picked up her mobile. After two rings, the line picked up. "Cassie, have we missed dinner?"

"No. Come home. Chicken is in the oven."

"Perfect. We're on our way."

"Dinner at your father's?" Sergei asked when she set her phone down.

"Yes, is that okay?"

"Of course. Whatever makes you happy."

"Thank you." Addison caressed his cheek. Sergei took her hand and kissed her fingers. She started the car and put them back on the freeway, taking Sergei's hand and intertwining their fingers. The entire drive home, she kept her emotions locked down. *You can't break down now.*

AS THEY PULLED INTO HER FATHER'S DRIVEWAY, CASSIE opened the door and stood on the porch. She pulled Addison into her warm embrace and held her tight. She kissed her forehead, and then pulled away and looked into her eyes.

"Everything okay, honey?"

Addison shook her head in defeat. "Eric wants a divorce."

"Damn. I'm sorry."

"Yeah, lousy timing." Addison stood, wringing her hands.

"Maybe they'll work it out." Cassie's voice held a note of optimism.

"He moved out today." Addison sighed.

"Shit." Cassie sounded defeated.

Sergei's head swung from one to the other while following their exchange.

"I'm sorry. Come in. I'll pour you a glass of wine." Cassie linked her arm in Addison's and led her into the house, Sergei trailing close behind.

The dining table was already set with four place

settings, including wine glasses. While Addison and Sergei took a seat, Eli poured them wine and Cassie brought in the chicken cacciatore, placing it in the center of the table.

"I'm sorry to hear about Eric. Did you talk to your mother?" Eli asked.

"No, she was in her room when I got there. The girls were on the couch crying, and Savannah suggested I wait to talk to Mama."

"That's probably for the best," Cassie said.

Addison nodded. She didn't have the energy to think about it anymore.

They finished the dinner with small talk. After her second glass of wine, the tension in her shoulders loosened enough for her to relax. "I'm exhausted. I think I'll head to bed early."

"Good night, honey," Cassie said.

Addison kissed her cheek, then her father's. As she walked by his chair, she touched Sergei's shoulder.

"Good night, *dorogaya*."

Upstairs, Addison slipped on her nightshirt and crawled under the covers. Tears flowed as she lay her head on the pillow.

She was frustrated with herself for expecting more from her mother. Her entire childhood had been about pleasing her. She never seemed to gain her mother's approval; even now she had hoped that things would be different. She stared at the slowly darkening sky through the window.

Her mother's drama once again consumed her. Even in childhood, life had revolved around it. The tension, the mood swings, the comings and goings of people in her life.

Her mother would only smother her dreams if given a chance. Addison had the opportunity for genuine happiness with a man who loved her unconditionally, enough to find her even after she'd left him behind. The time had come for her to take a stand and build the future she wanted, not what was expected of her, or would make others happy. *No more excuses.*

CHAPTER 31

Duty Calls

Addison

A ddison stood in the hot shower for longer than usual. The water pounded her back, easing the sleep from her muscles. She hoped Sergei found a better night's sleep in his room down the hall. After she combed out her hair, she threw on jeans and a pullover sweater before making her way downstairs.

Sergei was at the counter, drinking coffee with her father while Cassie cooked breakfast.

"Good morning," she called, stepping into the kitchen. She pecked her father's cheek, and then Sergei's, before pulling out a barstool.

Eli poured her a cup of coffee while Cassie served up the pancakes. The bacon and scrambled eggs were already on the counter. They served themselves, settling down to eat.

"What are your plans for the day?" Eli asked.

"I promised Beth I would come back today," Addison replied.

Eli nodded over his steaming cup of coffee.

Addison swallowed the lump of eggs in her throat as she turned to Sergei. "Would you mind staying here? I need to deal with this drama first."

"Are you sure?"

"I am. Can you start the search for apartments in the area?"

He smiled and patted her hand. "Of course," Sergei said.

"We're glad that you'll be closer to home," Cassie said.

Cassie and her father were taking it far better than she'd anticipated. Then again, they rarely seemed to get as worked up as she expected. Her father seemed to temper his responses to give her the balance she craved. Her mother's attitude was as predictable as her father's in many ways, though in absolute opposite directions if she were honest with herself.

ADDISON WALKED INTO HER MOTHER'S HOUSE, catching Savannah in the kitchen, making the girls a macaroni and cheese bake for lunch. Beth and

Raleigh were sitting at the table, wearing mopey expressions.

"Hey, sis."

Savannah turned to her and gave her a quick nod before turning back to the stove.

The girls jumped up from their seats and wrapped their arms around her, their faces split into wide, toothy grins. She ruffled their messy heads and kissed them before they dropped back into their chairs.

"How's Mama?"

"Still in bed," Beth said.

"How are you, bee?"

"I miss Daddy." Beth lowered her eyes.

"I'm sorry, honey."

"Do you think we'll get to see Daddy again?"

"Of course, sweetheart." Addison almost choked on her words.

"Raleigh doesn't see her daddy anymore," Beth said.

Raleigh twisted her head. "And Quinby and Savi never saw their daddy again after he went away."

Addison glanced up and caught Savannah's gaze. Her sister's eyes were full of unshed tears, and her shoulders were stiff. She hated seeing the pain etched on her face and the sadness in Beth's voice.

"I know, but maybe this time will be different." The words were thick on her tongue.

Beth and Raleigh had seen what the three older girls had gone through, and knew it wasn't that simple. She gazed into the other room. The memories that swirled through her mind gave her doubts. If Mama behaved true to form, she would punish Eric for leaving, as she had her father. If Eric acted as Luke or Rafe had, he may have no intention of looking back now that he'd walked away.

Either way, her heart broke. For all her sisters, because her father was the only one who had been willing to stand up to Mama. Raleigh had already gone through this with her father, though she was even younger than Beth when he left. In many ways, Eric was the only father she knew. She knew in her heart that her sisters resented her relationship with her father because they didn't have one with theirs.

Shaking her head, she turned her attention back to her sisters. Savannah was dishing up macaroni and cheese bake onto plates at the stove when Tandy made her entrance. Addison bit her cheek. Savannah passed around three plates of the macaroni and cheese and then gave Tandy a steaming cup of coffee before turning back to the stove.

Addison peered at her mother under her lashes, seated across from her in baggy sweats and a stretched-out t-shirt. Her hair was matted to the side of her head. Lines streaked down her cheek from where she'd slept on it.

Tandy glared at Addison over the lip of her coffee cup. "Where's the foreigner?"

Taken aback by the venom in her mother's voice.

She sucked in a breath. "I thought it best to wait to introduce you."

"When are you bringing him over?"

"We could come by tomorrow." Addison glanced up at her sister's back. Savannah was stiff as a board, hands in soapy water at the sink.

"What is he going to do here?"

"We'll be going to school—"

"Humph." Tandy took a sip of coffee and grimaced.

"What is he studying?" Savannah asked.

"He'll be finishing his doctorate."

"He's going to be a doctor?" Tandy's brow arched.

"No," Savannah and Addison said in unison.

Tandy glowered at her.

"He'll be getting a PhD in mechanical and electrical engineering."

Tandy's tone changed. "So, he'll be a grease monkey like your father, but with a fancy degree."

Addison tensed. "No. More like a scientist."

"Doesn't he need a master's first?" Savannah asked.

Beth and Raleigh were digging into their lunch, attention on their plates. They hadn't spoken a word since Tandy had come out of her room.

"He received his master's while I was in Russia."

Savannah nodded while Tandy continued to glower at her.

"What's he going to do after you graduate?"

"We're getting married."

All eyes turned to her. Even Beth and Raleigh stopped eating and stared at her.

"You're getting married, sissy?" Beth asked.

"I am, but not until next summer."

The girls, accepting this information, returned to their plates.

"Where are you going to live?" Tandy's penetrating gaze made her squirm in her seat.

"Sergei is looking for an apartment near the school today," came the evasive reply.

"And are you going to live with him?"

"Yes."

"Humph."

Beth and Raleigh finished their lunch. Savannah washed the dishes and put them in the drying rack on the counter to drip dry.

Addison stood and leaned in to kiss her mother's cheek. "I'm heading out. I'll stop by on Friday." Her mother nodded. Savannah gave her a weak smile.

"Where are you staying?" Tandy asked.

"At Dad's."

"With your boyfriend."

"Yes."

"And your father's okay with that?"

"Of course."

"Humph. I bet she must love that." Tandy's eyes narrowed.

Addison bit her tongue. Walking around the table, she stood between the girls. She kissed the tops of their heads and then hurried toward the door. Addison was just too tired to fight, so she let her mother have the last word.

SERGEI'S ATTENTION WAS FOCUSED ON THE LAPTOP screen on the counter when Addison returned. There was a steaming cup of coffee was by his hand, the aroma of the Hawaiian blend Cassie favored filling the air. *Amazing the amount of coffee, he imbibes daily.*

"How did the visit go?" Sergei asked, rotating in his chair to face her.

"Fine." Addison's shoulders drooped.

Sergei's brow arched, and his eyes narrowed. He extended his hand to her.

Addison took his hand and let him pull her to him. "I hate seeing my sisters hurting," she said.

"Do they know what happened? Why he left?" he asked.

"Not that anyone is saying."

He separated his legs, bringing her in closer to him. "I'm sorry," he whispered into her ear as he wrapped her in his arms.

Her head resting on his chest, thoughts of her mother and the drama surrounding her disappeared. She hated being weak. It frustrated her to be unable to help her sisters.

Cassie walked in as Sergei kissed the top of her head.

"Things that bad at your mom's?" she asked.

"Not really. It's just hard watching Beth and Raleigh struggle. Beth asked me if she would still see her dad now that he's moved out."

Cassie pinched the bridge of her nose as her eye twitched. A tight smile in Addison's direction said what words couldn't.

"What did you say?" Sergei asked.

"Of course. But then she reminded me of how Savi and Quinby hadn't seen their father since he'd left. That Raleigh rarely saw Rafe since the divorce."

"Ouch." Cassie shook her head. "That's got to bother them."

"Oh, they resent me. I have no doubt. I feel it sometimes sneaking through, though they've never said as much to me. Not that I blame them, either."

Sergei gave her a quizzical glance. She sighed. It was impossible for him to relate, considering his close-knit family. He could never imagine the level of dysfunction that reigned in her family.

"I was thinking kabobs for dinner." Cassie suggested.

"Perfect. Need help?" Addison asked.

"Sure."

The three of them set up areas to work and began cutting up the steak. She put the cubes of meat in the pan of a marinade and then slid it into the oven on low.

At Sergei's confused look, Cassie laughed. "It will grill faster, without over-cooking the vegetables and shrimp."

"What a great idea."

"She's full of little tricks like that." Addison scrubbed her hands in the sink.

Cassie grinned as she came up beside her and dipped her hands under the running water. Sergei moved into her space at the sink and, with a few splashes, had Cassie laughing at his antics. He was completely at ease with her stepmother.

This warmed Addison's heart. She said a silent prayer her mother would come around, eventually.

Eli came in and kissed Cassie before turning to the refrigerator to pull out a beer. "Sergei, would you like one?"

"Sure."

Eli pulled a second beer out and popped the tops before handing one over. "I'll go start the grill." He headed to the French doors and stepped outside. Sergei followed him as Cassie pulled the meat out of the oven to cool.

Addison peeked out the kitchen window to see the men chatting outside.

Cassie put a hand on her shoulder. "They look relaxed."

"They do. I'm glad. I've been so worried. Mama hasn't made it any easier."

"I'm sorry, Addy. I hope she comes around."

Addison stared at the men. Sergei had left his life behind to be here with her, and the least her mother could do was act like he was a person and not a cockroach under her shoe. She hadn't even met him, but she'd made her opinions of him clear each time his name was mentioned.

"Come, let's get these veggies diced up, and the kabobs assembled."

Addison nodded and turned away from the window.

They worked in tandem, sliding shrimp or meat and a variety of vegetables on each stick before setting it aside. They had just finished the last one when Eli came in. He grabbed a couple more beers from the refrigerator before taking the tray of kabobs back outside with him.

DINNER HAD BEEN PLEASANT. HER FATHER AND CASSIE had turned in early to get enough rest for work the next day. After a movie, Sergei had suggested they do the same. They'd climbed the stairs together before he kissed her goodnight and headed to his room. She slipped under the covers with a new paperback. Twenty minutes later, frustrated that the book hadn't distracted her from Tandy, she set it aside and shut the lamp off. Moonlight crept in through the shutters, bathing the room in an eerie glow.

She plumped up the pillow and closed her eyes.

CHAPTER 32

Facing Her Demons

Addison

Addison threw the covers back and stretched. There was no point remaining in bed. Sleep eluded her. After lying in the dark most of the night, tossing and turning, she stood and slipped on a heavy fleece robe. Her bare feet padded on the cool hardwood floor as she made her way downstairs.

She made a cup of tea and settled down on the couch with her notebook. Her thoughts returned to her mother. Not that her mother's behavior was unusual, it wasn't. It wasn't that Addison was unfamiliar with it, as it had been directed at her, her father, and her stepmother.

For some strange reason, she thought if she approached it differently, she could change her mother's opinion of Sergei. If she did that, things might be more comfortable for everyone. She hadn't expected to fall in love with him. And even when she realized she had, she spent months preparing to say goodbye to him when she left Russia. Now he was here, and she owed it to him to do everything in her power to make things with her mother go smoothly.

She set her tea on the table beside her and lay the notebook on her lap. Flipping it open to the middle, a blank page stared up at her. Drawing a line down the middle, she scrawled Pros and Cons across the top of the page. She tapped the pen against her bottom lip, pondering her relationship from an outside perspective.

Pros:

- Incredibly sexy
- A great kisser
- Great sense of humor
- Dependable
- Willing to participate in my interests
- Came to America to be with me

Cons:

- He may want to go back to Russia
- Russian Orthodox

- Cultural differences

She crossed out the top two pros on the list with a giggle. Though they mattered to her, they wouldn't endear Sergei to her mother.

"Why are you up so early?"

Addison jumped, causing her pen to slide to the floor. It rolled to a stop by her foot.

"Are you okay?" Sergei bent over and picked up her pen. He set it down on her notebook before he dropped onto the couch beside her. She clipped the pen to the notebook.

"What are you working on in the middle of the night?" he asked.

"The sun should be coming up in less than an hour."

The wrinkles on Sergei's forehead deepened as he pursed his lips.

"What?" Addison tilted her head and gave him a sidelong glance.

"You are evasive. That is not like you."

"Sorry. I was putting my thoughts together."

"Can I see?"

Addison chewed on her bottom lip as she handed over the notebook. The page she'd been scribbling notes on was on top.

"Hmm. It is good to see there are more pros than cons."

"I didn't work on it for long."

Sergei cocked his brow at her. She smiled. "I didn't mean it like that. I'd just started it when you came down."

Sergei nodded. His eyes were glued to the list in his hands. Taking the pen, he began adding his own notes to the bottom of the list.

A glance down at her empty cup, she patted his hand and lifted from the couch. "Would you like some tea?"

Sergei nodded, his attention still on the notebook.

Grabbing her cup, she went into the kitchen to make more tea. A few minutes later, she returned with two steaming mugs and handed one to him. After taking her place beside him, he slid the notebook back onto her lap.

Looking down, she laughed.

"Ouch." The tea sloshed onto her thumb, marking the skin a bright pink where it burned. He took her hand in his and brought the burnt digit to his lips, where he pressed a soft kiss to the area.

Sergei had made his additions to the list. His point of view made her heart swell. She sipped her tea, inhaling the scent of the refreshing mint blend deep into her lungs.

Pros:

- Incredibly sexy (***Good to know***)
- A great kisser (***This too***)
- Great sense of humor
- Dependable
- Willing to take part in my interests
- Came to America to be together (***Yes***)
- **Adores her**
- **A romantic**
- **Extremely intelligent**
- **Comes from a close-knit family**
- **Dependable**
- **Patient**
- **A great older brother**

Cons:

- He may want to go back to Russia (***We can visit my family and they can visit America***)
- Russian Orthodox (***Children can be your religion***)
- Cultural differences

"So why did you cross off 'great kisser'? Do I need more practice?" Sergei winked at her.

Addison swatted his arm playfully. "Not at all, silly. I was trying to think of things that would matter to Mama. Though I adore you, and yes, you are a fantastic kisser, Mama's expectations of you will be quite different."

Sergei nodded, his grin still wide as ever. "I am glad to see it at the top of the list, nonetheless."

Addison laughed. "You're incorrigible."

Sergei leaned over and kissed her cheek. "I work hard at it. Just so you know."

"I believe it."

"*Dorogaya*, you worry too much. Things with your mother will be fine."

"Did you mean it about not going back to Russia?" Addison struggled to be honest, even with herself, about her fears that he wouldn't stay. She hadn't been willing to stay in Russia even though she loved him, and it would only be fair if he felt the same way about America.

"You are my world. If I need to, I will remind you of that every day for the rest of your life." Sergei kissed the tips of her fingers.

"You may have to." Addison shook her head.

"I had a feeling you would turn my world on its ear the moment I first saw you."

"Did you know I would complicate it as well?"

"You have not complicated my life. You have enriched it beyond measure. You have brightened my days and filled my heart with joy." Sergei turned her hand over in his and kissed her palm.

"You make me a better person." Addison caressed his cheek.

Sergei scooted over and wrapped his arm around her shoulder, bringing her closer to him. She lay her head back against his arm, enjoying the warmth that seeped into her. His support and quiet strength reminded her of her father. No matter the storms that raged from her mother, her father had always been a beacon of light for her. Addison would need to draw on that strength when she faced her mother.

Lost in their quiet thoughts, enjoying the nearness of each other, they hadn't heard her father come downstairs.

"What has the two of you out of bed so early? Is everything all right?"

"Yes, just thinking of how to approach Mama so that she'll accept Sergei and be happy for us."

Eli chuckled. "Good luck with that."

"Seriously. Do you have any suggestions?"

"Hmm. I'm afraid the person to ask about gaining your mother's acceptance would be Cassie."

Addison stared back at him. The blank expression on his face gave her no clue what he was thinking.

"Ask me what?" Cassie walked into the kitchen. Addison smiled as she watched her begin the morning routine of grinding the coffee beans and preparing the coffee pot. The sun had made an appearance through the shades, its light dancing against the windows and reflecting through the room.

"Dad suggested asking you how to make my mother like Sergei."

"Hmm. Maybe stab him in the eye?"

Sergei looked at her, aghast. His hand flew up to cover his eyes.

"She's joking. I think." Eli chuckled.

Cassie's face was set in stone. The expression on Sergei's face made it clear he wasn't convinced.

Eli was laughing again. The gurgling sounds coming from the coffee pot broke the tension, hints of roasted nuts and vanilla tingling her senses awake.

"Sweetheart, I've been married to your father for well over fifteen years. Your mother still loathes me with a passion that is unmatched. So, humor is your only option."

Sergei's eyes grew wide.

"That's true. So, basically, you're saying I'm doomed," Addison said.

"I'm saying that you need to do as your father, and I have done. Separate church and state."

Sergei leaned into her and whispered into her ear, "church and state?"

"I kept my relationships and life here at my father's separate from that of my mother's. My friends didn't overlap, my hobbies—it was like living in a bubble."

"That sounds horrible."

"But necessary. It helped to contain the drama from

spilling over here. This was my sanctuary. I had a life at my mother's to deal with when I was there, and when I came here, I checked it at the door as much as possible."

"So, how do we separate church and state?" Sergei asked.

Addison took his empty tea mug from him and set it on the side table next to hers.

Cassie carried over two cups of the freshly brewed coffee and handed one to Eli seated at the table, then over to the couch to Sergei.

"I suggest you live your life focused on your own happiness. When you have to deal with Tandy, do so with respect, then back away and shut the door behind you."

She turned back to the kitchen and returned a moment later with two more steaming mugs. After handing one to Addison, she stood next to Eli and leaned into the arm of the couch he was sitting on.

"You can't change your mother, honey. To maintain a relationship with her, accept that and focus your efforts in and around it," Eli suggested.

"Great, I'm taking Sergei over there today to meet her. I'm not feeling all that secure in that."

"You'll be fine. Introduce him as your fiancé, making it clear your decision is made. Don't give her an inch," Eli offered.

Cassie rested her hand on the back of Eli's neck as they sipped their coffee in silence.

Addison pondered this new insight, putting her feelings firmly in check.

Twisting to face her in the passenger seat, Sergei asked, "Are you ready for this?"

"The question is, are you ready for this?"

"Of course. No worries."

Addison stared at him. Words failed her. *How the hell is he so calm?*

"Addison, it will be fine."

Wiping her clammy hands on her jeans, she closed her eyes and took a deep breath. Less manic, she leaned in and kissed his cheek. "Okay then, let's get this over with."

She flung the door open and stepped out. When Sergei walked around the car, he took her hand, and they crossed the street to her mother's house.

She rapped on the door twice before twisting the knob and pushing it open.

The television blared from the family room, assaulting her ears even from the entryway. Holding Sergei's hand, she led him further into the house. She took in the mood; her mother sat in the oversized recliner draped in a heavy quilt, while Savannah and Quinby huddled together under a blanket on the dusty old couch across the room. Her youngest sisters sat on the floor, close to a small space heater that pushed out the only warmth in the room. All attention was directed at the television. Gripping Sergei's hand tighter, she took a step forward. Beth and

Raleigh turned their heads and squealed when they caught sight of her.

"Sissy!" Beth reached her first, and she threw her arms around Addison's waist.

Raleigh came at her in a rush. Standing at Addison's side, she put her arms around Beth's back and her hip.

Grateful for the welcome from her youngest sisters, she hugged the girls tighter to her.

"Bethany, Raleigh, I want you to meet my fiancé, Sergei."

"What's a fiancé?"

Sergei chuckled. Kneeling, he took one of Raleigh's hands and said, "It means that I am going to marry your sister."

"You'll be our brother?" Raleigh asked.

"Would you like that?" Addison asked.

"Are you going to stand in the hall the whole time? Come in here," Tandy demanded.

Addison flinched. Sergei's eyes widened as Raleigh tugged at his hand to lift him up. This brought a smile to Addison's face. Her sisters accepted Sergei in an instant. Steeling her shoulders, she reached for Sergei's hand while Raleigh held his other. Beth, still attached to her side, released her waist and took her empty hand. What a sight they made, the four of them linked together, and what a wide entourage. Sergei pressed up against her as he tried to give the girl's space from the wall.

They ambled into the family room as a unit. And the moment her mother's eyes met hers, her lip curled.

"Mama, this is Sergei. My fiancé."

"Ma'am, I am happy to meet you," Sergei said.

The look Tandy gave them could have frozen time. It certainly dropped the temperature in the room. A shiver tore through Addison, more from her mother's expression than the frigid temperature in the house.

Tandy stood. "Lunch is ready."

Addison released Sergei's hand as Raleigh pulled him toward the kitchen. She patted Beth and nudged her to follow Sergei and Raleigh.

Savannah and Quinby waited until the little ones were out of earshot before they came and hugged Addison.

"She's in a mood today," Quinby whispered.

"What's new?" Addison rolled her eyes.

"Knock it off, you two. Mama's going through a rough time, and the girls don't need you to add to the tension." Savannah's tone was terse.

Addison rolled her eyes. Quinby giggled. Savannah scowled at them both.

"Are you planning on eating with your family?" Tandy called from the kitchen.

"What's for lunch?" Addison asked.

"Hamburger Helper. She found a box in the back

of the cupboard, and we had hamburger in the freezer."

She couldn't stop the groan from escaping. Less about the food choice, and more because she knew it was an unavoidable ripple of Eric's leaving. Reaching into her purse, she pulled all the cash from her wallet and pushed it into Savannah's hand. It wasn't much, but it would have to do. It was all she had.

"Tell her you found it in the laundry. You know the drill." Addison pursed her lips as Savannah nodded and slid the wad of cash into her back pocket.

"What drill?" Quinby asked.

Addison shook her head and headed for the kitchen without answering. Savannah whispered, "I'll tell you later," as they followed behind her.

In the kitchen, Tandy was scooping the pasta from the pan onto the paper plates the girls held up, showing Sergei how it was done.

He stood behind them, a paper plate in his hand.

"Sorry for the paper, our dishwasher broke," Tandy said.

"I understand. My mother has young children at home, too. It is hard to keep up with their messes, no?"

Addison could have hugged him. Tandy gave him a slight nod.

After the girls and Sergei were served, Tandy made a plate and sat at the table. Addison fixed a plate and nudged Quinby to take the seat closest to their mother, while she handed another to Savannah. Taking the footstool, she set it between her sisters and sat down.

The tension was thick, but her sisters kept up a litany of questions for Sergei to help ease some of it.

Her mother remained quiet for most of the meal, the bags under her eyes hinting at her stress.

Sergei ate without complaint, answering all the questions the girls threw at him.

"Are you going to take Addison back to Russia with you?" Raleigh asked.

Beth's lip trembled.

"No, I will stay here, in America."

Tandy's eyes narrowed.

"You don't plan to go home?" Savannah asked.

"Sure. To visit. Often, I hope. I have family there. And little ones like you," Sergei said, looking at the girls.

Tandy glared at Addison. "You have children?" The question was meant for Sergei.

"No. No. My siblings are young. Like Beth," he said.

Savannah's shoulders relaxed. She had also clearly misunderstood him at first.

"How will you afford that?" Tandy asked.

Addison froze, her fork dangling in mid-air. *Shit.* Conversations about affording a luxury such as travel never went well.

"I can only hope to afford it someday," Sergei said without missing a beat.

Quinby bit her lip and elbowed Addison. Glancing at the fork in the air, Addison quickly set it back on her plate.

Tandy wasn't appeased. "And what of work? Do you think you will find work easily here?"

"My education is almost complete. I hope to work at the university while I finish. After that, we will see."

"Fancy degrees aren't everything," Tandy said.

"I agree. I may be able to teach here. If not, I can work with Addison's father."

Crap. He just stepped into a pile of it, mentioning her father. She bit her tongue.

"Hopefully, you'll do a better job supporting Addison than he did," Tandy replied.

Addison swallowed the blood in her mouth. Her tongue ached from the bite.

Sergei nodded. "That is my plan."

Beth and Raleigh, oblivious to the undertones of the conversation, continued asking the questions they felt important.

"Will you make babies with my sister?" Beth asked.

"Someday—"

"I have to finish school first, Beth," Addison cut in.

Savannah choked on a mouthful of pasta. Addison pounded her on the back. "Ugh. Thanks."

"But you said you already finished school," Raleigh said.

"I want to study more."

"Yuck, I hate school," Beth said.

Everyone at the table laughed. Addison looked down at the half-full plate; her appetite was long gone. She hated to waste food, but there was no way she could finish it.

Quinby came to her rescue. "You going to eat that?" she asked and speared a piece of the hamburger from her plate.

Addison slid the plate in front of her sister. "All yours."

Quinby dug in like a starving waif, her ability to eat through anything apparent.

Her sisters kept the questions coming while Addison began clearing off the table. Taking the empty plates from Quinby, then walking around the table letting everyone stack theirs on top of her pile, she dumped it all in the garbage bin. Emptying the remaining food into a container, she then slid the frying pan into the sink filled with hot, soapy water. While it soaked, she scrubbed the counter and stove. Savannah took the towel and wiped the table.

"Thank you for lunch, Mama. We should be going."

"Fine," Tandy said.

"It was a pleasure to meet all of you." Sergei stood from the table and pushed the chair back in.

Beth jumped up and hugged him. "I like you."

"Please come back soon," Raleigh said.

Quinby and Savannah shook his hand before Beth walked him out of the kitchen. Tandy remained seated and didn't say goodbye. Addison leaned in and kissed her mother's cheek before following her sisters to the door.

Things would only get worse for them all, with Eric gone.

Sergei held her hand as she drove them back to her father's. She remained stiff and quiet from the moment they arrived at her mother's. The anxiety rolled off her in waves, yet he was helpless to change it.

"I liked your sisters." He hoped to reach her past the wall he sensed between them. "I hope I did not embarrass you."

"Oh, Sergei," Addison cried. "Of course, you didn't embarrass me. I couldn't be prouder of you. I'm sorry my mother was so nasty."

"She is unhappy. Her husband has left her, and she is worried for her children," he said.

Addison did not reply, though he could feel her tense up. She slid her hand into his and kept her gaze on the road as she drove.

Sergei let her be. Her shoulders were not as stiff

as before, and her hand was soft in his. She was relaxing from her visit, and that was all he could ask.

As soon as they returned to her father's home, she relaxed further.

Addison set her purse down on the counter. "I'm going to take a nap. I'll see you later?" she said.

Sergei nodded and walked to the stove. He could use a vodka, but out of respect for her family, he would drink tea. The faucet protruding from the wall, dumping boiling water into his cup, was like a miracle spout.

Alone in the kitchen, he sipped his tea. Lunch with her mother was not the disaster he had expected. Not that he would ever admit his concerns to Addison. Her mother was rough around the edges, but not impossible to navigate. He made a few missteps during the meal. He sensed it instantly, from the tension in the room to the shared glances between Addison and her sisters, or the way her mother's lips tightened ever so slightly.

"Penny for your thoughts," Eli said. Cassie came in behind him, carrying more shopping bags.

"Here, let me help." Sergei slid off his stool and took the bags from Cassie. "Addison is napping."

"Rough lunch?" Cassie asked as she began pulling food from the bags and putting it in the refrigerator.

"It was okay," Sergei said.

Eli placed the bags on the table and peeked into Addison's purse.

Before Sergei could question this blatant invasion of privacy, Eli looked him in the eye. "She did it again," he said. He pulled his wallet out and handed Cassie a one-hundred-dollar bill folded in half. Cassie kissed him and folded the money in half again, and slipped it into Addison's wallet and zipped it closed.

"What is that?" Sergei asked.

"You should explain," Eli said. "She doesn't even know I know."

"Don't you think it's time she did?" Cassie asked.

Sergei's eyes followed the exchange, still unclear what he'd missed.

"It's always been a thing between you," Eli responded. "Like a bond."

"Honey, she was seven."

"Okay," Eli said. "I still want to leave this to you. But if Sergei is going to become her husband, he deserves to understand."

Sergei bobbed his head. He didn't understand any of what transpired with the hundred-dollar bill.

Without another word, Eli went and grabbed a bottle of vodka from the cabinet and brought it to the kitchen table and set it down. Cassie handed him the jug of cranberry juice from the open icebox door, and he set it on the table. He put three tall tumblers full of ice next to the juice and began pouring vodka into the glasses.

"Do you like cranberry juice?" he asked.

"I do not know," Sergei responded.

"Well, give this a try, and if not, you can drink it straight," Eli said.

Sergei shrugged. This was an interesting exchange.

Eli and Cassie sat down across from him, and each held up their drinks. "To understanding this family!" Eli said.

"So, when Addison was really little—after Rafe left—we learned that he'd taken all the money out of their account. Tandy immediately filed for more child support from us."

"Why you and not Rafe?"

"I was Tandy's first target always. It never mattered why."

Perplexed, Sergei only nodded.

"She dropped it shortly after, but when the phone was disconnected, we knew she was broke."

"I caught Addison going through my purse a couple of weeks later. Money had disappeared before, but I couldn't prove it was her, so I left it alone," Cassie said.

Sergei took a huge gulp from his glass. *Not bad.*

"I walked into the room, and she was forced to face me. I asked her why she was stealing from me, and she cried." Cassie took a sip of her drink. "I asked her what she could want, that she felt she couldn't ask us for it. Didn't we buy her everything she needed?"

"She admitted the money was for her sisters." Eli was watching him as he stared at Cassie, and back to Eli.

"Once she explained about the food, we made an agreement that she would ask in the future and never steal from us again."

"Do you believe her?" Sergei asked.

"I do. I talked it over with Eli, and we agreed to limit the amount of cash in our wallets, just in case."

"So, you did not trust her?" Sergei asked. He took a smaller drink this time.

"We wanted to test her first. Cassie made a point of giving her twenty dollars every time she visited us for the weekend. It wasn't much, but it would be enough to start."

"A few weeks later, she admitted she hadn't told her mother the money came from us," Cassie said.

"How did she explain it to her mother?"

"Apparently, she confessed to Savannah, who told her to stop stealing. Her sister told her that if she stole from us, she might lose us, and Savannah didn't want her to lose a father, too."

"I like Savannah," Sergei said.

"I love Savannah, as I do Addison. After that, we gave her more, with the understanding she was hiding it for her mother to find."

"Why not give it directly to Tandy?"

"Pride," Cassie and Eli replied in unison.

"Tandy wouldn't have taken the money as a hand-out. If she felt she was pulling a fast one on me, sure, but never if it made me the good guy."

"Her children needed food. Pride should not matter."

"Tandy doesn't work that way."

"So, we made a point to give Addison about a hundred bucks a month for a few months, until Tandy started getting food stamps," Eli said.

"But she doesn't know you know she's giving your money to her mother?"

"No. I wanted it to be her shared secret with Cassie."

"When she reached high school, it started up again," Cassie said.

"And her own money by then," Eli said.

"Her own money?"

"Babysitting money, or cash she got as gifts."

The shadows falling on the counter as the sunset caught Sergei's eye. He glanced out the kitchen window to see the gray sky darken further.

"I'd better get dinner started." Cassie left the table and began moving about the kitchen.

"Anyway, whenever there's a financial hardship, Savannah and Addison have worked together to ease some of the burden."

"How do you know she did it today?"

"I gave her forty dollars last night, and it wasn't there today," Eli said.

"Why did you give her cash?"

"She mentioned she needed to go to the bank yesterday, and I knew she would forget once she told me she was taking you to meet her mother. So, I handed her the cash and told her to pay me back later."

"We try to make sure all of us have a little cash at all times, in case of emergencies," Cassie called from across the room.

Sergei nodded.

Sounds of footsteps on the stairs echoed through the kitchen.

Eli looked at Sergei and shook his head. The conversation was over.

"Hey, what's for dinner?" Addison asked. She leaned against her father, kissing his cheek as he wrapped an arm around her.

Cassie stood in front of the open ice box. "What did you have for lunch?"

"Hamburger Helper."

"Gross," Eli said.

Sergei laughed. "Is that what that was? I have never had that before."

"Hmm. Really, what kind?" Cassie asked.

"I think it was the pizza kind." Addison grinned.

"Okay, so no pasta."

Cassie continued to rummage through the

groceries, deciding on dinner while Addison joined them at the table. She took a sip of Sergei's drink.

"Really, Dad?"

"Hey, it was a compromise. I can't drink that stuff straight up."

"Note to self, Eli does not drink plain vodka," Sergei said.

Addison grinned. "It grows on you."

"How about sushi?" Cassie asked.

Addison jumped from her chair. "Yes! I'll go get my shoes on."

Eli chuckled. "Sergei, do you like sushi?"

"Of course."

"Good. Just so you know, sushi gets very expensive when you take Addison."

"Come on, let's go." Addison pulled Sergei from the table and led the way to the garage.

CHAPTER 33

New Digs

Addison

Addison was excited. They were moving into their apartment in the morning. A friend of her father's had a vacancy in the duplex he owned. The past three weeks had been filled with mad shopping sprees to find the basics to fill their new home. They'd hit the discount stores, and the thrift stores, eventually ending up at the local consignment shops for the essential furniture like a couch and kitchen table. Sergei wouldn't compromise on a bed, saying that a good night's sleep was vital to his well-being, so that had been their one splurge.

They could always look into better quality items later. Her mother wasn't thrilled with any of their plans. Not living together, or even the fact that she was back in North Carolina. During her last visit, her mother told her that she should focus on school, and not on playing house. And certainly not rushing down the aisle.

Sergei was settling into America faster than she had his homeland the year before. Then again, he had lived on foreign soil as a child, so he was accustomed to the change. She might have traveled with her father and Cassie growing up, but that wasn't the same as immersing yourself into a new culture for years at a time.

Armed with boxes, they walked into the apartment to wait for the furniture to be delivered and the cable and Internet to be installed.

Addison hung their clothes in the closet, set up the bathroom, and put her feminine touch on the little things while decorating. There was only one week left before the Spring semester started, so this would be the last chance for them to relax before studying.

Once the couch was delivered and the TV set up, she plopped down on the soft leather with a loud sigh. Sergei came over with two bottles of beer and sat beside her. After handing her one, he pulled the cheap wooden coffee table closer and lifted his feet to it. Leaning back, he laid his free arm over Addison's shoulders, pulling her to him.

"What do you think about ordering a pizza and making it an early night?"

"I like it." Sergei pulled her closer and kissed her brow.

Addison leaned into his embrace and kissed his lips. When Sergei deepened the kiss, all thoughts of food were momentarily forgotten. He was here, in North Carolina, with her. The unlikeliness of it still amazed her. She'd said goodbye to him in Saint Petersburg. She had accepted that their time had passed and that their short romance belonged in the past. She never doubted he belonged in Russia. Not after seeing how wonderful his family was, and how close he was to them. Never in a million years had she suspected Sophie would collude with Sergei and surprise her in France. Or that she would be getting married in autumn.

She pulled away first and picked up her mobile phone from the coffee table. She hit the speed dial for the local pizzeria and waited for them to answer. After placing the order, she snuggled back into his arms and waited for dinner to come to them.

CHAPTER 34

The Day Time Stood Still

Sergei

S ergei sat on the couch with Zara at his side, and Alexi on the floor at his feet. Having his family here to spend quality time with him before the wedding was the greatest gift they could have given him. When they arrived on Saturday, they had met Addison's mother and sisters for dinner that evening. Though a memorable experience in all the wrong ways, his family had taken it all in stride and made him proud. After breakfast, Eli went to his repair shop, taking his father and Viktor with him. Mikhail had taken the dogs out for a walk. American cartoons were on the television, and the kids' giggles competed with the laughter coming from the kitchen. Glancing over his shoulder, he could see Addison sitting on the island, talking to Cassie and his mother.

He couldn't hear their conversation, only the occasional bouts of laughter from the women.

Cassie had taken his parents and siblings under her wing and made everyone feel at home and welcome, just as she had with him all those months ago. The warm reception his family received from Eli and Cassie was marked by the opposite of Addison's mother. Dinner with her over the weekend had been tense and uncomfortable. Why they had expected her to treat his family with any more respect or warmth when she barely managed civility towards him, he would never know.

Their wedding was in five days. Nerves were frayed, with everyone uptight and short-tempered.

He was enjoying this quiet time with the twins, keeping out of the way until they went to lunch and finished running errands for the final wedding preparations. Sergei sat on the couch in his future in-laws' home, letting the women bond in the other room. He soaked up the time he had with the little ones. It was an ideal way to spend the morning.

"Addy, come quick!" Alexi hollered. This shout pulled Sergei from his musing as the women hurried into the room.

The cartoons were no longer on the screen. Instead, an image of a tall building replaced it, a mass of dark-gray smoke streaming out of its side.

"What happened to the cartoons?" Sergei looked at his brother in confusion.

"What's up, Alexi?" Addison asked.

He hadn't heard his fiancée approach, so when her voice came from directly behind him, he jumped.

"Addy, where is that building?" Alexi asked, his small hand pointing at the image on the television.

Addison stood behind the couch while Cassie and his mother flanked her sides.

"Manhattan." Cassie's voice was low, barely audible.

"Where is that?" Alexi pressed.

"It's in New York City," Addison said.

"What happened?" Lena looked from the television to Alexi.

"A plane crashed into the building," Alexi said.

From his peripheral vision, Sergei watched, concerned, as the color drained from first Cassie's face, then Addison's.

"Oh, God. Tamsen," the women said simultaneously.

"Excuse me," Cassie said. She patted Addison's arm before turning to backtrack to the kitchen, and moments later, she was dialing the phone. The telltale beeps echoed in the silent room.

"What is Tamsen?" Sergei asked Addison.

"She's Cassie's best friend. They work together. Tamsen's office is in that building."

"How can you tell?" Alexi asked. He looked up at them, his eyes wide.

"The World Trade Center buildings are square

and distinctive. And they're some of the tallest in the country."

His mother leaned against the back of the couch beside her and ruffled Zara's hair. Addison lay her hand on his shoulder. It had a slight shudder as it rested against his neck. His breath caught in his chest.

Taking the remote from the arm of the couch, he turned up the volume.

"...*It appears a plane has hit the World Trade Center Tower...*" the television blared. The sudden outburst of noise made him flinch.

"Sorry," he said. He pressed the volume down, not meaning for it to be so loud.

Addison stood behind him, solid other than the slight tremble that came from her hand.

"Is that going to happen here?" Alexi said from the floor. His voice had a slight hitch.

"No, that's far away," Addison said.

Sergei caught the hesitation as she spoke. He turned to catch her eye. "Are you okay?"

"Hmm? Yes. I'm just trying to wrap my head around a plane in a building, and I'm worried about Tamsen. She's family."

Sergei laced his fingers through hers and held her hand on his shoulder.

"Do they know why the plane hit the building?" Addison asked.

"Which one?" Alexi asked.

Another image filled the screen, showing more

smoke pouring from the side of the building. The image shifted from the top of the building to the street level, where dozens of people stood staring up at the fire. Panning back up to the top of the building, the camera zoomed in. At first, the angle of the image made no sense. The fires were much higher than before. Clearly, the fire couldn't have spread up so many floors so quickly.

"Which one? You? You mean which building?"

"*...A second 737 has crashed into the side of the World Trade Center...*"

"Two?" Addison squeaked.

Sergei could feel her weight as she leaned heavily against the back of the couch. He gave her hand a gentle squeeze.

"*...There's a gaping hole in the side and smoke coming out of the building. Emergency vehicles are racing to the scene...*"

Cassie returned a few moments later. The cordless house phone clutched in one hand, her mobile phone in her other. Standing next to Addison, her face was an ashen color. "I can't get through. I tried her desk, her cell phone, and the house. I even tried Drew's numbers." Her voice cracked.

"*In a few moments, the president is going to speak from the school in Florida where he had been scheduled to read to children.*"

Addison wrapped her arm around Cassie's waist. "Call Dad and have him come home. I'll call the shops and cancel our appointments for today," she said.

A stone-faced Cassie wordlessly dialed on the cordless.

"Addison, what do you need me to do?" Lena asked.

"We have missing family in New York, and until we know they're safe, we wouldn't feel comfortable spending the day shopping."

"That can wait. We just finished preparing the lasagna for dinner, and it is resting in the refrigerator. What else can I do?"

"We're looking at an unprecedented death toll, as more than fifty thousand people work in those two buildings."

Tears trickled down Addison's face as she shook her head. "I just don't know. We—We shouldn't scare the kids."

His mother nodded and patted Zara's head. "Doch, let me make those calls. Zara, come. Help me bake cookies."

Zara scrambled up, and his mother picked her up and over the back of the couch, and off they went into the kitchen.

Addison moved around the couch and sat down beside him, leaning into his side.

"Alexi, could you go help *Mamochka*?"

"But—" Alexi cried.

"Please. I'll play with you later."

Alexi pulled himself off the floor, nodded, and shuffled out of the room.

They sat in silence and continued to watch the horrors on the television. The event was surreal.

Suddenly, music played on the television as it went blank, then the news station's logo appeared in the center, and a red banner crossed the screen with the words 'Breaking News' inside.

"*We are breaking into the special live coverage of what's happening at the World Trade Center in New York to tell you what's happening right now in Virginia.*"

Addison stood staring at the television, her breath caught in her throat.

"*Reports of an explosion… the Pentagon is being evacuated as we speak, and we are being told that the White House may be under an evacuation order as well. Whatever it was, near the heliport, there's billowing black smoke… Workers reported rumbles. We don't know the cause of the smoke at this time.*"

"Oh God," Addison said.

"*Reports now say that one of the two planes that crashed into the World Trade Center towers was hijacked shortly after takeoff from Boston. President Bush has called the World Trade Center an apparent terrorist attack.*"

"What's happening to us?" Addison covered her mouth with her hand.

Sergei pulled her closer and held her tight. He was unsure what else he could do to comfort her.

"*Witnesses are saying it was an aircraft that crashed into the west side of the Pentagon. That's what we're seeing in Arlington, Virginia."*

Images continued to rotate of the World Trade Center fires in a small square to the right-hand side, while a live view of the Pentagon was in a square to the upper left side of the screen.

"All airplane traffic has been shut down nationwide by the Federal Aviation Administration, in reaction to what appears to be a terrorist attack on the United States."

There was a commotion in the other room as Eli came in, followed by his father and brothers. From his seat, he saw Eli exchange looks with Cassie, who shook her head. She cried, heart-wrenching sobs wracking her body as Eli wrapped his arms around her. She still could not reach her friend.

Viktor convinced the twins to change into their swimsuits. Joined by Mikhail, they went outside to play in the pool. Once aware it wasn't an accident, but an active terrorist attack on the country, no one wanted the little ones to know anything more.

An aerial view of the area was muddled as gray filled the screen, billowing plumes of dark smoke. Buildings could barely be seen through the thick clouds.

"It is not officially confirmed, but rumors are that part of the tower has collapsed."

The images on the television changed back to the Pentagon scene.

"*We're in a lockdown at this time. All government build-ings have been evacuated. Mark, are you there?*"

"*Thanks, Karen, yes, I'm here. I think I can answer the question earlier about the second explosion. It wasn't an explo-sion that was heard, it was the sonic boom of jet fighters being launched out of Andrews Air Force Base. One, maybe two fighters—it's most likely only as a precautionary measure. They are patrolling the skies over Washington.*"

Another reporter's voice spoke through the images of an empty grassy area being displayed. "*All the monu-ments and museums have been shut down and evacuated at the National Mall. We're just keeping our eyes and ears open right now.*"

"*That was Kevin Stroberg, reporting from the National Mall.*"

"*Karen, we're told all communications are down, landlines are down, cell phones are down.*"

"*Thanks, Mark.*"

The screen returned to the newsroom, where a man and woman sat somberly.

"*What we're getting across the wire now is confirmation that one of the Trade Center buildings has collapsed.*" The woman on the screen addressed the camera.

Addison whimpered. Her hand still covered her mouth, and she leaned into him.

The news station showed replays of the twin towers being hit.

Sergei was sure the images of the airplane

entering the side of that tall building would haunt his dreams for a long time.

The tv screen was filled with a street view, where fire trucks, ambulances, and news vans were being maneuvered farther away from the building on fire.

The chaos was confusing. Sergei wasn't familiar with these locations, but he couldn't recall ever seeing so much destruction portrayed anywhere that wasn't an active war zone.

"*Earlier the president spoke, saying today is a national tragedy. The president will be returning to Washington shortly,*" the news anchor said in the studio.

The flashing from place-to-place confused Sergei even more. So many people talking over each other and around each other, and nothing was getting any clearer for him.

"*They believe these events are connected. FBI, at the scene at the Pentagon, is telling us that there's concern about a hijacked plane on its way to the Pentagon,*" the reporter named George said.

Back at the studio, the woman spoke again. "*We have confirmation that the second tower collapsed shortly after being struck by that airplane.*"

Even though the screen was full of smoke, it was clear that the two World Trade Center towers they had been showing all morning were gone.

An image of the Statue of Liberty looked so small compared to the heavy smoke billowing from the center of Manhattan. The aerial views they were showing were from a distance, as close as they could safely get because of the smoke.

As he held a rigid Addison in his arms, watching the television, Eli comforted a crying Cassie in the kitchen. He had never felt so helpless as he did this morning. Even when Addison had left him behind in Russia and returned to her home, there was a feeling of determination and purpose within him. Today, there were none of those feelings. The morning's events had jarred everyone's sense of peace.

The jangling of the phone pealed through the quiet house like a bullhorn. They turned to face the kitchen when the phone rang, watching Cassie as she answered.

"Hello?" Cassie's voice was scratchy from all the crying she'd done. She physically sagged into Eli as she held the phone to her ear.

"I'm so glad you're safe. I've been terrified…"

Addison let out the breath she'd been holding, her entire body relaxing into his arms.

"Drew? Dax?"

Sergei arched a brow at Addison, but she just smiled and kissed his hand.

"Good. Good."

Cassie listened again, wiping at the tears streaming down her face.

"No planes, I understand. Drive. Just come as soon as you can."

They watched in silence at the one-sided conversation, though the tension in the room had lessened dramatically since Cassie answered the phone.

"I love you. Drive safe." Cassie ended the call and set the phone down on the kitchen island. "She's safe. Drew had Dax with him and they're safe. Drew doesn't want to risk staying in New York. The three of them are going to drive down tonight while they can still get out."

Eli hugged her tight to his chest, while his father placed a hand on his mother's shoulders. Addison scrambled up from the couch to hug Cassie.

Sergei turned the television volume down as far as it would go and followed Addison into the kitchen.

Her family was safe. The world was falling apart around them, and he knew there would be much more sadness to follow, but for now, he wanted to join her in the happiness that her loved ones were okay.

CHAPTER 35

An Altered World

Addison

Addison sat beside Sergei at the kitchen table as the dawning morning filtered through the blinds, drinking their second pot of coffee. Her father and Cassie, as well as Sergei's parents, were at the table speaking in hushed voices about what to expect after the tragedies that had befallen the country.

The prior day had tested their faith in humanity, while at the same time renewing it. Stories continued throughout the day about the horrors inflicted upon them, mixed with those of the amazing first-responders and everyday citizens who stepped up with an untold bravery to assist their fellow men. Their hearts had been cracked, and their souls were battered, but by the end of the day, one thing had been made abundantly clear through the sorrow, and pain, and tears. The terrorists had failed in their mission.

Men and women had stood strong, had come together to help each other get out of the buildings safely. Strangers rushed to the scene to search through the rubble of the buildings for anyone they could find. The day started with heartbreak, and yet through it all, heroes continued to emerge.

The adults had trudged to bed late in the night, only to wake long before sunrise. Nerves were wound tight in between the periodic phone calls from Tamsen and Drew. They were on their way. Traffic was worse than they had expected, but they weren't concerned. With only four days left before the wedding, guilt had set in. It no longer felt appropriate to celebrate while so much of the country was in shock and mourning.

When the phone rang, they took turns racing toward it. It was a minor consolation to be in control of something.

"Hello?" Addison said. She was breathless from her sprint from the table to the counter where the phone had been placed last.

"Addison, darling, we've just crossed into North Carolina. We should be there by lunchtime," Tamsen said.

"Wonderful, drive safe. We'll see you soon. Love you," Addison said.

"Love you, too."

Addison disconnected the phone. It had become a necessity to say, "I love you" to each other as often as the opportunity presented itself.

"Tamsen will be here in a couple of hours," Addison said.

"We should get showered and dressed before the kids wake up. Then I'll make breakfast," Cassie said. She was addressing Eli, but it applied to them all.

"What should we do for breakfast?" Lena asked.

"Hmm. I hadn't given it much thought. Anything the twins might enjoy?" Cassie answered.

"How about a quiche? We could set that to bake while we are getting dressed," Lena suggested.

"Sergei and I will head over to the apartment to get cleaned up," Addison said.

"Hurry back," Nikolai said, as he headed up the stairs to shower.

"Be safe." Eli wrapped her in his firm embrace and kissed her forehead.

"We will. Love you," Addison called out.

Sergei held her hand tight as they left the house, and he helped her into the car.

THEY HAD DRIVEN BACK TO THEIR APARTMENT IN silence, even turning off the radio for a moment of peace from the constant barrage they had endured the day before.

Once inside their apartment, the blinking light on the answering machine caught her attention. There were five unanswered calls.

"Addison, have you been watching the news? Call me."

Addison deleted the first message from her mother.

"Addison, this is the second time I've called you. Answer the phone."

Just like the first message, the second one was deleted swiftly.

"Addison, I've been trying to reach you all day. Where are you?"

Addison shook her head. Her mother was persistent, if nothing else. If it had been important, her mother would have called her cell phone.

"Addison, I've been calling you all day. Call me back, damn it."

Addison glanced at Sergei, who rolled his eyes at her mother's terse message before she deleted it as well.

"Addison, I don't understand why you're ignoring me…"

This time Sergei walked over and deleted the message with a forceful push of the button.

"Talk to me, *lubov moya.* You've been pretty quiet since yesterday."

"I'm sorry. I'm just overwhelmed," Addison said.

"Why does she call so many times? Is she worried about family?"

Addison groaned. "No. My mother has no friends

or family in New York and we're far away from what happened."

"She seems determined to talk to you, so why did she not call your mobile?" Sergei asked.

"I think she wanted to make sure I was alone when she talked to me."

"What difference does that make?" Sergei's brow arched.

"My gut tells me she wants me to cancel the wedding." Addison slumped against him.

"Really?"

"It's just a feeling I have."

"Is that why you are avoiding her?"

"Not avoiding her, she never called my cell. I just have to call her back."

"Take a shower with me," Sergei said.

"I don't think now's the time for amorous intentions." Addison laughed.

"Come, let me hold you in my arms. You can call your mother after the shower. It will make you feel better. We can comfort each other."

Addison nodded.

Stripping off her clothes and leaving a pile on the floor, Addison joined Sergei in the steaming mist of the shower. He enveloped her body in his arms and held her tight against him while the water pounded off his shoulders.

They stood entwined together for a few long

moments while the steam swirled around them and licked their skin.

Sergei kissed the top of her head, and then turned her body, facing away from him before easing her back towards him. He lathered her hair with shampoo and rubbed her scalp with gentle fingers.

She leaned into him, absorbing his quiet strength and support. He hummed a melody she didn't recognize as his hands massaged her neck and shoulders, trailing the frothy shampoo with each touch. His gentle caresses unknotted her tense muscles as he went. In his typical thoughtful way, he knew what she needed before she did.

When he was done, keeping his arms around her, he stepped back, bringing her directly under the spray. The hot water washed the shampoo from her hair and body as Sergei continued to work magic with his fingers.

Once her skin squeaked, he propped her against the shower wall before he quickly washed his hair and soaped up his body.

The cold tile pulled her from the sleepy state that he had relaxed her into. She pulled her hair over her shoulder and twisted the excess water from it.

Sergei shut the water off and shook his hair like a dog, spraying her with droplets as they flew from his head. She laughed. He did that to her. It was his sense of humor and the ease with which he could lighten a dark mood that drew her to him the most.

He slid open the shower curtain, letting a rush of cold air in as he reached for a towel. She shivered as her skin pebbled in gooseflesh. After pulling the towel off the rack, he leaned in and wrapped her in it. The oversized Egyptian cotton bath sheets warmed her at once as he rubbed his hands over her covered body.

She stepped out of the shower and handed the second towel from the rack to Sergei. She took a smaller towel from the shelf and twisted her hair into it and then padded her way into their bedroom. Slipping on a pair of loose cargo pants and a light-knit sweater, she dumped her damp towels into the hamper before returning to the bathroom.

Addison leaned against the doorjamb as Sergei exited the shower with the towel in his hands. When they were alone, he often eschewed modesty. Taking in his naked body, her body grew warm. He had a magnificent body. His morning runs helped maintain his muscles.

Eyes twinkling, he winked at her as he came closer, leaving a chaste kiss on her cheek as he passed, causing her to smile. Unlike many twenty-something-year-old men, Sergei was always the perfect gentleman and never in a rush to jump her bones. Her heart swelled as she considered just how lucky she was that he was hers.

While he dressed in their bedroom, Addison combed the tangles from her hair and twisted it into a messy bun at the nape of her neck.

The phone rang, its shrill bells cutting through the peace.

"It's your mother," Sergei said.

"How could you know that?"

"Her calls have the most persistent rings I've ever heard."

Addison laughed. "The phone rings the same for everyone who calls."

Letting out a heavy sigh, she tossed the brush onto the counter and headed to the kitchen.

"I'm telling you, it's her. You better answer it. She will keep calling until you do."

Addison groaned. "True."

Pulling the cordless from the wall, Addison answered the phone.

"It's about time you answered your phone."

Addison dropped onto the sofa and put her feet on the table. It would not be a quick conversation, she was sure.

"Hello, Mother."

"Where have you been?"

"At Dad's."

"The whole day and night?" Tandy's voice had an edge to it.

"Yes."

"Did you watch the news?"

"Yup."

"Are you going to cancel the wedding?"

Addison closed her eyes. Her head dropped back

onto the couch. She knew the moment Sergei entered the room. Even without seeing him, she could feel his soothing aura.

"I don't know, Mama. Yesterday was a bit over-whelming."

"I think it's a sign that you should at the very least postpone it."

Of course, you do.

"When are you going to decide?"

"Mama, if anything changes, you'll be the first to know. For now, everything remains scheduled for Saturday."

Tandy let out a sound of disgust, and Addison couldn't stop her shoulders from creeping up into her neck.

Sergei came and pulled her feet into his lap. With his thumbs, he pressed into the centers of her arches.

"Mama, was there anything you needed?"

"Do I need a reason to talk to my daughter?"

Addison ground her teeth. Sergei's hands shook as he laughed at her. She knew he could hear her mother through the handset.

"Of course not, Mama, but you called five times yesterday. I figured it must be something important."

"If you thought it was important, you would have called me back."

"I just got home today."

"I'm glad I did, since you didn't answer yesterday."

"Sorry."

Sergei pressed on her feet, a little harder than before. It was his way of letting her know how much he hated when she let her mother put her on the defensive, though he wouldn't say anything while her mom could hear. No matter how much he disagreed with Tandy or disliked her methods, he was the complete example of respect and consideration around her.

"They've shut down the airports, you know."

"Yes, but Sergei's family is already here. So, we should still have a wedding."

"Do you think that's appropriate?"

You *sound like a broken record.* Addison's gut clenched. She hated when she was right. As much as she loved her mother, once again, this was an excuse to cancel the wedding.

"Mama, I've got to go. I'll call you back tomorrow."

"Where are you off to again in such a hurry?"

"I'm going to have breakfast at Dad's. Tamsen and her family are arriving today."

"Who's Tamsen?"

"Cassie's friend."

"So, why do you need to be there?"

Trying not to lose her cool, Addison bit her lip, breathing in deeply before responding. "Because she just left New York City. Because she's here for my wedding. Because she's family."

"She's not your family," Tandy said.

"Mama, she's a part of Dad and Cassie's family, so yes, she's a part of mine as well."

"She's not blood, is all I'm saying…" Tandy said.

"Blood isn't everything, Mama."

Sergei continued to press on her feet and gave her the raised eyebrow, so she knew it was past time to end the call.

"Mama, I'll try to call you tomorrow. Otherwise, I'll see you on Friday night for the rehearsal dinner."

"Fine. I'll talk to you later."

Addison pressed the off button and let the phone drop to her lap.

"*Lubov moya*, why do you let her push your buttons? She just cares."

Sure, about herself. With an exhausted sigh, Addison pulled her feet from his lap and sat up straight. "She's my mother, and I don't have it in me to fight with her today. Not after everything that happened yesterday. I'm just spent."

Sergei leaned in and kissed her nose. "This too shall pass, love. This too shall pass."

Addison nodded, afraid that the tears and sorrow pent up inside would overflow if she said anything else. "I'm not canceling my wedding." She lifted her chin in stubborn defiance.

"Oh, so now you want to marry me?" Sergei kissed her lips.

"Not funny."

Sergei grinned. "Come, let us get back to the house. Your Tamsen is coming."

"You'll like her. She's a lot like Cassie."

Sergei stood, grasped her hand, and pulled her to her feet. They slipped on their shoes and headed back to her father's house for breakfast.

CHAPTER 36

Skipping Through Landmines

Addison

A ddison's frantic pacing stopped the moment her mother waltzed in. Her stomach hit her knees with a force that almost made them buckle. Tandy was already dolled up, not a surprise since she had an aversion to others' opinions on how she should dress or apply her makeup. It was clear why someone might have tried to convince her that her choices were not advisable. Addison caught Cassie's eye and shook her head.

The red dress flared out just above the knees. The three-inch black suede heels were higher than anything she had ever seen her mother wear. She'd probably break her neck in them, which would inevitably create a scene; then again, that was one of Tandy's specialties.

With the powder-blue eyeshadow, she half-expected to see a can of Aqua Net sticking out of her mother's purse. Her hair was teased and curled like she'd just stepped out of the 1980s. The amount of hairspray used surely had poked an additional hole in the ozone layer. Her mother did have an odd sense of style, but it suited her.

Addison sighed. There were no words. From the expression on Cassie's face, she didn't have any either.

This was typical of her mother. As far back as she could remember, Tandy needed constant confirmation of her importance. When she wasn't getting her quota from her husband or boyfriend, she was demanding it from her daughters.

Quinby hugged her before scooting off to a corner so that Raleigh and Beth could hug her. She took a deep breath. Though they were more than an hour late, at least the girls were showered, and their hair was clean, so Addison was grateful.

After hugs and kisses, Lena led the three girls into the other room, so Sophie could pamper them with Zara, while Tandy stood off to the side, aloof. Sophie and Bertrand's arrival early that morning had saved the day. There was something to be said about private jets and the ability to change plans on the fly.

The room cleared, and Addison found herself alone with Cassie and Tandy. The tension ratcheted, making her teeth clench. Cassie was seated on a plush couch, taking in the scene in her usual quiet calmness.

Her mother, on the other hand, was the furthest from calm.

"I'm telling you, this is a bad omen. This is not a week for celebration," Tandy said, her fists on her hips, a scowl on her face. "I don't care what anyone says. A terrorist attack days before your wedding is just as bad as rain."

"Mama, the wedding was planned long before the attacks happened."

"You should have postponed."

"Tandy…" Cassie's voice was tight.

"What? I'm entitled to my opinion."

"Mama, can you go check on how things are going outside?"

"Why don't you send Cassie? She shouldn't be in here, anyway."

"Mama." Addison's patience was at an end.

"Fine." Tandy gritted her teeth and stormed out, a slight wobble in her ankles.

"Savannah, can you go with her? Please."

Her sister nodded and quietly slipped out to follow their mother.

Addison dropped onto the smaller couch with her head between her knees, trying not to hyperventilate. The dressing room seemed to shrink. The gray-green-painted walls appeared to spin, and her skin was clammy. The deep breaths helped keep the croissant she'd eaten for breakfast in her stomach. Her heart thudded in her chest. Until a few days ago, she'd thought everyone had been paranoid for flying in early.

Lena had returned while she had been sending her mother away. She was perched on the small couch beside her, rubbing her back.

Cassie stepped out of the room to get her some water.

"It is okay, child. It will all work out," Lena said.

"Maybe Mama's right," Addison hiccupped. "Maybe this is a bad idea. We should have postponed this."

Cassie walked in then and handed over a glass of water. She kneeled in front of her, placing Addison's hands in hers. She's wiped away the lone tear that traveled down Addison's cheek. "Honey, I know you're scared. But I've seen you with Sergei. You love him."

Addison bobbed her head.

Lena continued to rub small circles on her shoulders. The gesture was comforting, and Addison's breathing calmed.

"Sergei loves you as well," Lena said.

Addison nodded again. "Yes, I know."

"That's all you need. Love and faith in each other," Cassie said.

"I agree." Lena patted her hands.

Addison was grateful for these two strong women. What had seemed to be an abundance of over-cautiousness turned out to be either a premonition or just an extremely wise choice, but who could have imagined the Twin Towers would tumble? The United States had not experienced a terrorist attack of this magnitude in its lifetime. She had sat in front of the television, riveted the entire day. Everyone had. There had been no words to convey the horror they witnessed. Then, when they grounded all flights, both international and domestic flights were affected, Sergei's Russian family and friends were stranded. Some were diverted to Canada, while others were held up at Heathrow. Most had made their new flights, but there was still concern that they would be diverted again before landing in Raleigh.

Cassie and Eli had opened their home to Sergei's family, not letting them sit in a hotel for two weeks in a strange place. She'd spent yesterday with Mama and her sisters. Hating every second of it, but everyone had dismissed her desire to stay in the apartment with Sergei the night before the wedding, telling her it was bad luck.

"I know what you need," Cassie said. She shared a conspiratorial wink with Lena as she slowly rose to her feet.

"What?" Addison wiped at her face.

"You just need to hear Sergei's voice. It will put things into perspective for you," Cassie suggested.

"Wait. What? We can't see each other today!" Addison cried.

"Cassie is right. We could blindfold him, and you could sit on the other side of the door," Lena said.

"We'll go get him and give you a few minutes to yourself." Cassie leaned down and kissed the top of her head. Across the room, Lena gave Cassie a sideways glance.

"Come now, let us get you set up next to the door." Lena stood and reached a hand out to Addison, helping her stand. After Addison was seated on a chair, her back to the wall against the doorjamb, Cassie and Lena slipped out of the room in search of the groom.

She leaned her head against the wall and closed her eyes against the tears. Cassie and Lena talked softly while standing on the other side of the room, but Addison could hear snippets of their conversation.

"Do you worry Tandy will poison Addison against you?"

Addison tensed. She hadn't wanted Sergei's family to be hurt by her mother, yet her mother had gone out of her way to be difficult.

"Her entire childhood we lived with that fear. Addison's a grown woman now. It's up to her to maintain the relationships she finds value in. If she chooses not to have a relationship with us anymore, it will break our hearts, but it would be her decision at this point, not her mothers."

Though this was true, Addison doubted the simplicity of it where her mother was concerned.

Lena sighed. Thought her voice belied her true feelings. "I worry she will be poisoned against my son."

"I don't," Cassie said.

"Why?" Lena asked.

"Because I've seen them together. Sergei is a wonderful man. I'm sure you're very proud of him."

"Yes." Lena's tone relaxed.

"No matter what Tandy does, she can't change that. He's a calm anchor for Addison, especially against Tandy's raging tides."

"I have never met someone so much about herself."

Cassie laughed. "I understand. I felt the same way when I first met her. In time, you'll learn to accept her as a necessary evil to ignore, but you'll come to ignore her for the most part, like I do."

Lena chuckled. "I like it. Addison is so lucky to have you in her life to give her balance."

"And now she has you and Sergei, and together we'll balance her just fine."

"Thank you, I feel better," Lena said.

"She's a lot to take in. It's best to do it in small doses!"

"I agree." Lena gave a hearty laugh.

Addison closed her eyes and forced her breaths to slow as Cassie and Lena's voices drifted further away.

Twenty minutes later, Cassie returned with Sergei in tow.

There was a thump against the wall as he leaned into it and slid to the floor, reaching around the doorway in search of her hand.

"*Lubov moya*, are you having second thoughts?" he asked.

"No! Yes. I don't know," Addison choked.

"About marrying me?" Sergei's gentle squeeze to her hand could be felt in her heart.

"No!" Addison said. Her voice squeaked.

"Talk to me."

"It's the wedding and this week, and maybe it's a bad idea. Most of your family and friends can't make it."

"There's always the option of Christmas in Saint Petersburg. We would visit everyone who could not come."

Addison sniffled. "Maybe Mama's right. Maybe what happened this week was a sign that we should wait."

"I have waited my whole life for you. I will wait for you forever." Sergei's thumb caressed her palm as he spoke.

"Oh, Sergei." Addison burst into tears. "I love you so much."

"*Solnyshka*, before you, there was only darkness. You fill my soul."

Her eyes overflowed. She glanced up to see Cassie

and Lena were holding hands with tears flowing freely down their cheeks.

Addison took his hand and brought it to her lips. "Let's do this."

The tension now broken, everyone laughed.

"Are you sure?" he asked.

"I'll be the one in white. You can't miss me."

"I only have eyes for you."

ADDISON'S SISTERS AND SOPHIE WERE BRIDESMAIDS. Savannah and Sophie had been responsible for putting the girls together that morning. While Savannah focused on everyone's hair, Sophie had taken care of the makeup. When it was done, Quinby had slathered glittery lotion all over everyone's arms, shoulders, and chests. Addison had been primped and pampered beyond her wildest expectations. They were still giggling as they held up Addison's dress. The strapless ivory ball gown—with a gentle sweetheart neckline and corset-style, dipped low in the back— would have given Cinderella a run for her money.

Savannah made a puddle of the dress in the middle of the room, opening a large hole in the center. Thousands of tiny intricately hand-sewn beaded crystals covered the corded lace-appliqué bodice, flowing organza skirt, and chapel-length train.

As Addison pulled her sundress over her head and

let it drop to the floor, she stepped into the circle of fabric at her feet. The ladies slid the dress up her long legs and laced the back tight.

"Ugh! Leave room for me to breathe." Addison laughed.

"Oh no, there's no room for that. The dress will fall to your ankles!" Sophie laughed.

"Stand tall and smile your way through it," Savannah suggested.

"Breathing's overrated," Quinby agreed.

"So, how do I say my vows without breathing?" Addison asked.

"Carefully!" the three women said simultaneously, and another fit of giggles ensued.

She twirled around in place, taking in her image in the mirrors. The ensemble was breathtaking in its simplicity.

Addison had been a nervous wreck, with her mother giving her a hard time for celebrating after a week filled with so much death and the guilt that so many were unable to attend, but her sisters and Sophie had made it all worth the effort. *Thank Heaven I didn't cancel the wedding.*

She glanced around the room, taking in the laughing women decked out in deep plum chiffon gowns that flowed to their ankles. They were stunning. Their feet were enclosed in matching glitter-infused, slip-on strappy silver sandals, with a three-inch Lucite heel, a gift from Cassie. The women each wore a comb encrusted with hundreds of tiny sparkling crystals in their dolled-up hair, a gift from Lena.

This was where the similarities ended, and their individual styles emerged. The dresses remained the same fabric and color on the bottom; however, their unique personalities were reflected by their choice of styles on the top of their dresses.

Savannah had chosen a deep V-neck that opened in front and back, while Quinby's gown rose up and tied at the back of her neck, a t-strap flowing down her back. Raleigh was across the room, fiddling with Beth's hair. The delicate silver-braided spaghetti straps kept slipping off her small shoulders, pulling on the soft square-neck bodice.

Sophie was her maid of honor. With a glass of Champagne in her hand, she danced around the room, making everyone laugh. She had to keep yanking up the strapless bodice.

"Come here," Savannah laughed as she pulled Sophie close and tightened the sheer layer of gently scrunched overlay that went up and over her right shoulder before tying it to a glittering silver satin sash decorating the empire waist.

They radiated enthusiasm and happiness.

CHAPTER 37

The Longest Walk

Addison

Addison watched from her perch behind a wall of lilies and roses. She was hidden from view, but could see everything in a small room off to the side of the main church.

The theme from Tchaikovsky's ballet, "Sleeping Beauty," played as the girls began their walk to the altar. Because the ceremony was inside an enormous church, there were three aisles of seats instead of the usual two sides with a single center aisle. The wedding party alternated between the left aisle and the right. Parting at the altar, the bridesmaids headed to their positions on the left and the groomsmen stepped over to their spot on the right.

Raleigh, as a junior bridesmaid, led the procession

from the right. Her short, brunette hair had been curled in soft ringlets, the comb pulling the bangs back from her forehead and off to the side. Tamsen's stepson Dax walked beside her, looking awkward in his tuxedo.

Quinby followed, coming from the left aisle, her jet-black hair braided into a crown that surrounded her head like a halo. Her comb was at the top of her head, sparkling like a mini tiara. Sergei's brother Mikhail joined her, holding her hand like a star-struck schoolboy.

Savannah walked down next, from the right side. Her skin sparkled from a glitter-infused lotion. Her deep ebony hair was pinned up and twisted around her head, the silver comb pushing it up in the back. The comb was centered, giving off the most sparkle when hit by light. Viktor had melted her stiff reserve and had her grinning broadly as they came down the aisle together, as though carrying a shared secret.

Addison fidgeted, getting anxious again.

Sophie kissed her cheek, before taking her place on the left, her short straight bob gleaming in the lights. When Pyotr whispered something in her ear as they parted, her giggles filled the air like twinkling bells; she almost floated to her position.

Sergei stood stiffly in front of the altar, next to the preacher.

The bridesmaids reached their places, their

bouquets of white and deep-purple calla lilies with sprays of lavender as filler held tight against their waists. Bluntly cut ends peeked from the bottom of a large satin ribbon wrapped around the stems.

She kissed the cheeks of her two flower girls before they headed down the aisle. Bethany and Zara were darlings in matching white dresses with a sheer illusion neckline in front and back. White silk rose petals were sewn into the tulle and floated at the bottom, bouncing with each step of the silver-glittered sandals. A set of matching combs nestled in their curls. Each carried a white wicker basket with a plum ribbon laced through it, filled with white and purple rose petals they dropped at their feet as they floated down the aisle together. Alexi looked dashing in his little suit. He walked down the aisle between the two little girls. When they reached the front, they separated and stood on each side of the aisle.

This is what being a princess is like. Addison's heart swelled as she prepared for her journey down the aisle. The gentle sounds of Jeremiah Clarke's "Trumpet Voluntary" filled the air. The coordinator set it up, so she walked down four stone steps to meet her father at the bottom. He looked smashing, all cleaned up and standing tall.

"Hi, Dad." Addison looked up to his beaming eyes.

"Hey, kiddo. You ready?" her father whispered.

"Absolutely," Addison said. She patted the lace appliqué, smoothing it into place.

Eli kissed her cheek and her curled hair that flowed around her shoulders. He touched the comb, which glittered against her copper highlights.

"You are beautiful as always," he said.

In the same silver sandals as the bridesmaids, she floated down the stone pathway strewn with rose petals on her father's arm. The satin lining glided against her bare legs.

As her father guided her down the aisle, Addison took in the crowd gathered, but once Sergei came into view, nothing else mattered. Everything and everyone blurred as he smiled at her.

Eli passed her hand to Sergei as she turned to face him. Her father kissed her cheek as the chattering of the guests and the birds chirping faded around her. Her beating heart thrummed in her chest. The love in his eyes penetrated through all her reservations. There was no room for doubt, standing there with her hand in his.

They had written their vows, making them personal and simple. It was important to Sergei's family that they marry in the church. However, being obligated to an organized religion was not how they planned to live their everyday lives. Their vows to each other were more about the connection they felt for one another.

The unity candle before them was a custom-made

creation in soft white and cream shades. In a stunning display of carved ribbons that climbed from the bottom to the tapered top, the huge candle stood centered between two matching tapers. The already-lit tapers flickered with impatience for them to join the flames together to light the larger center candle. Addison's hand shook as she held the dripping taper over to join her fire with Sergei's.

When the priest completed his sermon and pronounced them husband and wife, Sergei gave her the softest kiss. Her heart skipped, and he winked at her.

The world returned in vivid color and sounds in stereo. They faced the cheers as they walked up the aisle on the right, Addison's arm tucked into Sergei's.

The receiving line seemed endless as people gathered and formed a line to greet them. After the first dozen guests had passed her, gushing about the ceremony, or her dress, Addison tuned it all out. In a daze, her attention drifted around the room. A botanical garden couldn't beat the fragrances floating around her. The flowers filled the room with beauty.

The guests left the church, heading to the reception, while their families and their wedding party remained behind to take the obligatory photographs.

More pictures followed, family gathered, friends swarmed, and group after group of people to be included. Cassie and her father had done a remarkable job of moving people into place at the right times to keep things moving smoothly and to keep her mother happy.

"When are we going to take a family picture?" Tandy asked.

Addison's stomach lurched. Hysteria set in as bile rose in her throat. Her parents had never been a family, and she wasn't about to take a picture that her mother could hug to her bosom to remember times gone by. Panicking, she glanced over at her father. He gave her a brief smile.

Eli calmly whispered in her mother's ear, and she gave a stiff nod. Tandy stood by and did the obligatory photos with her daughters and the bride. The only picture taken of Addison's entire family included her sisters standing between her mother and father, with Cassie standing by her father's side. Her mother was not amused.

The photographer finished up, and the wedding party departed. Addison held her new husband's hand tight as they were escorted out to the car to head to the reception.

WALKING INTO THE BALLROOM, ADDISON TOOK IN THE enormous displays of flowers that surrounded her, filling the room with color. Exotic bouquets of birds of paradise, stargazer lilies, white roses, sprays of lavender, and poppy pods were placed at intervals around the dining room. They complemented the rust colors of autumn that surrounded them.

Music from the violinist and pianist filled the rooms as they played soft, classical ballads. They sat down at the head table, and guests joined them to grab a picture and chat with them before dinner started.

After they filled their plates, they returned to the long head table facing the room and ate.

A twenty-six-inch ice sculpture of a couple doing the tango sat next to the cake display. The cake itself was a four-piece ensemble, separately stacked in angles. The individual square cakes each sat atop a square silver plate. A glass block filled with white calla lilies separated each of the plates to give it more height. Small purple, white, and silver-colored candied flowers topped the cakes.

As DINNER WOUND DOWN, THE MUSIC CHANGED AGAIN. The beginning strains of Elvis Presley could be heard as the disc jockey invited them to the dance floor for the first dance. Sergei stood and held out his hand. His warm hand enclosed hers as he tucked it into the crook of his elbow and led her to the dance floor. With his typical grace, sweeping her into his arms as Elvis continued to croon, "Can't Help Falling in Love," Sergei held her close.

His musky cologne and the tea-tree shampoo he

used centered her. It was like coming home after a long day. Addison inhaled deeply, trying to permanently etch his scent into her brain.

Sergei laughed. "What do you smell, *lubov moya*?"

Addison lifted her head from his shoulder and peered into his eyes. "You. Only you."

Sergei laughed again and hugged her tighter to him as he continued to spin her about the dance floor. The flashes continued to go off around her, the relentless stream almost blinding her. If she never had to take another picture for the rest of her life, it would be too soon.

Every whirl gave Addison a new vantage point of the room, the guests, and the beautiful decorations surrounding her. Sergei's arms held her tight as they moved to the music.

Being in his arms, knowing that their whole life was ahead of them, filled her with joy. Even her mother couldn't dampen that with her sour mood.

Addison was so caught up in the dance she was startled when Sergei pulled away, handing her over to her father in a smooth transition for the father-daughter dance.

"Hey, sweetheart, how's my girl?" Eli asked.

"I'm great, Dad."

"You look so beautiful," he whispered into her ear.

Addison held on in a tighter hug. "Thank you, Dad."

As the song ended, Eli returned her to Sergei's waiting arms.

Champagne flowed as they danced and laughed well into the night. As the party drew to a close, Addison and Sergei walked in the middle of two lines of guests holding sparklers above their heads, cheering as they passed.

A Rose by Any Other Name

EPILOGUE

Nine Months Later
Addison

A ddison's long chestnut hair was sopping wet, and tendrils glued to the side of her face. Beads of sweat dripped down her forehead and into her eyes. Another contraction seized her, and she stiffened, taking in a shaky breath. She'd been pushing for over four hours. The room was stuffy and uncomfortably warm, though no one else seemed to notice. Sergei stood beside the bed, holding her hand, and wiping the sweat from her face with a damp, cool washcloth. Her mother stood on the other side of the bed.

"You should have come in earlier so that you could have gotten the epidural," Tandy said.

"I know, Mama." Addison gritted her teeth.

Sergei's brow arched at Cassie, who stood across the room by the window. She smiled in return. Addison caught the exchange and bit her lip. It had been a mistake thinking that having her mother and Cassie in the delivery room would be a good idea. It only seemed to make Cassie more uptight and her mother more domineering. She wondered if she would ever outgrow the need to be the peacekeeper to try to make everyone around her happy.

"Don't forget your breathing techniques," Tandy continued.

Addison grunted as another contraction rose within her.

"I had an epidural with all five of you girls. It didn't make the labor any easier, but it at least took the edge off," Tandy said.

Addison tuned her mother out. She wanted this over. She was two weeks past her due date and was beyond ready to evict her interloper.

"Push now. Give it all you've got, Addison," Dr. Patel said.

Teeth clenched, and eyes shut tight, Addison moaned and gave a final push. The doctor pulled the baby free of her and lifted him up for all to see. A shrill squeal filled the air.

"And you have a beautiful boy!" the doctor exclaimed.

The baby was covered in fluids and other

substances. His full head of black hair was slimed down and stuck to his head.

"Sergei, will you cut the cord?" The doctor held out a pair of large stainless-steel scissors.

Sergei took a hesitant step toward the foot of the bed and took a deep breath, taking the scissors from the doctor. With a snip, he cut the umbilical cord tethering the baby to Addison, and the nurse whisked the baby away to be cleaned up.

They laid the bundle on Addison's chest as Sergei came back to stand at the head of the bed, looking down at them. Cassie stood next to Sergei, and he put his arm around her. Tandy was on the other side of the bed.

Within moments, they took the baby away to the nursery to do whatever it was they did to newborn babies, leaving Addison drained and sweaty. Tandy offered to give her a sponge bath and Sergei and Cassie walked out of the room to tell the family in the waiting room the good news.

An hour later Addison was sitting up in her bed, the baby nestled in her arms, fast asleep. Her hair had been brushed and braided, and her face glowed.

Her father and Cassie came in, followed by Sergei. Her sisters Savannah, Quinby, and Raleigh strolled in a few moments later. Sophie would come the following week to spend time with her at home, as well as Sergei's family. His mother suggested coming later to spend time with them and the baby outside of the delivery room. Addison was grateful that her mother-in-law understood her so well.

Each took turns holding the baby and taking pictures with him.

"So, tell us. What's his name?" Savannah asked.

She'd agreed with Sergei to keep the baby's name and sex a secret until he was born, to avoid the well-meaning suggestions of what to name him.

Addison glanced up at her husband with a grin. With the baby in his arms, he winked back at her. "We've named him Maxim James Petrova," she said.

"What kind of name is that?" Tandy said between gritted teeth.

"It is from his grandfathers. We chose the middle names of each of our fathers," Sergei explained.

Addison ignored her mother's attitude, instead focusing on the look of pride that filled her father's eyes. This took away some of the sting from her mother's comment.

Sergei smiled in the genuine way that made her grateful for his love. "Don't worry, Mother, we plan to do the same for our daughter when the time comes."

Addison smothered a smile behind the soft head of her son, as Sergei had looked at Cassie when he'd spoken, though her mother assumed automatically he had only been addressing her. It was clear from the wide-eyed expression on Cassie's face that she hadn't made the same assumption. Her mother, however, was too wrapped up in her self-importance to even consider Cassie.

The wink Sergei gave her as he leaned down and first kissed his son's head and then her forehead made her grin widen. In such a short time, her husband had not only learned to soothe her frazzled nerves but to also smooth her mother's often-ruffled feathers.

Each day, she was grateful for his thoughtful and generous love.

Sergei, always in tune with her thoughts, stroked her cheek. Looking down at her son, and back up at her husband and the love shining in his eyes, she felt a sense of wholeness she had never known.

———

*I WANTED TO TAKE A MINUTE TO THANK YOU FOR TAKING the time to read **Her Guarded Heart**.*

*I hope you enjoyed **Addison and Sergei's** story as much as I enjoyed writing it. If you did, I would greatly appreciate you leaving a review on the review site of your choice. You can leave a review on Amazon by clicking here: **Amazon Review***

Reviews are crucial for any author and a line or two about your experience can make a huge difference in helping other readers find this book.

———

Did you like the story of **Addison and Sergei?**
Then you'll **LOVE Book 2** of this series,
Her Heart's Desire.
Sophie and Claude's Story.

SHE'S TAKING ON THE REINS OF THE FAMILY HORSE-breeding business. When scandal threatens her home, can she win the race to happily ever after?

Sophie Compte is impatient to settle down. Used to butting heads with her stubborn childhood sweetheart, the wealthy young Frenchwoman is certain she can convince him to bury his pride and finally propose. But while she's busy trying to persuade the driven veterinarian to get down on one knee, a long-standing client taints the farm's reputation with ugly accusations of fraud.

Horrified when a private investigator uncovers links to her beloved, Sophie digs deeper into the rumors threatening everything she holds dear. And as race-enhancing drugs are discovered on the property, the looming clouds of disgrace make her even more determined to defy the risks and get to the bottom of the mystery.

Can she uncover the truth without losing it all?

Her Heart's Desire is the witty second book in the Letting Love In romantic women's fiction series. If you like opinionated characters, intriguing twists, and sweet endings, then you'll adore Dawn Baca's page-turning drama.

Read **Her Heart's Desire** for a passionate triumph today!
Start reading **Her Heart's Desire** now!

Do you like **FREEBIE** books?
Sign up for my newsletter and get
***His Heart's Burden* for Free!**

To read my blog, get the latest news, future release dates, or to join my ARC team sign up for my newsletter at *www.DawnBaca.com.*

Also by Dawn Baca

WOMEN'S ROMANTIC FICTION

The Letting Love In Series

- **His Heart's Burden** —
  (*books2read.com/HisHeartsBurden*)
- **Her Guarded Heart** —
  (*books2read.com/HerGuardedHeart*)
- **Her Heart's Desire** —
  (*books2read.com/HerHeartsDesire*)
- **His Hearts Promise** —
  (*books2read.com/HisHeartsPromise*)
- **Her Heart's Wish** — *(Coming Spring 2026)*
- **Her Heart's Secret** — *(Coming Spring 2026)*
- **Her Lonely Heart** — *(Coming Winter 2026)*
- **His Forgotten Heart** — *(Coming Winter 2027)*
- **Her Fighting Heart** — *(Coming Winter 2027)*
- **His Racing Heart** — *(Coming Winter 2027)*
- **Her Jaded Heart** — *(Coming Winter 2027)*

CONTEMPORARY ROMANCE

- **Windswept Whispers** —
  (*books2read.com/WindsweptWhispers*)

HOLIDAY STORIES

(Coming Winter 2025)

- **Merry and Bright** —
  books2read.com/MerrynBright)

INTERNATIONAL COZY MYSTERIES

The Travel Visa Mysteries

(Coming Summer 2025)

- **Betrayal by the Bay** —
  books2read.com/BetrayalbytheBay)
- **Ended on Easter Island** —
  books2read.com/EndedonEasterIsland
- **Suspense on the Serengeti** — *books2read.com/SuspenseontheSerengeti*

Acknowledgments

Words could never convey the depths of my gratitude. To my amazing critique partners and editors, who are not only fantastic friends but also amazing authors in their own right:

Amabel Daniels, RB Austin, Esti Bega, Casey Hagen, Deb Julienne, Bobbi Antonelli-Szabo, Marnita Jondle, Meg Adams, Angela Evans, Kim Huther, Wendee Mullikin, Michelle Read, Amber Downey, Emilee Franssen Beck, Rachel Lamb and Rebecca Snider.

Thank you to Sherry Franssen Breinig and Jennifer Sosh who helped fix the errors that you came across. You ladies help me make the world go round.

This book would not be half of what it is today without all of your love, dedication and support. Thank you for helping me keep the faith and for making my writing better and stronger, and for all of the hard work that went into shaping this story into the best it could be.

Love to you all,
Dawn

About the Author

An insatiable reader of all genres since her childhood, Dawn is a globetrotter hungry to discover new places and experience unique adventures.

She can be found indulging in her husband's first love of summer camping in the mountains or luxuriating in the open seas while cruising to exotic destinations during the frigid winter months.

When she's not jet-setting she can be found in Central Valley California with her family and their many rescue animals.

To read her blog, get the latest news, future release dates, or to join her ARC team sign up for her newsletter at *www.DawnBaca.com.*

Social Media

facebook.com/DawnMBaca

x.com/BacaDawn

youtube.com/DawnBaca

pinterest.com/dawnmbaca

instagram.com/dawnbaca

amazon.com/author/dawnbaca

bookbub.com/profile/dawn-baca

goodreads.com/dawnbaca

tiktok.com/@bacadawn

Paperback ISBN: 978-1-7329615-0-0
Cover: 100 Covers
Blurb: Best Page Forward
Editor: Wendee Mullikin
Chapter Image by lukasdedi on Freepik

 Created with Vellum

Contents

www.ingramcontent.com/pod-product-compliance
Lightning Source LLC
Chambersburg PA
CBHW051314250626
47155CB00007B/2321